DOCTOR
Dreamy

Alana Jade

Doctor Dreamy

Alana Jade

This book is a work of fiction. Any references to real events, real people, and real places are used fictitiously. Other names, characters, places and incidents are products of the Author's imagination and any resemblance to persons, living or dead, actual events, organizations or places is entirely coincidental.

Disclaimer: The material in this book contains graphic language and sexual content and is intended for mature audiences, ages 18 and older.

ISBN 13: 978-0645112429

Editing by Kay at Swish Design & Editing
Proofreading by Nicki at Swish Design & Editing
Formatting by Swish Design & Editing
Cover design by Sarah Paige at Opium House Creatives
Cover image Copyright 2021

DEDICATION

To my mum. My best friend. My person.
Thank you for being the best mum a girl could have.

DOCTOR Dreamy

CHAPTER 1

CHELSEA

Relaxing into my couch, I kick my shoes off and place my throbbing feet on my coffee table. This isn't something I usually do, but I'm exhausted.

I've just come off an eighteen-hour shift at the hospital on a Friday night. Normally, I don't do longer than twelve, but a colleague needed to leave partway into her shift as her daughter got sick, and, of course, me being me, I couldn't say no.

Releasing my long brown hair from the bun it's been pinned in since yesterday afternoon, my scalp screams hallelujah as the tension is instantly eased. I run my fingers through my gold-flecked locks, untangling any knots which have formed before placing my hands behind my head and sinking into the plush cushions of my couch.

Usually, after an overnight shift, I head straight to bed because, for a doctor, sleep is precious. But today, I'm going to enjoy a few minutes on the piece of furniture I spent a small fortune on but rarely use and relish in the fact that I don't have another shift until Monday evening. The shift in the ER was much more stressful than any previous shift, and it really has me doubting if I want to pursue trauma medicine.

As a resident, I usually have to work weekends and all the shitty shifts that no one else wants to do, but I requested this weekend off as it's my younger cousin's wedding, and my parents told me that if I didn't attend, they'd be crushed. There's nothing better than parental guilt, especially when you're an only child.

I'd love nothing more than a strong coffee right now, but I can't be bothered moving, and it's probably not a good idea to have caffeine. I need to try and get some sleep before my cousin's nuptials later today.

After Sara announced her engagement, part of me was perhaps slightly disappointed that I wasn't asked to be in the bridal party, especially since we're each other's only cousins, but in many ways, I was relieved. I didn't have to do any form of diet, so I'd look perfect for wedding photos, I didn't have to wrap myself in pastel colors and plaster a smile on my face in a room full of people I don't know. I'm more than happy to be a guest at the wedding and to pass my congratulations on and leave at a decent hour so I can have a nice sleep-in on Sunday morning for the first time in months.

Glancing around my small apartment's living room-kitchen area, I notice my black and tan lace dress hanging on a hook over the door to my bedroom. A grin spreads across my face as I take in the beauty of my online purchase. Not once have I purchased a dress online that fits me in every single perfect way, but this one is as though it was made for me.

Hauling myself up from the couch, I walk to the kitchen to get myself a glass of water before heading to my bedroom and placing it on my nightstand. The bed is too inviting to ignore, and I flop down on the mattress.

Wriggling on my comforter, I quickly find a comfortable spot and lose my fight to keep my eyes open.

A noise from the living room makes me jump and it takes me several seconds to register what noise it is. My cell. It must be the alarm as the noise has now stopped.

Taking a quick look at the clock on my nightstand—it's after midday.

So much for a power nap before a shower.

Groaning, I lift myself from my comfortable spot before heading to my bathroom, peeling pieces of clothing off on the way and dropping them to the floor.

Besides sleep and coffee, hot showers relax me, washing away the job's stress. There have only been a few times I've opted for sleep over a shower after work, and today was one of them.

As much as I love being a doctor and constantly thinking on my feet, along with juggling multiple patients each shift, I do find it stressful when I need to inform the family of a patient's death or if I can't determine a diagnosis. I'm constantly told that eventually I'll thrive on the stress of the job. Perhaps that will kick in after I complete my fellowship.

Last night was also the supervising doctor's final shift, who I reported to for the last two years. Dr. Alex Arthur has been a fantastic supervisor, and I'm going to miss her unique way of getting the best out of me.

For now, I'll report to another doctor before Dr. Arthur's replacement starts in a week. I haven't been told the replacement's name yet, only that the doctor is a brilliant surgeon.

Stepping under the steaming water, I begin to quickly wash my hair to style it for the wedding from wet rather than attempting to do it while dry.

As I quickly wash my face under the showerhead, the faint

strums of my cell's ringtone sound through my apartment. Furrowing my brows and letting out a long sigh, I choose to ignore the call, preferring to enjoy my shower for thirty seconds more.

As soon as the noise stops, it starts again.

Groaning, I step from the shower and swipe my towel from the rail. I collect the second towel from the rail and wrap it around my head.

It's probably Mom, making sure I'm not still at work.

But what if it's the hospital regarding a patient from my shift? It can't be, they'd page if there was an issue.

It stops ringing just as I reach the device.

Picking it up from the table, I check the missed calls. *Sara.*

Why would she be calling me, especially on her wedding day?

Before I get the chance to tap to call her back, it begins to ring again.

Swiping across the screen, I bring the cell to my ear.

"Hey," I answer.

"Chels, I'm so glad you finally picked up. You weren't asleep, were you?" Sara mumbles.

"No, I was in the shower and about to get ready for *your* wedding. Is everything all right?" I ask.

She doesn't reply. Only soft sobs are heard down the line.

Shit. Has she broken up with Matthew?

Sara has always been known for drama. If she had a scratch, it was a laceration. But there's something about her voice this time that tells me she isn't being melodramatic.

"Umm, not really. We've already started getting ready for the wedding because, you know, brides so want to be woken up at four in the morning on their wedding day." Sara lets out a fake chuckle down the phone as I intently listen to her.

"Wow, why so early?" I ask.

"Hair and makeup, and, of course, the photographer will be

here in two hours."

"Right. But why are you upset? It should be the happiest day of your life. You didn't argue with Matt, did you?"

"Oh geez, no. Nothing like that. Matty is my everything," she gushes down the line.

"Sweetie, you aren't making any sense." I'm trying to remain calm with my cousin, but she's not being very forthcoming with the information or why she's upset, and I'm beginning to lose my cool.

"Sorry, Chels. I'm so stressed about this wedding, but I'm ringing because one of my bridesmaids had a car accident this morning on the way to Mom and Dad's place to get ready."

"Oh shit. I'm so sorry to hear that. Is she okay?"

How awful for Sara to have something so tragic happen on her special day.

"Yeah, she'll be fine, but she's got a concussion, a possible broken rib, and a broken ankle. I begged her to still come to the wedding, but she said that the doctors have told her she isn't going anywhere today."

"Well, yeah, she won't be going anywhere for a little while. She probably needs scans and depending on how bad the break is, maybe surgery," I try to explain, rolling my eyes at my cousin's lack of compassion.

Sara lets out a loud groan down the line. "Why did this have to happen to me?"

My eyes involuntarily roll again. I'm glad that my cousin, the bridezilla, can't see me doing that. Otherwise, I may be in her firing line next.

"Maybe one of your friends can fill in for her?" I suggest.

"That's why I'm calling. I've called the other girls who might have been able to fit into Peaches' dress, but they've all given me some bullshit excuse. The conversation ended with me telling them not to come to the wedding if they aren't going to help me

5

in my moment of need."

Moment of need? Does she hear how ridiculous she sounds?

"So, I'm calling my best cousin..."

"Sara, I'm your only cousin," I interrupt.

She giggles down the phone. "I know... still makes you the best. Will you stand next to me today as I tell everyone I'll love Matty forever and a day?"

"Umm..." I reply.

I can't be a bridesmaid. I've had minimal sleep, I haven't waxed in forever, and my hair needs coloring.

"Don't you dare tell me no, Chelsea?" I can picture Sara's pout now.

"I... umm... Sara, I'm the last person you want next to you. I'm not bridesmaid ready. I haven't washed my hair properly in weeks, and it desperately needs a cut."

"All that shit doesn't matter. Your hair will be pinned. But I'll need you here in twenty minutes."

"Sara, I'm not sure."

"Please, Chels. Please."

My stomach knots. I don't want to do this. I don't.

"Please," she squeaks down the line. Her tone's the same as when she used to try to get me to do things I didn't want to do as a child.

No, Chelsea. Say no.

"Chels?"

"Fine! I'll have a shower and be over to your parents' as soon as I can."

"Yay, thank you. Make it twenty minutes, and I'll pair you with Matty's best friend, Cameron. He's mighty fine."

I chuckle at her rather unusual threat. "It's fine, Sara. Pair me with whoever. I'll get there as soon as I can."

"He's a doctor, too. The girls call him Doctor Dreamy because he really is. Maybe you guys will hit it off. Although you'll probably have to fight Amanda for him."

A huge "hell yeah" sounds in the background of the call.

The last thing I need is a guy, I remind myself, but a small part of me thinks that it'd be nice to get to know a man again. It's been years now and for a good reason.

"Sara, get off the line, so I can get ready." I laugh.

She giggles. "Thank you, Chelsea. I love you."

"I love you, too."

Ending the call, I throw my phone on the couch and run my hand through my hair.

Why one earth did I say yes?

Nerves rumble low in my belly. I take a deep breath before blowing it out, but it doesn't settle my stomach, so I repeat the action.

What the hell have I agreed to?

CHAPTER
2

CAMERON

After straightening my bowtie in the mirror, I run my hand over my dark hair before smoothing the crease from my dark navy suit jacket.

Of all colors for my best friend to choose for his wedding suits, he selects the color I wear almost every day. In all fairness to Matthew, though, I'm sure he had little to no input into much of the wedding planning.

"All ready, buddy?" Matthew grins as he slaps me across the back.

"Sure am."

"Not used to seeing you with a smooth face," he teases.

"There aren't many people I'd shave it off for..." I smile. "You're lucky, buddy."

"And I appreciate it... well, Sara does. I couldn't care less what your facial hair is like." He chuckles.

I'm glad Sara appreciates it, but I have to admit it took a few weeks for them to convince me to be clean-shaven for their wedding. I rather like my well-groomed beard, and it'll be coming back once this wedding is over.

"What about you? Ready to commit to the same girl for the rest of your life?" I cheekily quip.

"More than you know."

We've been friends since high school. Matthew went off to law school, and I became a doctor. But we've always remained good friends, including when we shared the shittiest apartment in all of San Francisco.

He met Sara, his wife-to-be, when she was a freshman—he was helping a professor as his research assistant while he applied for associate positions at firms—and they've been inseparable ever since, even though she dropped out of law to pursue fashion.

"Have you heard from the girls?" I ask.

"Fucking drama at Sara's folks today. One of the bridesmaids had a damn car accident on the way to the hotel this morning. Sara was in panic mode, but I got a text from her a few minutes ago, and apparently, it's all sorted."

"Glad it's sorted, but that poor girl who had the accident. Do you know where she was taken? I can make a call and check on her."

"No idea, man. She's fine but is staying overnight in the hospital. Sara's cousin is her replacement."

"The last-minute replacement bridesmaid... wow. I wouldn't have thought that could happen. I guess some people jump at the chance to be in a bridal party."

"Guess so. I'm hoping that's the last of our rule of three bad-luck incidents today."

"Rule of three?" I ask, no idea what he's talking about.

"You know how things happen in threes. Well, my shoelace broke, then Brad lost his vest, and we had to make an emergency call to the store to get another one, and then the car accident. That's all that can happen now."

"Right." I smile at him, wanting to laugh at his silly superstition.

"The photographer has left Sara's parents and will be here shortly to start taking photos of us. I'll go and grab the other guys. Do you mind tidying up in here a little?"

Offering a nod in reply as Matthew leaves the hotel suite, I look around for this supposed mess in the room. A couple of my suit hangers are on the bed along with the suit bag and plastic bag containing my shoes on the floor. Hardly a mess.

My guess is that it's not him who's worried about the state of the room today. Sara will be wanting everything magazine-worthy for the photographer.

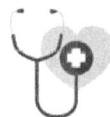

Time flashes by, and before we know it, we're standing at the altar, Matthew rocking back and forth on his feet.

"You all right, buddy?" I whisper through a plastered-on smile.

"Shitting myself, actually," he mumbles back, trying not to move his lips as the photographer and videographer run back and forth, attempting to get the right angles for us.

The music changes from soft windchimes to Beethoven's "Ode to Joy" as the bridesmaids begin to make their grand entrance.

The first couple of girls walk down the aisle with fake smiles on their faces. Their peroxide blonde hair is swept into some fancy hairstyle, and the makeup has been caked on their faces. There's nothing natural about them at all. Matthew warned me they are extremely flirty girls.

The second to last girl walks down and she's a lot more natural. Hardly any makeup and natural-looking soft brown hair. Her face is void of a smile, and she stumbles several times in the shoes she's wearing. I begin to wonder if this is the replacement bridesmaid as she seems nothing like the others.

"Wow," I gasp to myself.

By the time she steps up to the altar, I don't even notice the Maid of Honor making her way down the aisle. My eyes are fixated on girl three.

She puffs out a breath before her eyes wander around the room, taking in all the grandeur surrounding us. But eventually, she looks toward us, and the second our eyes connect, it's as though a fire has been lit inside of me.

The music changes again to Pachebel's "Canon in D Major," the only song Matthew used to play on the piano, and I break the connection with this gorgeous girl and flick my head toward the other end of the aisle. The doors open, and Sara stands there on the arm of her father. She looks gorgeous.

Throughout the ceremony, I can't help but glance at the bridesmaid, who seems to be looking at me each time I glimpse across. I mouth, "Hi," to her at one point just before Sara and Matthew say their vows. Her cheeks flush pink before she looks away.

A short time later, the reverend pronounces Matthew and Sara as husband and wife. The ceremony was lovely, and there was a threat of a tear from my eye as Matthew professed his undying love for Sara. You could feel the love radiating from both of them in the room, and I am so proud of my best friend.

I've never been interested in settling down. My job as a doctor keeps me more than busy, but on the odd occasion, I do find myself wondering if my dream girl is out there somewhere. Weddings don't usually evoke this kind of emotion from me, but this time, I'm standing next to my best friend, so maybe that's why I'm feeling different.

The bridesmaid who's caught my eye stands amongst the other girls, her smile beaming. As Sara and Matthew share their first kiss as husband and wife, the other bridesmaids fumble for a tissue as their overly dramatic sobs are loudly heard, but not her, not the one who's caught my eye, she's still proudly watching on, her grin has not faltered.

As we line up to leave the ceremony, the wedding planner asks us to collect the bridesmaid's arm we are escorting back down the aisle.

"Amanda, you'll swap with Chelsea for the rest of the day," Sara barks as she quickly turns around.

"What?" the girl next to me scoffs. "Are you fucking kidding me? I don't want to give this one up," she mutters under her breath, just loud enough for me to hear.

Sara narrows her eyes at Amanda before plastering a sweet smile on her face and looks back toward the congregation happily cheering for the newly married couple.

"This is such crap," the bridesmaid says as she unhooks her arm from mine. "Maybe we'll get to dance later, sexy." She beams at me before moving down the line. I offer a sympathetic smile as she walks away, but I'm secretly glad she's gone. I've only met her once before, but the amount of sexual innuendo that the woman delivers is unbelievable. Another girl wearing a matching fluffy dress in a different shade of pink, slides her arm into the crook of mine all the while laughing.

"What's so funny?" I ask as I glance down at her.

It's her, the natural beauty.

"I was just called a bitch by her." She tries to cover her face with her bouquet to calm herself down.

"And that's funny?"

"I'm the replacement. My cousin is the bride. She told me I was to be partnered with you. It was part of her *deal,* but it appears that Amanda didn't want to part with you, though."

"I'm in hot demand." I chuckle.

"Seems that way."

She looks up at me, her flowers still covering part of her face. Her pale blue eyes lock with mine, and she instantly stops laughing.

"I'm Cameron." I grin.

"Chelsea," she quietly replies as she lowers her bouquet.

Something stirs low in me. A feeling I haven't felt for quite some time. Chelsea is gorgeous, and I'll be thanking Sara later for changing my partner at the last minute.

The bride and groom begin their walk back down the aisle, and we wait for our cue from the wedding planner before following them. I place my hand on top of Chelsea's as we walk behind the happy couple. It's my way of helping her keep her balance. Chelsea wobbles in her heels and mumbles, "thank you" as we leave the church.

"Cam, have you met my beautiful cousin, Chelsea?" Sara squeals as we all wait for the congregation to leave the church.

"I have."

"Can I take these shoes off now, Sar?" Chelsea whines, forcing both Sara and me to laugh. "I'm not joking. I didn't even wear heels to my prom."

"You can put your flats on at the reception, Chels. A little bit longer, okay?" Sara soothes before turning around and taking the arm of her new husband.

"They don't look very comfortable," I whisper to Chelsea.

"I've only had them on for an hour, and even then, I took them off in the car. My feet feel worse now than they do after a double shift at the hospital." She holds onto my arm as she reaches down and fiddles with the buckle of the shoe.

"Oh, you work in a hospital?" I ask, not wanting to presume her job.

"Yeah, I'm a doctor."

"What a coincidence. So am I." Chelsea looks up to me while still holding onto my arm and adjusting a strap on her shoe. She slowly starts to nod her head as a small smile appears on her face.

"I know, Sara told me." I feel as though she wants to add something else to her sentence but is holding back.

Before I can even reply, we're being asked to return to the cars so we can head to a nearby park for official photos. Sara and Matthew stay back to wait for their family and friends to gather outside the church and blow bubbles as the newlyweds run down the church stairs.

Extending my hand, Chelsea take it before moving to slide into the vehicle first but stumbles, and I madly rush to catch her before she hits the ground.

"Are you all right?" I ask, looking down at her in my arms. Warmth spreads over my body.

"I'm so clumsy in these damn heels." She laughs as her cheeks begin to turn slightly pink. "Thanks for catching me. Sara would've killed me if I dirtied my dress, although there's plenty of padding on it so I doubt I would be hurt."

I laugh. "That's what I'm here for."

The wedding planner attempts to hurry us into the cars as Sara and Matthew run through the bubbles down the stairs and into a waiting convertible.

Pulling the door closed behind me, I notice it's only Chelsea and myself in this car, the rest of the bridal party must have squeezed into the other limousine.

"Just us." I smile.

"Good, I can take these shoes off for five minutes." She laughs. "As long as you don't tell my cousin."

"My lips are sealed." I slightly loosen my shirt's collar hoping to let some fresh air in and cool my body down.

"Are you in bridal parties often?" Chelsea asks.

Turning from the window to look at her, I notice her nose is screwed up. "That's an odd question." A chuckle escapes me.

"Geez, I don't know where that came from. I guess I'm trying to make small talk." She groans as she places her hand on the frill of the neckline of her dress. "Why do they make ugly bridesmaid dresses?"

"It's so you don't upstage the bride... although, in my eyes, you could wear a paper bag and do that today."

I'm shocked by my brazenness.

That's a come-on if I ever heard one, Cameron!

Her cheeks flush at my comment. "You're too kind. I must look like a mess, though. I've barely slept. I worked eighteen hours overnight."

"Shit. I hate those shifts. Second-year resident?"

"Fourth, actually," she replies.

"Well, you look lovely. Between you and me, I know this thing will end around ten tonight. If you're anything like me, the earlier, the better."

"Yes." She laughs. "The bonus is I get to sleep in tomorrow."

"Me, too."

Chelsea is easy to talk to, and I'm finding it fantastic that she understands a doctor's life and how we appreciate the small things like a sleep-in or hot coffee.

A tap on the window has both of us twisting our necks to see who it is. Our peace is shattered by the Maid of Honor and Matthew's cousin, Pete, joining us.

As Amanda slides in, I can just hear Chelsea groan, and she turns to look out her window. I stifle a laugh.

The car has been transformed into a mass of two-toned pink fabric as Amanda tries to constrict her dress so she can see.

"Wow, shoes off already, Chelsea. Wait until I tell Sara," Amanda snides.

Chelsea slowly turns back toward Amanda. "How old are you, Amanda? You're going to tattle on me to *my* cousin over shoes. We're all over twenty-five here, aren't we, not six-year-olds."

15

"I'm trying to make it a perfect day for my best friend," Amanda snaps.

"Sara isn't here. I'm resting my feet now, so I don't have to midway through the photos. I don't need some friend of *my* cousin's who's on some weird bridesmaid power trip to tell me what to do."

Amanda instantly huffs before crossing her arms across her chest and looking out the window. I look to Pete, who's got a grin on his face, and he rolls his eyes at the drama before us. He's barely of drinking age, and according to Matthew, he doesn't go out, so to witness this would've been eye-opening for him.

The way Chelsea just put Amanda in her place has me wanting to congratulate her. In other instances I've seen like this, usually the other bridesmaids just go along with what the Maid of Honor says, but Chelsea is different, and I love that.

Placing my hand over all the layers covering her knee, a smile plays on my lips as she gazes up at me. It's my way of hoping she calms down.

I'm going to enjoy getting to know Chelsea tonight.

CHAPTER 3

CHELSEA

What the hell did I think when I agreed to be a part of Sara's day? I certainly didn't sign up for any crap from Amanda.

Even having our photos taken in the park, she kept mumbling things about me to the other girls. This isn't high school. They are meant to be mature women, but obviously, their brains are still set to fifteen years ago.

Maybe my reacting to their stupidity is lowering me to their level, but I can't stand this sort of behavior, and I shouldn't have to put up with it.

Being tripped on the way back to the cars was the final straw. Of course, it was assumed I'd stumble in the grass in my heels, but I saw Amber's foot jut out a little too far as we walked. Luckily, Cameron was there in seconds to help me back up. We laughed it off, but inside, I'm still seething.

Sure, I know of these girls, given they're my cousin's friends, but I don't know them well. Only what Sara has told me about them. They are a strong click from high school. Click girls don't welcome outsiders too easily, and that's blatantly obvious by their behavior today.

Willing myself to calm down, I gently touch the pinned pieces of my hair, pushing the hairpins in further so it feels a little more secure.

It was the quickest I've ever seen hair and makeup being done today. The moment I arrived at Sara's parents' house, I was shoved in a swivel chair and pushed and pulled in under ten minutes with four people working on me. I said no to heavy makeup and fake lashes, telling them I have allergies. No one questioned it because I'm a doctor. The other girls applied way too much, though, and I'm glad I kept mine toned down. I did feel amazing when the stylist and makeup artist were done, but I was desperate for a coffee.

But there was no time for that. My aunt kept saying over and over that water was my only option today before they asked me to step into the most hideous pink dress I've ever seen—scoop neck with a layer of tulle creating a frill that feels like it's sitting just under my chin. The dress is shorter in the front and longer in the back, but the girl who's meant to be wearing it must have been slightly taller than me, so it sits a little further down my legs than the other girls. It fits reasonably well but these ruffles are so over the top.

Were ruffles ever in fashion? Maybe in the mid-eighties. Trust Sara to add an eighties flair to her wedding.

This was me helping my cousin in a moment of need. My uncle, Mom's brother, pulled me to him for a big hug just as we were leaving, thanking me for coming aboard at the last moment.

But what I didn't sign up for is the other bridesmaids being nasty. It's not my fault the girl had a car accident. Bitchy girls annoy me so much, and I'm surprised that Sara is friends with these girls. Sara's dramatic but not bitchy at all. I need to suck it up now and maintain a look of happiness on my face. Once I'm home, I'll never have to see these assholes again.

Taking a deep breath, I startle slightly as I feel Cameron's hand on my knee, over my dress. A glance confirms his hand there, and then I shift my eyes to look at him. A small but sweet smile is on his lips, and I can feel the tension begin to leave my body.

"I'll grab you a drink the moment we get to the hotel," he whispers before his smile grows to a grin.

"Thank you. That will be perfect."

If Sara had told me that I'd meet the nicest guy at her wedding, I would've laughed in her face. It's so stereotypical. Guys always appear nicer when you're at a wedding. Maybe it's the pheromones in the air, the suits guys wear that make them look ridiculously handsome, or a persona they put on. But with Cameron, I can tell this is no act. He's a down-to-earth guy, very easy on the eye, exceptionally charming, and he understands the pressures of my job.

There have been no awkward silences between us. I don't feel that we're forcing ourselves to talk or laugh like some of the other couples in the bridal party.

In one of the photos they had us pose for, the photographer told us to act as though one of us had just said something funny. It could've been completely fake, but all Cameron had to do was mention my stilettos, and we both started laughing. Not a chuckle, a real belly laugh.

The moment we arrive at the reception, we're herded into a room to the side of the hotel's ballroom, and Cameron and I make a beeline for the tray of champagne flutes.

I've never seen such grandeur before, and I've been to quite a few weddings. Large bouquets of white, peach, and pink roses are placed on every flat surface available. Each room seems to have a chandelier positioned just right so the lights surrounding it reflect in the crystals. Sara's outdone herself with the details of this wedding. It's every little girl's dream and exactly how my cousin had planned her big day.

"Are you staying here tonight?" Cameron asks as they line us up for our grand entrance into the reception.

"Apparently so." I see him from the corner of my eye, and my heart flutters as I wonder if he's insinuating anything.

I had no plans to stay at the hotel tonight, but Sara told me that she'd booked a room for each of her bridesmaids as a thank you, so I may as well use it. It saves me from having to try to get an Uber later.

The wedding planner is encouraging us to dance as we enter the room. I laugh at her ridiculous request. Sara has made me wear the heels until we're formally introduced.

Yeah, 'cause I can so dance in these shoes, I think to myself.

A sudden burst of laughter escapes Cameron as he offers me his arm, and I gratefully accept it.

"Couldn't have you struggling with your shoes."

"Thank you."

"Aren't you lucky that I don't like to dance? I'm happy to walk in," he mumbles.

"Oh, thank God for that," I reply, slightly louder than I should have. I cover my face with my bouquet as one of the bridesmaids turns around to shoot me a dirty look.

Sara leans in from behind me. "I'm not dancing either. Matthew will twirl me halfway, but that's it. Then we can both wear our ballet flats when we sit down." She giggles.

"You have some, too?" I ask.

"Duh! I love my shoes, but I have a blister the size of an island on my foot right now," Sara complains. She suddenly twists her head toward her new husband and groans, "If they haven't swapped Peaches' and Chelsea's names over, I'm not paying them for tonight."

Shaking my head at my cousin's complaining, the other

couples make their way inside the reception room, dancing as they go to a Bruno Mars' number, and then it's Cameron and my turn next.

Taking a deep breath, I slowly blow it out. I'm not a fan of being the center of attention. While all the other girls in the bridal party are lapping it up, I'm dreading this thirty-second walk.

Cameron notices my puffed cheeks and jagged breath and rubs his free hand on my arm linked with his.

"Ready?" he asks.

"As I'll ever be," I reply before taking another deep breath.

"Best man, Cameron Chase, and Bridesmaid, Chelsea Mitchell," the announcer booms through the speakers.

I'm not sure if it's the sight of three hundred people looking at us as the ballroom doors open or the fact that Cameron is still lightly rubbing my arm that has my stomach jumping all over the place.

It's the longest thirty seconds of my life as we walk across the dance floor, me gripping onto Cameron's arm for dear life. The dance floor isn't as slippery as I imagined, possibly since I've worn these shoes on a concrete surface now and 'broken' them in.

Noticing my parents sitting at a table next to the dance floor, my mom raises her eyebrows at the sight of me with Cameron. I shoot her a look as though to say, "Don't start, please."

Her dream is to marry me off and for me to give her grandchildren. Even though I've often told her I still have plenty of time for all of that, and I want to concentrate on my career for now, she still manages to sneak a comment into a conversation from time to time.

My parents were unable to have any more children after me. Mom had complications with my birth, and they were forced to do a hysterectomy not long after I was born. Mom has always said I'm their everything, and they only want the very best for me in life. They gave me the best start possible, and I'm hoping that I make them proud.

We were told we're meant to split as we reach the other side of the dance floor and walk to opposites sides of the bridal table as girls are on one side and the guys on the other. But Cameron walks with me, and I'm so grateful to him.

"You don't have to," I whisper while trying to keep the plastered smile on my face.

"I couldn't let go," he replies. "I'd never forgive myself if you fell."

A smile pulls at my lips as he walks me around the back of the table to my seat. I notice that Amanda is already sitting where I should be. Our place cards have been switched around.

"Looks like you get the chair next to the bride, too," she groans.

If she hadn't been such a bitch earlier, I would have told her to swap them back. Glancing up at Cameron, a smirk plays on my lips as I shrug my shoulders.

He leans down, his lips hovering near my ear. "You're one spot closer to me."

Before letting me go, he leans forward and brushes his lips against my cheek. My breath catches in my chest.

My cheeks begin to feel warm as he lets go of my arm and walks to his chair only three seats away from me.

Did he just kiss my cheek?

Why are you acting like it's never happened before? It's a friendly gesture, that's all.

Frozen on the spot, the crackle of the microphone over the speaker shocks me back to reality, and I stand behind my chair as Sara and Matthew are introduced. The glass of champagne on the table is much too alluring, so I grab it, taking a big sip.

Watching as Sara and Matthew slowly walk inside the room,

the guests erupt in applause. As they hit the middle of the dance floor, Matthew twirls Sara as she had told me, but they then break out into a little dance number they've prepared.

It's less than thirty seconds long, and Sara remains on the spot most of the time, her puffed skirt swaying from side to side, mimicking movement. But at the end, Matthew dips Sara, and they finish with a passionate kiss in the middle of the dance floor. A chorus of ooh's and ahh's echoes throughout the ballroom.

As Matthew and Sara sit down, they begin to serve our meals.

Time flies as the reception goes on, and after the awkward Maid of Honor speech is done by Amanda, who gushes a million times at how lucky Sara is and how beautiful she looks, Cameron stands and fumbles with his suit jacket as a panicked look washes over his face.

"Umm, looks like we have a bit of a technical difficulty here, folks." He laughs down the microphone. "The Best Man has lost his speech, but lucky in this day and age, that I took a photo of it on my cell. Please bear with me."

Pulling out his device, he scrolls through it quickly as though he's desperate to find this speech. He taps on the screen before using both fingers to try to maximize it but looks to be struggling.

"You know what... I'll do it from memory." He chuckles as the wedding guests laugh at his misfortune. "I promise I won't embarrass either of you. I had many witty comments planned and a few stories from years gone by, but being here, at this moment, it doesn't seem right anymore. I only want to offer you both my congratulations and thank you for giving me such an important role in your wedding. I love you both. Let's clink our glasses and congratulate the newly married couple. To Sara and Matthew."

The guests all raise the glasses in front of them and repeat

Cameron's toast. Glasses clink as Sara and Matthew lean toward each other for a kiss.

Cameron pauses briefly for a drink. "To the groomsmen I had the honor of getting to know today. Matthew is lucky to have you guys by his side. To the bridesmaids, it was a rocky start this morning, worrying for your friend and finding a replacement bridesmaid, but you all look absolutely amazing today..."

A laugh catches in my throat, and it quickly turns into a snort. Sara shoots me a look before twisting back to Cameron. He's noticed my laugh at what he said, and his grin grows larger.

"To the bridal party," he calls, holding out his glass.

As I repeat the words, I can't help but giggle.

Cameron ends his speech before Sara and Matthew take turns delivering their speeches. If I were a betting woman, I'd have placed my life savings on Sara crying, and I would've made a small fortune from it.

Matthew tried his hardest to remain calm but broke down toward the end. I can only imagine what an emotional day a wedding is for the bride and groom, with months or years of planning for this special day and hoping upon hope that it all goes as planned. They had a very shaky start to the morning, but I feel that it's gone as well as any other wedding I've attended, not that I'm an expert in weddings by any means.

Sara leans toward me as I take another sip of my sparkling wine. I know I should slow down with the alcohol, but it's very easy to drink.

"Dancing now. We'll get up first, and then with the second song, each couple will be called to join us before our parents are called up."

Gulping down the wine, I slowly nod at Sara's information. Dread washes over me. However, the only bonus is that I now have my ballet flats on, and I have less of a chance of tripping than I did earlier tonight.

Glancing over at Cameron, I notice he's taken his suit jacket off. His crisp, white shirt fitting his body perfectly and showing off his fine physique.

Having watched Sara and Matthew do their first official dance as a married couple, Cameron leans over and whispers, "Care to dance?" He extends a hand for me.

Slowly twisting my head to look at him, I take his hand before saying, "Yes."

He helps me from my seat, and we wait until we're called to the dance floor. Seconds later, Cameron leads me to the dance floor before taking me into the waltz position. It's a slow song from the movie *Twilight* which is Sara's favorite. Cameron and I begin to move as the chorus plays through the speakers.

His hand splays on the small of my back, and my breath hitches at his touch. I lean into his shoulder, the woodsy scent of his aftershave a complete turn-on.

"Hmm," I whisper as he moves me around the floor.

My eyes flutter closed as I allow myself to get lost in this moment. He brings our clasped hands to his chest and rests his cheek on the top of my head. Even though we're on a dance floor with many other people, this moment between us is intimate and something I've never experienced before. I never want this song to end.

"Enjoying this?" he asks.

"I am. It's nice." I cringe at my comment. "I thought you said you can't dance."

"Don't dance… I never said I can't."

Our feet barely move as we sway along to the music. He lightly caresses his thumb against my back, and my heart skips a beat. In these three minutes that we've been dancing, I can feel there's a sweet passion between us. The lust I felt for him earlier is now gone. There's a chemistry between Cameron and me.

As the song ends, Cameron leans down and whispers in my

Alana Jade

ear, "Would you like to go and get some fresh air?"

I nod my reply as words fail me right now. My heart is beating erratically as he slides his hand into mine, our fingers interlocking.

That was some dance with this amazing man, and I'm looking forward to spending a few minutes alone with him.

Maybe it's the sparkling wine letting my walls come down or the wedding talk, but what's between Cameron and me is something I'd never thought I'd experience in such a short time of knowing someone.

This dance has been the fuel to the fire between us. Regardless of what happens tonight, I hope I can remember this sweetness between us, a far cry from the last male I was interested in.

The way I was treated by a guy in my freshman year of college was disgusting and turned me off men for the longest time. Sure, I've begun seeing men after that, but I never felt anything more than friendship for them, plus study and then work always got in the way.

I owe it to myself to see what happens between Cameron and me. Perhaps have a little unattached fun. Isn't that what you do when you're in your twenties and single? But I'm going to embrace what we have right now. This has been nothing short of a divine pleasure.

CAMERON

Grasping at Chelsea's hand, I guide her out of the ballroom and to a small but secluded sitting area toward the back of the hotel.

"This area is really pretty," Chelsea remarks as she looks around at the golden drapes on the window, the same style as the ones drawn behind the bridal party's table. We both sit in the double dark leather chair in front of the window. I fix the cushion behind me slightly before laying back into it.

The area isn't as brightly lit as the ballroom but is much more suitable for getting to know someone.

We sit in silence for a few moments. Each time our eyes meet, we both awkwardly smile at each other before looking away. Deciding I need to break the ice, I think of a generic thing to say. "Glad the night's nearly over?"

"Yes and no."

"Both?" I laugh.

"Yes, because I can't wait to get out of this itchy dress," she groans, tugging at the frill around her neck."

"It doesn't look comfortable." I laugh.

"It's not the worst bridesmaid dress I've seen. A friend from med school got married about a year ago, and she had her girls wearing these lemon-yellow dresses with a large hat in the same color and a parasol. They all looked like Little Bo Peep." A roar of laugher escapes Chelsea, and her laugh is music to my ears.

"Doesn't sound appealing. And no?"

"Sorry?" she asks.

"You said yes and no... you didn't tell me what the no is."

My eyes fixate on her mouth as she draws in a corner. In my eyes, it's the sexiest move a woman can make, and it drives me wild.

Keep yourself calm, Cameron. You don't want to come across as desperate.

"Ah, well. Umm... no, because I'm kinda having a good time... with you." A pink hue forms on her cheeks as she looks away from me.

"I know what you mean. That's how I feel, too."

Chelsea clasps her hands together on her lap before slowly turning her head back to me. A smile pulls at the corner of her lips as our eyes connect.

"I'm going to do the manly thing and ask something I wouldn't normally ask."

"Okay," she whispers. Her eyes never leaving mine.

"Can I kiss you, Chelsea?"

Her smile grows, and she offers a quick nod as a reply.

Extending my hand to her face, I brush my fingers across her soft skin before cradling her ear and leaning toward her.

Her eyes flutter closed as our lips connect.

It's a soft, barely-there kiss, as though I'm testing to see whether she enjoys it or not.

Leaning back slightly, I search her face for a sign to continue, and I instantly see a smile growing on her lips.

Taking that as my yes, I lean in again. As we connect this time, my lips massage hers as I slide my hand to the back of her head and deepen our kiss.

Chelsea moans slightly, opening her mouth, and I run my tongue along her lips, hoping she opens a little wider.

As though someone is talking on a microphone, a noise from the ballroom has Chelsea pushing on my chest.

As we break apart, she looks up at me, slightly breathless. "Did you hear what they said?" Her brows furrowing.

"No, I didn't. I was kind of engrossed in what we were doing." I laugh.

But Chelsea's brows remain knitted together. "Maybe we'd better go and check. Bridesmaid and Best Man duty and all."

"As long as we can do that at least once more tonight." I smile.

She softens as her lips pull to one side. "I think we can arrange that. Do you... ah, maybe, want to come up to my room once the wedding wraps up?" she asks me, a slight slur noticeable in her voice.

"That'd be nice. But do you want to come to mine? I have a suite."

She nods. "Sure."

Heading back to the ballroom, we notice there's a big circle being formed. "Shit, Sara and Matthew are leaving. It's lucky we got back," she whispers as we try to find a spot amongst all the guests.

The goodbye circle hasn't been fully formed yet. Luckily for us they did have a lot of wedding guests, so it doesn't look like we were missed too much when they were getting ready.

Matthew gets to me first and throws his arms around my neck. I have no idea how many beers or wine he's had tonight, but he looks about as good as he did the night after he sat for his bar exams. As he mumbles incomprehensible things to me, I laugh at his behavior. If Sara expected a loved-up night with her new husband tonight, she might have a surprise in store for her.

Once he's finished with me, Sara hugs me and thanks me for being their Best Man.

"It's my pleasure," I reply. "You going to be okay with him tonight?"

She chuckles. "Yeah, I'll let him sleep it off for a couple of hours while I watch the next few episodes of *Project Runway*."

"Have a great time in Mykonos." I smile before placing a kiss on her cheek.

"Thanks, Cam," she replies before taking a step toward Chelsea.

They embrace for the longest time, both uttering words to each other that I can't hear. A tear falls from Chelsea's eye, and she quickly stops it before it hits Sara's dress.

They both mumble, "Love you," before Sara moves around the circle. It's lovely seeing cousins close. I never see mine and only ever hear from them when they want or need some free medical advice. It makes it slightly harder being an only child and not close with your extended family.

A short time later, we stand at the front of the large group waving goodbye to Sara and Matthew. They are staying in a suite at the hotel where we had photos taken this morning, and mine is two suites down from them.

Some of the guests come back into the ballroom and sit down or go back to the dance floor as others collect their belongings and say goodbye for the night.

I was sure Chelsea was right next to me, but as I look down to talk to her, she's disappeared. Searching the room, I notice she's hugging a couple who were sitting at the table with Sara's parents. They could be Chelsea's parents. She walks with her arms linked in each of the couple's and shows them out of the ballroom.

While I wait for her to come back, I grab myself a couple of beers and sit back at the bridal table. The other bridesmaids are nowhere in sight.

Thank God.

Most of the other groomsmen have left except for Matthew's cousin, who's looking a little green around the edges, and after his father comes over to tell him they are leaving, Pete dashes to the bathroom.

"Ah, to be young again," Matthew's uncle laughs.

Chuckling at what he says, I reply, "I'm not sure it's just for the young."

He looks at the beer bottles on the table in front of me. "Maybe you should stop for the night now, too. Anyway, I'd better go and find him before his mother does. Have a good night, bud."

"You, too."

Taking a swig of my beer, I look around for my suit jacket before noticing it slipped off the back of the chair and fell on the floor. Bending down to collect it, a familiar voice brings a smile to my face.

"Hey," she drawls.

"Hello. Where did you go?"

"Seeing my parents out. I gave them my room for the night, so Dad doesn't have to drive home tonight. His eyesight at night isn't as good as it used to be."

"My father has the beginning of nyctalopia, too. Even though we deal with life and death daily, nothing prepares you for watching your parents get a little older and their bodies starting to fail them."

"So true."

A waitress walks past with a tray of wine, and Chelsea takes two from her.

"So..." She grins at me, stumbles slightly then takes a sip from one of the glasses.

"So," I reply. "How many have you had?"

"Not many. Like four."

"You sure?"

"No, but I'll say four. I still know what I'm doing, though." She cheekily pokes out her tongue before taking another drink.

I can't talk. I've had more than my fair share of beer mixed with wine tonight. It's a wedding. You're expected to drink and celebrate.

"You now don't have a room for the night. Are you planning on going home?" I tease.

"Well, this handsome guy did suggest we'd go to his room. I'm hoping his offer is still valid." She nibbles at the corner of her lip.

My dick twitches in my pants.

Hell, yeah.

"It very much is. Want to finish our drinks, and we'll head out?"

She nods before her face contorts. "Ah shit, I'll have to swing by the room I was going to use. My parents are leaving my bag of things outside for me. They wanted me to stay at the wedding and enjoy the night rather than collecting it now."

"Won't they be suspicious of where you're staying?" I curiously ask.

"I'm in my late twenties. My dad doesn't care, and I'm sure if my mom thought I was hooking up with a random at Sara's wedding, she'd be secretly hoping I get pregnant." Her hand flies to her mouth at her overshare.

My eyes widen at her comment.

Pregnant?

She laughs at my expression. "I have no idea why I said that. Why do words seem to fly from my mouth when I'm around you? It's like I've known you forever, but it could be the alcohol." She giggles.

"I know what you mean," I whisper. My voice hasn't fully returned from the shock of her previous statement.

"Forget what I said before. I'm a doctor, I know how babies are made, and I'm on as many contraceptives as I can take to prevent it from happening."

"Glad that we got that straight. I'm the same. No kids yet." I laugh.

"I'm happy someone understands it because my mom sure as hell doesn't. Can I ask how old you are?"

"Forty-three."

"And you *still* don't want kids?" Her voice raises a decibel on the final word.

"I want them but not yet. I'd like to marry before kids come along. I'd love to add Chief to my title within the next few years as well."

"Yes, that's a highlight in a doctor's career, that's for sure."

Chelsea downs the rest of her wine as I take the final swig of my beer.

"Let's go." I smile.

This isn't me.

I don't take girls to my room, but I also haven't been this drunk in many years.

Chelsea links her fingers in mine as we walk from the ballroom and head to my suite.

I'm not sure if you can have these instant feelings for someone else or if it's the alcohol talking, but I sure as hell feel something drawing me toward Chelsea, and I'm keen to see where it may lead.

CHELSEA

A mix of nerves and excitement floods my body as we walk down the corridor toward Cameron's suite. The alcohol cursing through my body has only added another level to my emotions.

Cameron stops several times to push me up against the wall for a passionate kiss. Each time we break apart, my lips tingle, and I instantly wish they were back on mine.

"One-five-oh-eight." I find myself counting much louder than it is in my head as I swing the bag I just collected from my room, back and forth.

"Shh," Cameron hushes.

I'm giggly and slightly uneasy on my feet, but then again, I'm sure everyone who attended the wedding today assumed I was drunk from the moment I walked down the aisle in those ridiculous shoes.

"Here we are," Cameron announces.

While I'm sure he's at least tipsy, he's a lot more stable on his feet than I am, and he is acting as though he's not affected by the alcohol at all. I guess that's the difference between someone who's five-foot-eight and one-hundred and twenty-five pounds and someone who's easily six-foot-three and possibly two-hundred well-distributed pounds.

He unlocks the door and pushes it in before flicking the light switch on the inside wall. The room lights up, and a beautifully decorated suite is before us, from the dark beige carpet with the hotel's logo to the bouquet of roses matching the color of the ones in the wedding come into view. This is luxury.

Holding the door open for me, Cameron invites me inside with a wave of his hand. I place my duffel bag down on the carpet as I walk over to the plush couch and run my hands along the cushions. But it's the view that has caught my eye. San Francisco Bay is stunning at night. I'm not sure I've ever fully seen it at such a height.

Standing at the full-length window, I gaze out into the Bay and momentarily forget where I am and who I'm with.

Cameron walks up behind me and slides his arms around my waist, startling me.

"Sorry, I didn't mean to scare you," he apologizes as he nuzzles into the crook of my neck.

"It's fine. I was daydreaming," I reply, as I raise my shoulder and move my head to cradle his. My arm automatically slides over Cameron's as warmth spreads through my body.

Cameron kisses my shoulder before spinning me around and pressing me against the glass window. His gesture catches me off guard as I look down, and all I can see is how high up we are. As his lips find mine, I close my eyes, trying to block out my newfound fear of heights which has somewhat been made worse by the amount of alcohol in my system.

As much as I don't want to, I break our kiss and gently push on his chest.

"Are you all right?" he asks.

"Fine, just a little acrophobia. Do you mind if I use the

bathroom?" I ask, desperate to get away from the window.

Normally, I love views from a height, but I can never stand on the edge of a cliff and look down. Even images of people standing in ridiculous places and looking down give me the heebie-jeebies.

He nods as his lips twist into a smile. "Of course."

Standing in front of the bathroom mirror, I decide to wipe the residual lipstick from my mouth and tidy up the remainder of my makeup. A few smears have appeared over my face from Cameron and my make-out sessions.

After deciding that it looks as good as it will get, I head out of the bathroom. Walking back to Cameron, I decide to show some initiative and throw my arms around his neck before pulling him into a deep and needy kiss.

A gasp escapes him as he wraps his arms around my body and gently lifts me, carrying me over to the huge king-size bed.

Placing me down on top of the shiny white covers, he peppers kisses from my mouth down to my neck, over my body, and down to my toes before removing my ballet flats.

"Silly question, but how do you get all of this... ah, material off?" He laughs.

A chuckle escapes me as I stand back up and madly try to find the dress's side zipper and hope and pray it doesn't get stuck. Cameron holds the material taut as I slide the zipper down.

As the frills of tulle fall from my body, a wave of relief goes with it.

"Thank goodness," I cry.

"Funny, I was thinking of thanking God right now," he teases.

Standing before Cameron wearing nothing but my mismatched beige strapless bra and white panties, his eyes run from my head to my toes as though he's taking in every inch of my body.

"I think someone's too dressed," I quip.

He begins to unbutton his shirt, but I stop him.

"Let me," I mutter.

With each button I undo, I kiss down his chest, a ripple of muscle becoming more and more evident along with his golden tan.

"Hmm..." I murmur. "Someone loves the sun."

"That I do."

Sliding the shirt from his shoulders, I press my lips to his chest as his hands sweep up and down my sides.

A wave of goosebumps forms on my skin as I slightly wriggle at the ticklish sensation.

My hands slide down his body, following his masculine form, and stop at the waistband of his pants. Without looking, I wrestle with his belt buckle before realizing it's not a standard metal loop and pin, more like a clamp.

"This is difficult." I laugh.

"It's meant to be much easier to undo," he replies before adding a chuckle at the end.

"Can you tell I'm a little out of practice?" I whisper, embarrassed by my lack of belt skills.

"Don't worry. It's been a while for me, too." He hooks his finger under my chin to lift my head to meet his.

As our eyes meet, a smile creeps onto my lips as butterflies take flight low in my belly. He lowers his head to mine and presses the softest kiss on my lips as I finally undo the belt buckle and pull it out from the loops of his pants.

After undoing the button and finally the zipper, I slide the suit pants as far down as I can reach without breaking our kiss.

"Hmm..." he hums against my mouth.

He grips onto my hips as he gently steps me back toward the bed.

Cameron's kisses move to my cheek and ear before moving

down my neck as his hands slide up my back to the clasp of my bra.

"Hopefully, this isn't a difficult one," he mumbles into my collarbone. I smile as I tilt my neck to the side, allowing him better access.

With a flick of his fingers, my bra is undone, and he slides it out between us, holding it out as he drops it to the floor.

His hands instantly come back to my breasts, his warm palms massaging them as he continues to kiss along my shoulder.

A slow moan escapes my mouth as his thumb runs around my nipple before plucking at the soft pink peak.

I'm not sure I've ever had someone give such gentle attention to my breasts. The other guys I've been with have been rather rough, but not Cameron. Even the soft pinch on my nipple sends a shiver down my spine as blood rushes between my legs, making me desperate to get things moving.

Pushing against his chest again, I hook my fingers into the top of his tight-fitting boxer shorts and push them down, his dick springing free from its cotton confinement.

Slowly, I begin to lower myself down, playfully licking my lips as Cameron watches.

"Oh no, I want to pleasure you," he whispers.

"Let me do this first," I murmur as I sink to my knees.

The moment I wrap my fingers around his length, Cameron throws his head back and lets out a deep, guttural moan. My center tingles at the sound.

Gently moving my hand back and forth, I quickly form a rhythm before my tongue juts out and licks the bulbous head.

"Argh," he groans. "This is delightful torture."

Guiding his length into my mouth, I moan as it touches the back of my throat. As my tongue massages the underside of his dick, I gently suck him before pulling back and plunging his cock further into my mouth.

Cameron gently pushes on the back of my head so I can take a little more of him. I try to stop myself from gagging at the sensation. I'm not sure I've ever had one this size in my mouth before.

As I slowly move my mouth up and down his length, he begins to writhe.

"You'd better stop, or I'll come," he pants out.

I do as I'm asked and pull him from my mouth. Flicking my tongue over the tip, I savor the taste of his pre-cum.

Standing, I gently wipe any saliva or precum from my lips, knowing that the other men I've been with definitely don't want to taste themselves on my lips.

"Don't worry about that. I plan on doing the same to you in about thirty seconds."

My breath hitches at the thought. If he's half as good at licking me as he is with his kissing, then I'm in for a real treat.

CHAPTER 6

CAMERON

Gently pushing Chelsea down on the bed, I watch as her perfect breasts bounce before settling into place.

She's still much too dressed for my liking. I hook my fingers into the top of her panties and slide them down her legs. She lifts slightly to help me get them off completely.

Before moving toward her, I kick my shoes off and remove my pants and boxers.

Gently reaching out to touch her well-groomed mound, I swipe my finger down her center before bringing it back up and then parting her lips to expose one of the most beautiful pussies I've ever seen. It's taking all I have not to plunge deep into her now and bring her to the highest of highs, but I know that it's only fair to bring her to the brink first, just as she's done to me.

"Slide down here a little," I encourage, and she does as I ask.

Pushing her legs apart, I slide to my knees and swipe my finger over her middle again, spreading her juices.

Bringing a finger to my lips, I pop it into my mouth and taste her sweetness. Heaven.

Leaning forward between her legs, I gently spread her lips before nudging her clit with my nose. She jumps a little at the sensation.

"Are you all right?"

"Hmm," she moans.

My tongue flicks out over her clit before moving to her entrance and back again. Sucking her bud into my mouth, I tease it with my tongue and apply slightly more pressure.

"Oh," she pants as she arches her back from the bed.

Reaching out, I slide my hand up her abdomen to her breast as she flattens herself back onto the mattress. I gently roll her nipple between my thumb and finger before sliding my hand back down to her pussy.

Extending a finger, I gently tease her opening before carefully sliding inside.

Seeing her writhing about has my dick aching. He's as hard as he has ever been and needs some relief.

After adding a second finger, I pump in and out of her as I rub at her clit over and over. I then notice her knees are trying to come together, trapping my head like a vice.

"Want me to make you come, gorgeous?" I ask as I move my head back to her pussy, my voice creating vibrations against her center.

"Yes," she cries.

Driving my fingers into her several more times, I still them inside her before wiggling them back and forth, hitting her spot. Sucking in her clit much harder than before, I hum against it, and she instantly releases her legs as an orgasm washes over her.

"Ahh," she wails before going limp on the bed.

Releasing the pressure on her clit, I smile against her as I watch the tension turn to relaxation. Again, stilling my fingers, I wait until she has ridden out her orgasm before removing them and sucking them clean.

"How was that?" I ask her as I place my elbows onto the soft mattress between her legs and rest my head on my hands.

"Holy shit," she pants.

"You ain't seen nothing yet." I laugh.

Reaching out to my pants, I fumble for the pocket and fetch my wallet before pulling out a condom.

"Would you mind if I have a drink first?" she asks, "My mouth is dry." She silently chuckles at her own words.

"Of course," I reply as she sits up on the bed.

Standing, I walk to the mini bar and grab two bottles from the small refrigerator before walking back to Chelsea and handing her one.

We both crack the lid at the same time and down quite a bit of the bottle. Chelsea replaces her lid before crawling over to the side table and placing it down.

Walking around the other side, I place my bottle down before pushing back the covers on the bed and jumping in.

My hand works at my cock to get him as hard as can be again, but one look at Chelsea's sexy ass in the air, and he's ready to go.

Sliding the condom down my length, I squeeze the tip and adjust as need be before reaching out to Chelsea.

"Come here, sexy," I mutter.

She crawls over to me and massages my length before placing her lips over mine.

Encouraging her to lay down, she has other plans and pushes back the covers a little further before sliding her leg over the top of me.

Grabbing my cock, I begin to tease her entrance with it, running it back and forth.

Chelsea puffs slightly in frustration, the little pout adorable on her lips.

"All in good time, sweetheart." My lips twitch into a smile.

"I want you now, Cameron."

Holding onto my shoulders, she leans down to kiss me again before guiding my length inside of her. A moan escapes her as she takes as much as she can.

She stills for a moment, and I search her eyes with mine. Within seconds, she begins to move up and down my length, going a little deeper each time.

Screwing my eyes shut, I will myself to calm down. Her tight channel is getting me much too excited too fast.

Slow down, Cam... slow down, I think to myself.

After letting her be in control for a few minutes, I gently flip her onto her back, staying inside her as we move. I encourage her legs to bend at the knee and run my hands along them before leaning down and kissing Chelsea with force.

Sliding out of her, I push back in as deep as before, and her back instantly arches at the sensation—I know I've hit a sweet spot there.

Chelsea releases a satisfied moan before angling her hips so she can take me deeper again. As much as I'm trying to go slow to enjoy this, the alcohol in my system isn't going to allow me to hold out much longer.

Running my hand over her breast, I cup her face and bring my lips to hers. My kisses are much hotter than before as my release draws closer.

Her nails dig into my shoulder and run down my back as I feel her tighten around my cock. Surely, she's close as well.

Sliding hard and fast into her, her body begins to writhe beneath me.

"Close, sexy?" I pant against her lips.

"Hmm," she purrs.

Chelsea's hands grab my ass as I rest my elbows next to her body, my fingers brushing the loose strands of hair from her face. I want a perfect view when I bring her to orgasm.

"Open your eyes," I beg.

She does as I ask before her brows pull together.

"Cameron. Yes," she groans.

Crashing my lips to hers, I plunge into her two, maybe three times before she drags her knees up toward her and moans into my mouth. Her pussy grips me before releasing me as a gentle shake takes over her body, forcing her eyes to close.

Watching her release take hold, I push once more before I still and explode inside of her.

"Fuck," the word draws out as my heart beats out of my chest.

I haven't come inside a girl for a long time now, and I've almost forgotten how good it feels.

She milks me for everything I have, and I've never felt so good.

Still inside her, I allow her to ride out her orgasm, my cock still slightly spasming as her eyes flutter open, and a sweet smile spreads across her lips.

My arms begin to shake from resting my body weight on them for such a long time, and I decide to withdraw from Chelsea slowly before rolling on my side.

"Wow." She beams.

"You're telling me," I reply.

Sitting up slightly, I remove the condom and knot it before getting up from the bed to find a trash can.

"I think I could do that over and over." Chelsea laughs, her words slightly slurred as she reaches to where her bottle of water is located. She sits up slightly to have a drink.

Deciding that's a great idea, I throw the used condom in the trash can before heading to the table where my water is.

"I'm not sure I could do it over and over, but I could enjoy spending hours looking at you and your gorgeous body."

After taking a long drink, I place my bottle back down and crawl onto the bed. Placing my hands on either side of Chelsea's body, my lips find hers before pushing her back against the plush pillows.

As much as I'd love to take her again, right now, my cock isn't playing nice. He isn't even at half-mast. Perhaps this is my punishment for drinking too many beers.

"Maybe he needs some help." Chelsea grins.

"Perhaps this is what happens when middle-aged men drink too much at weddings." I chuckle.

"Hardly middle-aged. No, he just needs some encouragement." She playfully licks her lips.

Pushing against me, she rolls me over this time and begins to play with me. Her delicate fingers gently wrap around my cock and slowly massage him.

The night has been so much more than I ever expected it to be.

Chelsea is the surprise at this wedding.

But this is only one night.

Neither of us wants anything more.

Two grown adults are more than capable of having casual sex without feelings getting in the way. Can't they?

CHAPTER 7

CHELSEA

Lifting myself off Cameron, I flop onto the bed as he disposes of the second condom. His chest is rising and falling in quick succession.

My orgasm was nowhere near as strong as last time, but it still had me seeing stars.

I'm regretting drinking as much as I have tonight. It's made my already fatigued body absolutely exhausted. But in some ways, it's given me the courage to be bolder and take control, something I'd rarely do when sober.

After drinking the rest of the water from my bottle, I twist on my side to face Cameron. Usually, I'd be embarrassed at having my body on clear display with the lights on and drapes still open, but right now, I don't care.

Propping myself on my elbow, I take in every inch of his amazing body and begin to wish that this was something I saw daily.

But we haven't had a chance to speak about anything more. Sure, we live in the same city, and there's something between us, but it's a wedding fling with great sex—amazing, mind-blowing sex with a great guy I met at a wedding. Wedding flings don't last.

Trust you to start thinking too heavily, Chelsea.

Screwing my eyes shut to stop myself from thinking, I quickly open them again and notice Cameron is now mirroring my position on the bed.

"Getting tired?" he asks.

"Slightly, but I can hold out."

He leans forward and places a kiss on my lips before moving back to his side of the bed.

Reaching out, I run my fingers through the patch of gray and dark chest hairs before sliding my hand over his muscled abdomen.

"Do you think doctors know how to have fantastic sex because we know the body parts?" I blurt out. The words escape my lips before I've even processed them.

What the hell are you saying? It's as though every thought I have flies from my mouth, my filter having been removed.

Cameron roars with laughter.

"Possibly," he says between laughs. After a few moments, he calms down. "Do you have sex with doctors often?"

"No. Not at all. You're the first doctor I've been with, and it's the best sex I've ever had."

My mind screams at me to shut up, but I'm not able to.

"The best, hey?" He grins. "That's the nicest compliment I've ever had, so thank you."

"So, what happens from here?" I ask, willing myself to stop talking.

"We enjoy this night together and see how we feel in the morning."

A rush of disappointment floods my body. Am I just a bit of

fun for him? I was sure the feelings I felt earlier were being reciprocated.

He twists around and flicks a switch, and the two lamps on the side tables both switch off.

"Tired?" I ask, my lips twisting into a smile.

"Well, someone has completely exhausted me. It's what happens when you get old."

"Hardly old, Cameron. You're like, what, only fifteen years older than me?"

"Geez, thanks, Chelsea. That means I was a teenager when you were born." He chuckles.

"I didn't mean it like that. Ignore me... it's the alcohol. You probably think I'm the biggest idiot right now," I mumble.

"Hardly. I think it's cute. It's like you're telling it like it is."

My lips pull up at the side as I look away from Cameron.

"I might use the bathroom and then turn off the other lights," I tell Cameron, whose eyes look like they are getting heavier by the second.

"Thanks," he whispers.

Before I switch the last light off, I find my cell in my bag and turn on the flashlight. After flicking the switch, I make my way back to bed, only to find Cameron lightly snoring.

Even in the dim light of my flashlight, he looks so handsome, laying on his side with one arm tucked under his head. His dark hair with this one patch of silver is a mess but in such a sexy way.

Giggling to myself that I've tired him out, I switch the light off my phone and place it on the side table before crawling back into the bed and snuggling into Cameron.

Maybe I should've put my underwear back on, but part of me is hoping to be rolled over in the middle of the night and taken hard and fast, or maybe I'll crawl on top of him. I have to make the most of this one night of pleasure because I'm not sure when I'll get the opportunity to have a weekend off like this again in the foreseeable future.

My eyes grow heavy as Cameron's arm snakes around my waist, holding me against him. The heat radiating from him is enough to warrant not having a blanket over us.

As my eyes close, the buzz of my cell startles me.

Who in the hell is texting me at this time of the night?

It better not be Sara. Surely, she's still enjoying her wedding night. I certainly have.

Lightly groaning, I reach out and grab the device and slide the screen on, the brightness in the dark room almost burning my retinas.

Cameron groans before letting go of me and rolling over.

"Sorry," I whisper.

It's a message from my colleague, Ava. We're both residents at the hospital and are being supervised by Dr. Arthur.

Tapping the screen to open it, she's telling me about the new doctor who will be supervising us, encouraging me to google him.

Right at the end of the message, she's typed his name, and it takes me several seconds to process it.

Cameron Chase.

Are my eyes deceiving me?

Is this for real?

Reading the message over and over, it eventually sinks in.

Cameron will be my new supervising doctor at the hospital.

I've just slept with my new supervisor.

Holy shit.

Getting out of the bed, I walk to the small couch near the large window in the other room and flop onto it before opening my search engine and typing in his name.

Sure enough, a photo appears and confirms my worst fears. My stomach twists, and I begin to shake. The hospital has strict rules about staff forming relationships. But surely that doesn't count if you didn't know each other worked there.

Continuing to scroll down, page after page appears listing all the amazing things Cameron has done in his career as a surgeon at his last hospital. He's fantastic, but I already knew that.

I knew he was a doctor but never thought to ask where he worked or what his specialty is.

Questions begin to form in my mind. The more I think, the more I need to ask.

Will this mean the end of my residency? Will I need to complete my residency somewhere else?

I'm only glad that I'm staying in general surgery. I could've been paired with a vascular or orthopedic surgeon, specialties I'm not keen on pursuing.

Can I request a new supervisor? Or swap with someone? But what will I tell them as my reason?

All I know for sure is that I have two options right now. Crawl back into that bed and go to sleep, pretending I know nothing of this and enjoy the final few hours together or flee now, hoping he doesn't remember me when he starts at the hospital. I mean, it's a slim chance, and I don't think he knows my last name.

But he's seen much more than just your face, Chelsea.

Standing from the couch, I pace to the suite door and back to the couch, walking over and over, trying to find some clear thought in my mind.

Sleep isn't likely to happen for me now, even though my body is aching to rest.

The smart thing for me to do is collect all of my belongings and get out of here as quickly and quietly as I can.

However, it's the shit thing to do. We've had the most amazing night together, but if he knew the reason, he'd completely understand, I'm sure.

I'm doing this for both of us.

Switching the flashlight back on my cell, I dress in the clothes

I wore to Sara's house and tidy my hair before bundling my bridesmaid dress into the bag. While I can easily locate my ballet flats, I can't find the high-heeled shoes for the life of me, but they are one small sacrifice I'm more than willing to take.

Hooking my arm through the duffel bag, I walk back over to the bed and watch Cameron sleep for several minutes.

This was fun, but it was never going to be forever. One-night stands rarely are.

Bringing my fingers to my lips, I place a kiss on them before lowering it to Cameron's cheek, stopping short of touching his skin out of fear of waking him up.

"Bye, Cameron," I whisper as I turn to leave.

My chest feels heavy as the door clicks behind me.

Am I sad for leaving him? Yes.

But it's more than that. Maybe it's because I feel something for him.

It's only fear of missing out on something, Chelsea. Nothing more.

Walking down the corridor toward the elevator, a tear runs down my cheek. This feeling must be fear—fear for my career and training and what happens when Cameron realizes who I am.

In an instant, it's gone from the best night of my life to possibly the worst.

CHAPTER 8

CAMERON

The sun streaming in through the bedroom window wakes me from one of the best nights of sleep I've had in years. I'm rested, calm, and don't instantly feel like I have to down five cups of coffee to wake up.

Memories of the night before start to flood my mind, and a grin spreads across my face, even though my eyes aren't yet open.

Stretching out, I can't seem to feel anyone else in the bed with me. Either side of me is cool to the touch.

Rolling to my side, I reach out but again, nothing.

Has she already gotten up? Perhaps she's ordering room service for us.

Letting out a deep breath, I slowly pry my eyes open. The sun almost blinds me, and I quickly shut them again.

Carefully rolling to the other side, I begin to open my eyes again, testing how bright it is before eventually opening them.

I'm still lying on the side of the bed where I fell asleep. The bathroom door, which I'm now facing, is open, and the room is dark. The only sound I can hear within the suite is my feet moving against the bedsheet.

Where is she?

"Chelsea?" I croak before clearing my throat. "Chelsea?"

But there's no reply.

Did I dream the best night I've had in years? Definitely not.

Swinging my legs off the side of the bed, I haul myself up and scrub at my face. The slight prickle of my five o'clock shadow reminds me it's going to be annoying to grow my beard in again.

Glancing around the room, there's no sign of Chelsea at all. My brows furrow as I begin to wonder where she is.

Did she regret last night?

Did I do something to upset her?

Has she used me for sex?

Sure, she was drunk but not possibly drunk enough to spend the night in the bathroom.

My head pounds slightly as I stand, reminding me that I too had a bit too much to drink last night, but it's nothing a couple of Tylenol won't fix.

"Chelsea?" I call again.

But the silence is deafening.

Walking over to the small couch, I instantly notice her big, puffy pink dress is no longer there. This dress was something you couldn't miss.

Has she left?

My gut tells me she's long gone as I search the small suite. Perhaps she waited until I dozed off last night or woke in the middle of the night and panicked. I play our conversations over in my mind. I was sure we'd discussed having breakfast together this morning.

We both went into the night knowing it was a random bit of fun. There was no promise of forever or anything else. We were both consenting adults who had an itch to scratch and soothed each other's needs. It was nice to feel a sort of chemistry with someone again, though.

A wave of sadness washes over me as I collect the room service menu. I'm not exactly hungry, but I always make sure I have some form of food to start off the day, whether it be a protein shake or eggs and bacon. The latter is always a Sunday preference when I have the time, of course.

After placing my order, I have a quick shower and dress before packing my suit back into its clothing bag, another one to add to the collection at home. Luckily for me, they aren't like bridesmaid dresses that you wear once. Suits are much more universal, and I can easily change out a shirt or tie and wear this to a hospital benefit or other formal event.

As I collect my suit jacket from the floor, I instantly notice the sparkle of those stupid heels Chelsea was wearing yesterday. Hope surges through me before I realize I have no way of contacting her.

Sure, I could ask Matthew or Sara for it, but I'm not going to disturb newlyweds for a woman's number.

Shoving the shoes in my bag, I decide I'll wait until they return from their honeymoon to ask for Chelsea's number, or maybe I'll hand them back to Sara, and she can do as she pleases with them. Maybe this is how Chelsea wants it to be and doesn't want to see me again, and I have to accept that.

"I thought we had more of a connection than that," I tell myself.

The sad feeling is replaced by anger and a touch of hurt. If she wanted to use me, then that's fine, but I saw the look she gave me. There was more going on there.

She did the dog thing and ran from me in the middle of the night. She didn't even have the balls to wake me and say thank you or give me a bullshit excuse about why she has to go. She just left. Not once have I ever run on a girl in my life. Most of the time, we part ways before going to sleep, but on the odd occasion and we've both drifted off, we part amicably in the morning.

Calm down, Cameron. Breathe.

A knock sounds at the door, and I rush toward it, pulling it open. A small part of me wishes it's Chelsea, but I know better.

I'm greeted by a young man dressed in a deep burgundy-colored suit with a silver cart.

"Room service, sir," he quietly says.

Stepping aside to let him wheel the cart in, he places the tray with food covered on the small table in front of the couch before leaving.

The smell of coffee and bacon fills the room, and my mouth begins to water. Shaking my head, I puff a laugh at myself. So much for not being overly hungry. I'm suddenly ravenous.

Having eaten the food, I begin to wish I'd ordered two servings. I down the last of my coffee before checking my cell.

There's one text message from Matthew and an email from Maxim Walker, the new hospital's Chief of Surgery. Checking Matthew's first, I shake my head at my best friend's request.

> **Matthew:** *Thanks again, bro, for being my best man. We're off to the airport now. Can you collect my suit from the front desk on your way out? Sara's mom has already taken her dress, but they didn't take my suit. Hope you had a good night with Chelsea, man... let me know the details there.*

Deciding to play dumb, I give Matthew a generic reply.

> **Me:** *You're welcome. Have a safe flight. Yes, I'll collect your suit, and I'll drop it at your house. Spare key in the same place? Great wedding, man. Enjoy your*

honeymoon and talk to you WHEN YOU GET BACK.

Hesitating for a split second before I check the email, I contemplate checking my texts to see if there is one from Chelsea. But I scoff at my own stupid thought. We were too preoccupied to swap numbers last night, and even if we had, if she ran out on me in the middle of the night, why would she contact me now?

Taking a deep breath, I shake the last thought of Chelsea from my mind. She's gone, there's nothing I can do, and I'll move on with life, just as she has. Perhaps we should have had the conversation of what's next before hooking up. I'm only disappointed as I know we had a spark. Hopefully, I don't run into her at Matthew and Sara's house any time soon. That would be awkward for us both.

Sliding the email open, I give it a quick read. It's likely information about starting my new job—a job I'm more than excited about.

> **Dr. Maxim Walker:** *Morning, Cameron, and welcome to Mercy General. Your expertise is highly anticipated. We look forward to having you at our hospital. I have scheduled a meeting for us at 9 am on Monday the 15th in my office where we'll discuss your position and what's expected of you. Until then, Maxim.*

Throwing a glance at the clock to double-check the time, I decide to quickly respond to the Chief's email. The last thing I'd want to do is forget and end up in his bad books before I even start.

> **Me:** *Good morning, Dr. Walker. I'm looking forward to starting at Mercy General and learning your*

operations. I've added the meeting to my schedule for the 15th at 9 am, and I look forward to seeing you again. Best regards, Dr. Cameron Chase.

Polite, yet straight to the point. That's how I handle everything to do with my working life. When it comes to patients and their families, you're offering them hope. With fellow staff, you need to be civil as you have to work together as a team. Of course, I have disagreements from time to time and am often yelled or screamed at by desperate families, but I don't feel that you need to reverberate that negativity.

Learning from the best, my father, his favorite saying is, 'You catch more flies with honey than vinegar.' It's the way he projected himself as a doctor and eventually Chief of Surgery, and it's how I am as well.

Having collected my belongings, I do a final check of the room before heading down to the front desk to check out and collect the groom's suit.

This was a magical wedding, and the night that followed was even better. It's a shame it was tainted when I woke this morning. But I have a week off now before the new job starts, and I'm going to enjoy doing nothing in that time before life becomes hectic again.

CHELSEA

My head pounds as I roll over on the couch. It must be nearing lunchtime, but I don't care. All I want to do is sleep right now and pretend that the previous twenty-four hours hadn't happened.

Actually, that's a lie. Yesterday was absolutely fantastic. My only wish is that I hadn't checked that damn text message from Ava. I'd have remained oblivious to the fact that Cameron will be my new supervisor, starting sometime in the next month.

My stomach gurgles at the thought of seeing him again, and not knowing when makes it so much worse.

Even after telling myself over and over that leaving him last night was the best thing to do, I'm still wracked with guilt over doing something so low.

Guilt is something I shouldn't be feeling, though. It was a one night. We hadn't discussed the future. He used me for sex. Perhaps I used him as well, although I had real feelings behind it, I was sure he did too. But what's done is done, and I can't go back. Now I need to brace myself for what is possibly coming for me. I only wish I knew when he's starting at the hospital.

My cell dings on the coffee table, and I groan at the noise. I desperately want to ignore it. Today is a day off, a chance to recuperate and hope to God that I'm refreshed for my seven o'clock start tomorrow morning.

Deciding that I've put up with the pain in my head for much too long, I get up and head to the kitchen. Fumbling in my cupboard for Tylenol, I shake two tablets from the container before getting a glass of water to wash them down.

A bitter residue stays in my mouth even after I've swallowed the tablets, and I drink another glass of water to rid myself of the awful taste.

"Blah." I grimace and shake my head as I place my glass in the sink.

My cell begins to ring, and I groan as I walk back to the couch and swipe it up from the coffee table. It's Ava. I don't want to be talking about work stuff today with her.

My finger hovers over the swipe for a moment before I swipe the screen.

"Hey," I croak.

"Hey. How was last night?" she asks.

"It was a nice night. I ended up as a bridesmaid for my cousin... long story."

"A bridesmaid? Wow. It must have been a great night. You sound like shit today." She laughs.

"I had a glass of wine too many, I think. How could I resist the good stuff?" I half-chuckle a reply.

"I don't blame you. I'd have grabbed a bottle if it was the expensive shit. Take a couple of Tylenol. You'll be fine."

"Is that your professional opinion?" I tease as I flop onto the couch.

"Sure is. That, coffee, and greasy food always make my hangovers much better tolerated."

My stomach contorts at such a thought. There's no way in hell I can handle any form of food right now.

"Thanks, Dr. Saxon," I respond in a bubbly way.

Ava laughs at my tone. "You're welcome. Anyway, the reason I'm calling... did you get my text? Did you google him?"

My stomach flips at her question. I didn't need to google him. He was before me, naked, only twelve hours earlier.

"I got it, but I haven't had a chance to search him yet," I lie.

"Well, do it. You won't regret it. He's so fucking hot."

My eyes roll at her comment, anyone with a penis is attractive to Ava. As I begin to say something, an announcement over the PA sounds in the background.

"Are you at work?" I ask.

"Yeah, this is a break or whatever you want to call this fifteen-minute pause. Dr. Uwing keeps sending me off on random errands. He's nothing like Dr. Arthur." A tut comes through the device. "I can't wait for this new doctor. Surely, we'll both be placed with him."

Glad you're looking forward to it, I think to myself.

"Maybe. Or maybe they'll shuffle us all around. I wouldn't mind that." I place my elbow on my knee and rest my head on the hand holding the device.

Running my free hand through my hair, I realize it's still full of pins and hairspray from yesterday and feels like a mass of knots. That'll be fun to take out.

"Maybe..." A rustle sounds down the line before the rest of her sentence is mumbled. Another rustle sounds. "Shit, sorry, I gotta go. That was Dr. Uwing. I've been found. See you tomorrow."

"See..." I can't even finish my sentence before the line goes dead.

Placing the cell down next to me on the couch, I sit up straight and decide to tackle the bird's nest of my hair. Maybe if it weren't so knotted and tight, then my headache might ease—wishful thinking on my part.

A good forty minutes later, my couch is covered in hairpins, but my hair is smooth, and luckily, my headache has subsided slightly. It's probably mind over matter, but I'm beginning to feel a pang of hunger too. Perhaps the worst of this hangover is done with now.

After showering and washing the hairspray remnants from my hair, I feel much better and decide to have something small to eat. A banana sounds perfect.

As I eat the fruit, I decide to sort my clothing from yesterday, although there isn't exactly much to sort out—a dress that has taken up the majority of my duffel bag and a few toiletries.

Collecting a hanger for my dress, I pull it from the bag and laugh as I hang it up. How I wore this monstrosity for so long yesterday, I'll never know.

After hanging it up over my bedroom door, I wonder what I'm meant to do with this dress now. It's not mine, I know that, but I'm not sure Peaches was meant to keep it or if they were rented. What about the shoes that I've lost? Shit. I throw my banana peel away before grabbing my cell. Maybe one of the messages was from Sara with those instructions.

Sure enough, a message is on my cell from Sara.

Sara: *Hey cuz, thanks again for yesterday. I hope you had lots of FUN. When you can, please return to dress and shoes to Mom and Dad's. They'll have them dry-cleaned and store them. I'm dying to find out what happened but I'm boarding the plane soon. Will call you when I get back. Love you.*

It's pointless responding to her since she's probably somewhere over Ohio by now.

There's no chance in hell she'll be hearing the gory details from me, anyway. This secret is staying in the vault. But what if Cameron says something. Technically, he's got all the power in this situation. He's a supervising doctor, and I'm a resident. He could easily make up some bullshit and have me fired.

But I don't think he's like that. He was so kind, sweet, and caring.

"And you walked out on him without so much as a goodbye," I mutter out loud to myself.

Heading to my bedroom, I brush past the giant pom-pom hanging from my door and grab my laptop. Walking back to the couch, I power it up and search my emails for my employment contract. Perhaps it has some information in it about relationships.

Reading it over several times, there's only one sentence in one paragraph that sticks out to me.

The hospital prohibits any relationship between employees, residents, and students.

Shit.

This isn't good.

But technically, when Cameron and I got together, neither of us knew where each other worked. This all happened off hospital property. It's not like we were caught in a storeroom at the hospital. But if Cameron wants to be an ass here, he could spin it any which way he likes, and I could be screwed.

My stomach twists and turns. Nerves wash over me as I struggle to come up with any form of solution for this problem. If only I hadn't slept with him, none of this would be an issue now.

Should've used your head, not your vagina, Chelsea.

Shutting my laptop screen, I slide it off my lap and curl into a ball on the couch.

My eyes grow heavy again, and I decide to give into sleep.

This can now be a problem whenever Cameron starts at the hospital. Who knows, I may not end up with Cameron as a supervisor at all. Out of all the residents at Mercy General, the chances of landing him are slim.

For now, I need to sleep this hangover away and concentrate on the coming week at work.

CHAPTER 10

CAMERON

A Little Over A Week Later...

Fastening my shirt's top button before grabbing my lucky tie, I lift my collar and wrap the silk material around my neck, fastening it into a half-Windsor knot. Smoothing my collar back down, I look at myself in the full-length mirror in my bedroom. This look will do.

I'm all for making a good impression, but I have to admit I am looking forward to being handed a set of scrubs and a new white coat with my name and the hospital's logo embroidered on it. Well, at least I hope so. It's what happened at every other hospital I've worked at.

It is early in the morning, slightly before seven, but I've already been up for a good hour and a half. I enjoy a half-hour workout each morning as it wakes me up, even after only a few hours' sleep. Once my workout is complete, I shower and then take my time having my breakfast. I don't like starting the day rushing around, especially the first day of a new job.

I'm not due to start until nine when I have the meeting with the Chief, but I thought I'd get there a little earlier and have a look around. I've never actually been to Mercy General before, except for my interview.

Heading out to my kitchen, I make one more small coffee before sitting down at the table and scrolling through the morning's news on my cell.

Anxiety runs rampant in my body this morning, which is really unlike me. I'm not normally a nervous person. I need to remain cool and calm under very tense situations, so why am I concerned about today?

This is the hospital you've been wanting to work at, Cameron. You have big shoes to fill.

Putting it down to first-day nerves, I drink the final sip of my coffee before putting the cup in the sink.

My cell begins to vibrate on the glass tabletop.

Walking over to it, I smile as I see my dad's name flash across the screen.

"Hey, Pops," I answer.

"Hi, Cam. Just ringing to wish you good luck today." His voice crackles down the line. It's much weaker today than it has been lately, which always worries me.

My dad is now in his early seventies and was forced to retire six years ago as his voice became more and more hoarse, and then he developed a cough. He'd always put off seeing someone about it until one morning he coughed up blood, and Mom rushed him to the hospital. It turned out to be laryngeal cancer. Of course, he had surgery and a mixture of therapies and has been cancer-free for five years now, but it's never far from your mind.

"Thanks. I'm looking forward to it. How are you feeling?" I ask him.

"I'm fine."

"Your voice doesn't sound that way to me."

"I had a cold. Nothing major. Don't start, son. Your mother has been nagging at me, too," he warns. "I have a check-up this week, anyway. I'll mention it then."

"Be sure you do. Otherwise, I'll make the call to Bentley's office myself."

"Have a son who's a doctor they said. It'll be great to have him follow you, they said. What a load of horse crap."

I laugh down the line. He's a stubborn man, my father.

"Who's the chief at Mercy General now, anyway?" he asks.

Dad worked at Mercy for the last ten years of his career. He loved it there and was so pleased to hear I landed the position.

"Maxim Walker," I reply.

"He was in your position when I was there, a supervising surgeon. He's a ladies' man but also a bit of an ass, though, so watch him."

"Right."

"It's a good residency program they have, quite competitive to get into. So hopefully, you've been paired with someone competent and willing to learn." Dad begins to cough down the line.

"You all right, Pops?" I ask when he stops coughing.

"Yeah," he replies before gulping down some water. "Better let you go. Don't want you to be late. Have a good one, son. Love you, Cam. Mom says good luck."

"Thank you. Love you both."

Ending the call, I place the device in my pocket before grabbing what I need for the day and checking that my modest two-bedroom home is closed up. Heading out, I jump in my new-model Chevrolet Malibu and head over to the hospital.

On arrival, I punch the number I've been given into the parking lot keypad, and I'm allowed entry. *Phew, one less thing to worry about.* By the time I find a parking space and head to the main entrance, it's after eight, and I take a walk around the hospital, locating the cafeteria, ER, and where the operating suites are situated.

Not wanting to be late for my meeting with Dr. Walker, I head to his office toward the back of the hospital.

His PA sits at a large wooden desk as she types away on her computer. She seems rather young to be a PA for the Chief of Surgery.

"Hello." She smiles, flicking her blonde hair over her shoulder. Her long, red fingernails catching my eye. "I'm Maryella, Dr. Walker's PA. How can I help?"

"Good morning. I have a meeting—"

She cuts me off. "Dr. Chase to see Dr. Walker at nine?"

"Yes, that's correct." I smirk as I nod my head.

"I looked you up after I was told how handsome you are. Take a seat. He won't be too long." She smiles.

Doing as I'm told, I sit down in one of the chairs outside his large corner office. Frosted glass panels frame his area, and while I can't see his face, I can make out that someone is walking around in the office.

Several minutes later, the solid door is pulled open, and Dr. Walker steps out.

"Dr. Chase. Good to see you." He offers a curt nod.

"Dr. Walker," I reply, pressing my lips into a tight smile.

"Come in."

He holds the door open for me before calling to his PA, "Maryella, midday, my office?"

"Of course, Dr. Walker," she replies before a giggle escapes her mouth.

Dr. Walker quickly shakes his head before walking ahead of me. I'm sure I hear a soft grunt leave his mouth.

He shows me a chair, and I sit. I secretly hope this meeting doesn't last too long as I'm itching to get started. I didn't realize how much I miss performing surgeries after only one week away.

The glass-walled office is sterile. After all, it's within a hospital, with only one bookshelf to the side. His large mahogany desk is overbearing in this room. A few framed photos on a low cabinet would really brighten up the area. According to pictures I've seen, that's exactly how my dad had this office when he was here.

Dr. Walker gives me a brief outline of the hospital and how things are run before mentioning my employment contract.

It's pretty standard, just like the other hospitals I've worked at, except with one strict clause.

"Since taking my position as Chief, I've implemented some new policies. We have a complete non-fraternization policy at this hospital," Dr. Walker states.

"I understand."

"It leads to instant dismissal."

"You won't have a problem with that from me."

"I sure hope not. The doctor who you're replacing was found to be heavily involved in a relationship with her resident. There's a reason why we don't allow relationships. Patients need our full attention. This isn't some TV drama but real life. People are sick and need us."

Nodding my head, I want to reiterate that he won't have a problem with me, but he's obviously wanting to get this off his chest, so I allow him to do so.

He eventually stops about the relationships and begins talking about the residents who I'll be supervising.

"Both of these women are fine up-and-coming doctors. Dr. Arthur taught them well. Hopefully, you'll be able to see them through the rest of their residency."

Dr. Walker hands a piece of paper to me. Collecting it from the desk, I notice the names of Ava Saxon and Chelsea Mitchell.

Chelsea... why does she have to have the same name as the one I've been trying my hardest to forget for the last week or so? The Chelsea I know, her last name was Barker, though. Well, that's what I assumed given that was Sara's surname, and they are related.

My brows furrow as I notice Chelsea is a fourth-year resident. That's a coincidence.

The meeting concludes with Dr. Walker, and he escorts me out of the office before handing me two new white lab coats still wrapped in their plastic wrap.

"Dr. Elizabeth Atkins is on level two surgery right now. She's more than happy to show you around the hospital and will introduce you to your residents. Your hospital identification will be ready for you by lunch."

"Thank you," I reply.

Heading down to level two, I quickly find the department before asking for Dr. Atkins.

A bubbly woman greets me. Her deep brown hair is piled high on her head. Her deep ruby lipstick shocks me slightly as it's rare to see such boldness in a surgeon's appearance.

"Hello, Dr. Chase. I've been waiting to meet you. Your reputation precedes you."

"Thank you, Dr. Atkins."

She happily shows me around. The hospital's layout is quite good and makes it easy for someone to find their way without getting too lost. There's something about Dr. Atkins, though. It feels as though she's flirting with me. Perhaps she's just being nice to the new guy.

After placing my belongings in a spare locker, she then shows me the staff room area and the on-call rooms where we can sleep when we're on-call or between shifts. The bunk beds look much nicer here than they did at my last hospital. I'd have gotten more sleep on a cardboard box than there.

"I've just paged your residents to come and meet you. They have been practicing in the simulation lab since their shift began. They shouldn't be too long." She smiles as she takes a seat in the staff room. I take a seat opposite her. Her smiles are slightly more flirtatious than I think are acceptable, and I shift in my seat, uncomfortable with her manner.

"That's fine," I reply as I begin to read through the patient files that have been assigned to me. Pretty basic—appendicitis, gallbladder, and hernia to start with, along with any emergency procedures. The residents can definitely help if they've got time up in the simulation labs. For me, these are surgeries I can perform in my sleep, so to speak, but we all have to start somewhere. Perhaps they are giving me simple things, so I can prove my worth to these people.

Less than five minutes later, someone clears their throat near the doorway.

Looking up, a blonde-haired woman dressed in scrubs and holding a clipboard is standing in the doorway with another woman behind her. From where I'm seated, I can't quite see her.

"Hello, I'm Ava Saxon, and this is Chelsea Mitchell."

Chelsea steps out from behind her colleague to say hello, and my jaw nearly hits the floor.

Chelsea... *my Chelsea*. Well, the Chelsea who used me for a one-night stand.

Excitement starts to flood through my body, but I quickly quash it.

She ditched me, and a part of me hasn't fully recovered yet. I didn't think it was going to be one night only. She gave me the impression that she was completely into me, as I was her, but obviously, it was nothing more than sex.

Right now, I need to maintain my professionalism. I'm going to act as though we've never met before today.

"Ava, come with me. Chelsea, take a seat. This is your new

supervisor, Dr. Cameron Chase." Dr. Atkins leaves as Ava's mouth drops a little before turning and running after Elizabeth.

"Please sit." I motion to Chelsea. "We'll have a short chat if that's okay with you?" My tone is low and serious. I'm trying my hardest to pretend I don't know her.

Chelsea's blue eyes are wide as she slowly nods her answer. Does she think I want to discuss our night together? She's still as beautiful as I remember, even if she is wearing blue scrubs and her hair is wrapped in a tight bun.

Not now, Cameron. You need to forget anything you felt for her. She obviously has about you.

While I'd love nothing more than to find out why she left that night, this is definitely not the time and place for that. Maybe it never will be. Or perhaps I don't want to know the reason.

"Cameron," she whispers, but I quickly shut her down.

She does know who I am, though.

"Please don't address me by my first name. We don't know each other yet. Don't the residents call their supervisors doctor? At least in the beginning," I reply. "It's Dr. Chase."

"Sorry," she mumbles.

This is how I'm going to play it.

I don't know her at all.

We're strangers.

It's safer that way, especially after the lecture I received this morning and what my predecessor was fired for.

We will remain strictly professional.

If she has any objection as to how I handle this, then that's on her.

CHELSEA

How can he be acting this way? It's hurtful, but he does have to maintain his level of professionalism.

My heart is pounding against my ribs as I sit across from Cameron. My worst fear has come true. He's going to be my supervising doctor, and he's acting as though he has no clue who I am.

In the two minutes since I've sat down, he's not looked at me once. His head's been buried in a document in front of him.

I'd kill for him to look at me once, just once. I long for those eyes to meet with mine again.

But you ran out on him, Chelsea, my inner voice argues.

Since I last saw him, Cameron's grown a thicker beard, making him look more distinguished but somehow even more handsome.

A fleeting thought passes through my mind of when Cameron's five o'clock shadow was tickling my thighs.

Stop thinking about him, Chelsea.

Screwing my eyes shut, I quickly shake the thought from my

head as my stomach flops, making me feel a little ill. I can't think those things here. It could be dire for my career.

The stern tone of his voice as he asks each question is tinged with anger, and with each response, he cuts me off before I can finish my sentence. It's beginning to become annoying, not to mention coming across as extremely rude.

But do I deserve this? Maybe.

Who am I kidding? Of course, I do. He probably thinks I used him for sex. That I didn't care for him.

He's clearly pissed that I left him.

But I don't blame him.

It's been eating me alive, but all I'd like is one chance to explain myself. I did it for us.

"Dr. Chase, may I ask a question?"

"Of course," he replies, his eyes not leaving the sheet of paper in his hands.

"Is this how you act at work with people... you personally know?"

"Know? I'm sorry, I'm not sure what you mean?" He shakes his head but refuses to look at me. I can just see his eyes widen as his brows pull together, but not once does he look up.

My eyes widen in disbelief. There's no confusion. I was intimate with this man. The same man who brought me to the highest of highs only a little over a week ago.

"Cameron, come on... you know what I'm talking about," I plead.

A short conversation is all I want.

"I'm sorry, but I don't, and I won't remind you again about using my first name." He puffs a breath in frustration. My heart aches as he dismisses me.

Slowly lifting his head, his eyes connect with mine. Those sapphire eyes are piercing into my soul, sending me a warning not to push him.

But that spark is there between us, the same one we had when we locked eyes across the altar at my cousin's wedding.

"I apologize for overstepping, Dr. Chase," I mumble. "I was certain we knew each other. I was wrong, and it won't happen again."

"Mumbling isn't acceptable either, Dr. Mitchell. Surgeons need to be clear in their speech."

Why is he acting like such a bastard? Sucking in a deep breath, I succeed at fighting back my tears. I won't give him that satisfaction of seeing me cry. I'm bigger than that. It's unlike me to get emotional. I've worked hard on controlling my emotions since med school.

Well, two can play at that game. If he doesn't want to know me, then I won't know him.

It's probably for the best, after all.

Straightening myself in my seat, my fingers link, and I place them neatly in my lap as I listen to him tell me what he expects from his residents.

"Yes, Dr. Chase," I answer politely.

"Any questions?" he asks, lifting his head briefly from the paperwork.

"Not that I can think of."

"Great. Thank you. If you and... ah, Ava, can do another hour or two in the simulation lab for a hernia, I'd happily let one of you scrub in with me this afternoon. Please send in your colleague."

Standing, I thank him before walking as fast as I can from the staff room. I need to get out of here and take a moment to clear my head.

"Your turn." I plaster a fake grin on my face as I walk past Ava before heading to my locker.

Punching in my code, I pop the lock before swinging open the metal door. Luckily no one is around. Bunching a spare shirt into my mouth, I scream into it, hoping all my frustrations will leave my body. While it helps somewhat, I still feel tense, and the headache that was a little niggle earlier is now pounding against my skull.

Frantically searching for some Tylenol, I finally locate the foil package before popping two tablets out. After throwing them in my mouth, I take a long sip from my water bottle and gulp it all down, wishing that these tablets would take effect immediately.

Placing my bottle down, I turn around and slide down to the floor. My feelings are completely mixed. I'm not sure if I'm hurt, angry, or sad, or a combination of all of them. Hell, I was even a little happy to see him in the beginning, even if it was only for a fleeting moment.

What hurts the most is that he acts as though he doesn't know me. I know I did wrong, but we had something. I'm not sure what it was, but it would be nice to find out.

However, I ruined things.

I treated him like a meaningless fuck.

He has every right to be angry, and I'm hoping he can forgive me and move forward.

My career depends on that.

Pulling my legs to my chest, I wrap my arms around them as I place my head on my knees. I take several deep breaths to calm myself. I know I need to be back on the floor, do my time in the simulation lab before heading to the ER to see if any surgical cases are waiting for us.

My mind plays different scenarios over and over in my head, each one more and more stupid than the last. I need to find a way to make this situation work. Otherwise, I could find myself searching for another supervisor, or worse, finding a new hospital to finish my residency.

This isn't me. My thoughts are only on the job at work, but in the last half-hour, they have been anywhere but.

My pager vibrates against my hip, but I choose to ignore it until I can get my emotions and thoughts in check.

"Hey," a voice mutters from the doorway.

Lifting my head, I see Ava standing there.

"Hey," I reply.

"Are you all right? You've been acting funny since we were introduced to Dr. Chase."

"Funny? I don't think so," I protest, trying to hide my secret. It'd be disastrous if Ava were to find out what happened between us. She loves a good piece of gossip. I couldn't have that information falling into any senior doctor's hands.

"You were. Like you went quiet. I mean he's super cute, though. Don't you think?" Her lips twist, and she lightly nibbles on her lip.

"Not my type."

"Argh, boring," Ava groans. "We're so blessed to work in a hospital with so many hot doctors. Dr. May is another. His green eyes send shivers down my spine."

"Oh, please," I reply.

"Whatever. But are you sure you're all right?"

"I'm fine. I have a headache that won't let up."

"Do you need some painkillers?" she asks.

"I've just taken two Tylenol. I can't have anything stronger while on-call."

"Hope they work soon. Oh my God, did you hear why Dr. Arthur left?" Ava whispers.

"No, why? She transferred to a higher position job, didn't she?"

"Well, that's what she had us all believe. But according to Maryella, my cousin and Dr. Walker's PA, she said that Dr. Arthur was fired for a relationship with one of the residents."

"What?" I cry. "There's no way."

"Apparently, she's pregnant, too."

"That's a pile of horse shit. No way." I grimace at the gossip. I can't believe Ava is spreading things about a doctor who was an amazing supervisor to us.

"Well, it's what I heard."

"Don't spread stuff, Ava. You don't know the full story."

She rolls her eyes at me before unlocking her locker. "My cousin gets some good gossip where she works."

Idle gossip is awful, especially in the workplace, but I also have a pang of worry about it, especially if anyone ever found out about Cameron and me.

"Did you get the page?" she asks, changing the subject. "We have to go to ER for a consult with Dr. Chase in five. Possible splenectomy."

My eyes light up. I haven't been in the operating room for over a week now, not since Dr. Arthur had me assisting with a gallbladder removal. I'm really missing it.

"I'm going to enjoy this for now," Ava adds. "I'm being moved to a different supervisor tomorrow."

"What?" I cry. "That's shit."

"I know. Something about Dr. Chase only wants to supervise one resident."

Why can't it be me who got moved?

I pull myself up off the floor and give Ava a quick hug before checking my face in the mirror on my locker door before slamming it shut.

This is what I need to do. Focus on my job. Of course, I'll have to take instruction from Dr. Chase, but he can be my supervisor and nothing more. I'll prove to him that I can be professional and a great surgeon.

CHAPTER 12

CAMERON

Three Weeks Later...

Throwing my surgical gloves into the trash, I pull the cap from my head before heading to the door where I can wash up and change.

"Well done, Cameron. That was a tricky one," my colleague and anesthetist, Matilda, says as she completes her final checks. Spinning around, I nod at her compliment as she bats her eyelids several times, pulling her lips to one side and slightly tilts her head.

She's not the only female on staff who's been a little flirty with me since I started. But like with every other hospital I've worked at, I ignore it. The staff doesn't seem to take this non-fraternization rule too seriously around here, but I'd be too worried about stepping out of line. It seems like Maxim Walker is out to make an example of anyone he can catch.

"It wasn't easy. I'm glad I was able to cauterize every bleeder," I bluntly reply.

Leaving the room before the conversation continues, I grab a clean set of scrubs and head into the little alcove to change before washing up.

Daniel May, one of my colleagues, is hovering in the doorway as I turn to dry my hands.

"Great surgery, Cameron."

"Thanks, man. It was touch and go there for a little while, but we got there."

Daniel's a great guy, similar age to me but works as a trauma surgeon.

"That resident of yours is quite talented, isn't she?" Daniel states.

"That she is. She's got a good eye." I nod.

"Shame she didn't sign up for trauma. She looks well-composed. She could've done very well in my program."

"Ah, not everyone can be the fancy trauma surgeon around here," I joke.

Daniel steps into the room and begins to scrub in as I notice a patient is being wheeled into the operating room and begin to set up for another surgery. "I'll be done in a minute and will get out of your way."

"Appreciate that, man."

"Good case?" I ask, always keen to find out what other surgical cases are happening around the hospital.

"A hockey fight went wrong. Poor guy was impaled on a broken hockey stick."

"Holy shit. Good luck with that one," I reply before leaving the operating room.

He's right about Chelsea, though. She's proving to be quite a talented surgeon and an extremely quick learner. Her talents can be used anywhere in this hospital, and it's a blessing she's stayed with me in general surgery. Chelsea's more than happy to do the menial jobs and is always looking for extra, often staying back after shifts to follow up with patients. That's the sign of a good doctor in the making.

At first, it was extremely difficult to pretend as though I didn't know Chelsea. I often found myself looking for her, wanting to page her or catch myself watching her as she walks away from me.

Our hands have brushed against each other several times while in the operating room too. That spark between us is as strong as ever. But I quickly snap myself out of that and realize I have to treat her exactly the same as any other resident— professional all the way.

However, over the last week, mainly since I've allowed her near me in the OR and not just observing, I'm having porn-worthy dreams about Chelsea and me, one of them almost ending with me having a teenage-boy moment in my bed.

I've caught her looking at me on several occasions at work too. Not at the suture I'm using, or my method, but at me. It's caused my heart to skip a few beats, that's for sure.

But it's also painful—someone right in front of me who I'd love to ask on a date, but I can't, and I know I won't ever be able to do that.

She seems to hate me for the way I've treated her, anyway, although it's not unusual for a resident to hate on their supervising doctor. But our situation is quite different than most.

There's definitely some undeniable connection between us, an energy perhaps. It's been there since the wedding, even if she does think it's the worst thing in the world to be paired with me.

She's a beautiful human—compassionate, intelligent, and always the first to answer any question I ask. There's no doubt that Chelsea is gorgeous. I'm drawn to her as proven by our night together, and that pull is still here, if not stronger than before.

But I also need to build up trust here with the Chief and am determined to keep my nose clean. I'm not doing anything to jeopardize my place at this hospital. It hasn't exactly been an easy road to get here.

I've had to work in some of the country's toughest hospitals, where they had low budgets and many patients. I've done clinic work and bit my tongue every time a slightly more senior doctor told me I had a diagnosis wrong, even when it was right. But the last hospital I was at, here in San Francisco, was a step in the right direction. It helped to build me as a person and a surgeon, and now I'm determined to follow in my father's footsteps and become Chief of Surgery one day.

Stifling a yawn, I make my way down to the surgical ward to check on a few patients before heading to my car. It's been an exhausting fifteen-hour shift, barely a break between surgeries. Don't get me wrong, I love it, but I've worked eight days straight now. I'm looking forward to my day off soon.

It's late at night, around ten, as I walk toward my car and unlock it. I'm parked in another staff lot today as it's closer to where I exit the building, and much less chance of me getting stopped by an intern or nurse.

A groan followed by a few expletives from a female voice filters through the parking lot, startling me.

What the hell?

Fearing that someone is in danger, I search in the poor light for where the noise may be coming from before noticing someone forcefully kicking a car tire. A yelp sounds before they drop to the floor.

Placing my belongings in the back of my car, I race over to where the woman is. As I get closer, I notice it's Chelsea, but I'm too close to her now to back away.

"Are you all right, Chelsea?" I ask, keeping a little distance.

"Yes, I mean no. I don't know," she cries. Puffing her cheeks out, she takes several deep breaths, pained and frustrated. "Sorry, this isn't me. I don't usually let things like this get to me."

"What's wrong?" I take several steps toward her before crouching down. She looks up at me as another tear rolls down her cheeks. The blue in her eyes is somewhat brighter as though highlighted by the pink rim.

Even when upset, those are the eyes I see in my dreams. The eyes that have me waking up hard every morning, and the ones I threaten myself not to think about as she stands across from me in the operating room.

"The car won't start. So, I got frustrated and kicked the tire, and now I've injured my foot."

As Chelsea rubs at the top of her foot through her shoe, I notice she's wearing Asics—strong and durable running shoes—much like the ones I wear.

"I'm sure it's not severely injured. Those shoes are tough. Let me have a look," I offer.

"I'm fine," she replies with a grunt. There's the stubbornness that's been present since I started here. It's as though she wants to be nothing but a hard-ass around me. What she doesn't remember is that I've seen her soft side.

"Chelsea, it'll take a minute to check. I'm not leaving until I know you're all right or if I have to take you over to ER."

She rolls her eyes at my suggestion but withdraws her hands from her foot and allows me to gently remove her shoe. She winces as I roll the sock from her foot and place it on the concrete. I quickly glance at her as my hands touch the sole of her foot, gently checking for any apparent injuries.

"Where exactly is the pain?"

"My big toe."

The light is terrible in this parking lot, not safe at all. I dig my cell from my pocket and switch on the flashlight.

"Do you mind holding this?" I ask.

Chelsea takes the device from me, hovering the light over her injury.

"Everything looks fine. You may have broken your big toenail down the side. It's bleeding a little. You'll probably need to glue it together but be very careful that it doesn't grow into the skin."

"I'm sure it'll be fine. I probably overreacted. I was frustrated about the stupid car."

After carefully replacing her sock and then shoe, I take my cell from her and stand before switching the flashlight off.

Offering a sympathetic smile, I offer her my hand to help her stand. She looks at my outstretched palm for a moment before accepting it. The connection is the same as we had all those weeks ago at the wedding—the jolt of electricity and the tingle left on my skin as we break apart.

Chelsea must feel it too, as she quickly pulls her hand away from mine, stuffing it into her pocket.

"Thank you, Dr. Chase," she whispers.

"No problem. But what will we do about your car?"

"It's fine. I'll call for help and wait. Maybe I'll get an Uber home if they can't get it started."

"I can't leave you here on your own," I protest.

The strong need to protect her overcomes me, but I fight myself. She doesn't need me to protect her. *You're essentially strangers, remember, and you must remain that way.*

"I'll be all right, Dr. Chase."

"Cameron," I answer.

"Sorry?" she asks as her brows knit together.

"You can call me Cameron when we aren't at work."

"Thank you, Cameron, but I'm sure I'll be fine waiting here."

She crosses her arms across that sexy body. Besides the dreams I have, we make quite a good team at the hospital. She seems to know how I think and what my next move will be—something I find to be a fantastic quality.

"Let me drive you home. I'd feel better seeing you home safe."

Her head flicks away from me as she sucks in a deep breath.

"Chelsea, it's just a ride home. You can call a tow for the car."

"Cam, you know I can't get in your car." Her voice is barely a whisper, but her using my nickname has my dick twitching in my pants.

"And why's that?" I ask, knowing damn well why.

She lowers her voice before replying, "Because we'll have to discuss what happened at the wedding, or we won't be able to keep our hands off each other."

"Chelsea," I boom, feigning shock. I shouldn't have been so loud in calling her name. Perhaps it's my attempt to cover my ass in case anyone else is within earshot.

But who am I kidding, she's right. It's not a smart idea for me to give her a ride home. I'm not sure I can control myself if left alone with her.

No, I haven't forgiven her for bailing on me, but this connection between us is so strong. So much stronger than anything I've ever felt before.

"I'm sorry, Dr. Chase," she answers, her eyes darting over the parking lot but never connecting with me. "Thank you for your help."

Turning away from me, she takes a step toward the car, but I reach out and grab at her arm. She spins around to face me.

Let her go, Cameron. This will be trouble.

My feelings toward Chelsea outweigh the rational thoughts of my inner self.

As I take a couple of steps to her, Chelsea pushes herself hard against the car as though she's trying to flee but can't. Those perfectly pouting lips pop open slightly in shock.

"Grab your things. You're coming with me," I declare as my hand slides down and links with hers. "Now seems like the perfect time to speak about what happened."

Chelsea nods but doesn't say anything more, yet her eyes remain fixated on mine.

It's taking everything I have in me to refrain from kissing her right here and now, but this is definitely not the place.

"Cameron, this isn't a good idea," she mumbles.

"It's not, but I need to be alone with you."

Her breath hitches before she slides out between the car and me and collects her things.

After locking her car, we walk back to mine, and I open the passenger door for her. She slides in and fastens her seat belt as I push the door closed before heading back around to the driver's side.

My stomach twists at the situation as though I know I'm walking into a lion's den.

This can go one of two ways—a colleague giving another a ride home, or we can both give into the feelings we have and make a decision that may fuck up our careers.

Surely, sense will override emotion.

It has to.

CHAPTER 13

CHELSEA

Nerves have gotten the better of me as I watch Cameron walk around the car to his seat.

This isn't good and certainly isn't right, but I'm glad Cameron is giving up on this stupid idea of pretending not to know me and is wanting to have a conversation about what happened that night. Maybe it'll be what we both need to move forward with our lives and have a platonic relationship from here on. But a part of me hopes that he'll understand why I ran, and we'll kiss and make up, metaphorically of course.

But apart from all of that, I appreciate him giving me a ride home. This parking lot is creepy at night, and I didn't exactly want to be here alone with a car that wouldn't start.

My car isn't anything fancy. It was Mom's hand-me-down, and I've been meaning to look at purchasing a new one for over a year now. But, of course, being a doctor gets in the way of car shopping. This is the third time in a week it's broken down, and I'm beginning to think this is its end.

Trying to take my mind from the inevitable conversation

Cameron and I will have, I gaze about his car. I'm amazed that a surgeon would have such a modest car compared to Dr. Walker's penis- extension Jaguar.

It seems to do the job, as by the time Cameron has started the car and begins to drive out of the parking lot, I'm feeling calmer.

"I suppose I should type my address into your GPS," I blurt out, leaning forward in my seat. My parents have the same brand of car, so I know how to use the system.

"Before you do, I have a thought. What if we go back to my place—"

But I cut him off. "Oh no, I don't think that's a good idea."

What's he thinking?

"Hear me out, Chelsea. We need to talk. Much more than a fifteen-minute conversation in the car on the ride home. Come back to mine, I can make us coffee, and we can talk this out."

Hesitating, I wrack my brain trying to think of a million excuses that don't sound lame.

"I'm exhausted, Cameron."

That's the best you've got?

"I am, too. But this is important. We need to get past this... speed bump so we can move forward and be the great surgical team I think we can be."

My heart skips a beat. Not only has he just told me that he wants to move on from what happened at the wedding, but he's also told me that he thinks we make a good team. Holy fuck. A compliment from a superior is always something to feel very pleased about.

"Thank you. You're an amazing surgeon with a very interesting technique, one I hope to learn."

"One I'm looking forward to teaching."

"But going back to your place is dangerous," I whisper.

We sit silently for several minutes before Cameron pulls the car to the side of the road.

"So, where to?" he asks.

His words ring in my ears for several moments as my eyes dart left and right. I'm unsure what to do.

As the seconds tick on, he twists his head to look at me. "Chelsea?"

"Umm," I murmur, my fingers lightly tapping against my pants.

"A talk, a coffee, and then I'll take you home. That's all I'm asking. Nothing more. We can both remain professional."

As my nerves rise, I gulp them down before looking directly at Cameron. "Okay," I whisper.

"Great." He grins. He pulls away from the curb and heads in the opposite direction to where I need to go.

Professional. We can do that.

But that nervous excitement I felt the last time we were alone makes itself known, and I squeeze my legs together to try and quash it.

Leaning back in the seat, I close my eyes and concentrate on my breathing, willing myself to calm down. I don't get this nervous about anything. I've been taught how to, so why am I feeling like this now?

Fifteen minutes later, we pull into the driveway of a house. With no streetlight nearby and several trees growing on the sidewalk in front of the house, it's very hard to see much except for the black door of the garage.

Cameron leans toward me and collects a remote from the glove compartment. Pushing the button, the door of the garage begins to slide up.

"I'll leave the car out to take you home," he mentions as he drops the remote back where it came from before popping his car door.

Following his lead, I collect my bag before exiting the car.

Cameron walks into his garage and flicks on the light, so I can see where I'm going.

"Thank you," I call before walking into his home.

The garage door closes behind us as Cameron leads me up a few steps and into a darkened room.

"This is going to be a bit of a backward tour, unfortunately. This is my storage and laundry area. We'll actually walk through my bedroom before we come out to the living area."

I laugh at what he says. "It's a lovely storage area. Be grateful you have one, my apartment consists of one bedroom and my living area. That's basically it."

"I've done apartment living for too many years. I wanted a bit of space, so I bought this around two years ago now, and it's the best decision I have made."

Bought? Wow. I know it'll be many years before I can afford a house in San Francisco on my own. Surgeons make a ton more than residents, though.

He leads me through a hallway and flicks another switch. His bedroom lights up, and I immediately notice the soft gray palette mixed with stark white. It's an extremely masculine room, including a large-screen television mounted on the wall in front of the bed.

The manly scent of the woods combined with a hint of cinnamon infiltrates my nostrils, the same blend that turned me on so much only a month ago.

It's been hard to avoid that smell, especially when we both start a shift together, but I've found that rubbing a little scented lip balm under my nose has helped keep me in line. No one wants a resident to be a horny mess every shift.

"Lovely bedroom," I comment.

"Thank you. This room is finished. The spare bedroom upstairs is still a work in progress."

"So, you've renovated this house yourself?" I ask.

"Sort of. I paid someone to come in and make it as good as

they could. When I bought this place, it was old bathrooms and a run-down kitchen and living area away from everything else. Now I feel it flows much better, and my bedroom has access to the terrace as well as the living area."

"Sounds great," I reply.

"Let me show you."

He takes me to the living room. The large couch and television sit in front of the double glass doors which lead out to the terrace. The kitchen takes up the rest of the area with its stone countertops and wood doors. Three tall chairs sit at the counter.

This is the type of house I always envisioned living in. Something practical but great for entertaining, if I ever get time for that and perhaps one day, raising a child.

"Please, take a seat. I'll put some coffee on," Cameron says, breaking me from my thoughts.

"Do you mind if I kick off these shoes? My toe is still sore."

"Of course. I'll grab some peroxide and a bandage for you."

Sinking into his plush couch, a very similar color to mine, I remove my sock and shoe. The toenail doesn't look too good. I notice the nerves from earlier have vanished and have been replaced by a sense of calm, the same feeling I had when I first met Cameron.

"It won't be a moment." Cameron sits on the couch next to me, placing the first-aid items in front of us. "So," he starts.

"So," I repeat, not sure how we're going to start this conversation.

"Did you want me to clean it up for you?" he asks, looking at my toe.

"I'm a doctor, too. I can do it." I chuckle.

He watches me intently as I clean my toe and place the Band-Aid over the top. It'll do for now. I'll bandage it once I get home.

"I'll start and be blunt, Chelsea. Why did you leave that night?"

"I really didn't want to. I'd just had some of the most fun I've ever had, and—"

Cameron cuts me off. "I had a great night, too, which is why I can't understand what happened."

"Just after you'd fallen asleep, I received a text from Ava. I was about to doze off, and I thought I'd better check, in case on the off chance it was about a patient."

"As I would do," Cameron comments.

"So, I checked the text, and Ava was telling me all about the new supervisor starting... you... and how everyone calls you Doctor Dreamy."

A chuckle escapes Cameron as his brows come together. "Doctor Dreamy. Oh, for goodness' sake."

"Well, that's what they call you," I reply, as my cheeks begin to grow warm.

"Me? I call bullshit on that."

"Trust me, all the interns and residents do. Anyhow, reading on with the message, your name popped up on the screen, and I nearly died. I didn't want to wake you because I wasn't sure how you'd react. I just knew I had to get out of there... for both of our sakes."

"So, you ran because you were told I'd be your supervisor?" he repeats. His eyes widen at what I say.

"Yes. The moment I got home, I totally regretted it, but the damage was done."

"I understand why you left, but didn't you know that we'd see each other again? Didn't you think it would've been better if we were both in the know about working together?"

"After I got home, I realized that would've been the smart thing to do, but in the moment I panicked. The non-fraternization rule is well known around the hospital. Dr. Walker enforces it to the letter of the law. I was doing it for both our careers. I'll be forever sorry about it."

"What's done is done, but I can't tell you how surprised and shocked I was to see you when we were introduced, especially after just getting the lecture by Dr. Walker about no hospital romances. It would've been nice to have had a heads up."

"I understand," I reply. "I made a bad call. But trust me, it won't happen again."

Cameron stands and walks to the kitchen. "How do you like your coffee?"

"Black with two sugars, please," I slowly reply. I was sure he'd tell me to get an Uber home after telling him about my stupid decision.

Bringing two cups with him, he places them on the coasters on the glass table in front of the couch before settling back down.

"Thank you," I mumble as I collect my cup and take a small sip, the chestnut-colored liquid leaving a pleasant burn on my lips and in my mouth. A whispered moan escapes my lips as I savor the flavor. "I haven't had coffee this good in so long."

"Only the best here. I love good coffee. The stuff at the hospital is absolute shit." He laughs.

"Do you think you can forgive me, and we can move forward?" I blurt out after several minutes of silence as we drink our coffee.

Cameron places his cup down before turning to face me, his fingers reaching out and gently brushing my arm. Goosebumps immediately form along my skin as my breath hitches.

"I'm not concerned about the night of Matty and Sara's wedding... that's in the past. And yes, we can move forward. I'm more concerned about the now. This thing between us." His voice is barely a whisper at the end.

Without giving me a chance to respond, Cameron shifts forward and gently places his lips on mine. The feelings from a month ago return with a vengeance, and I quickly find myself kissing Cameron back.

Something that feels so good is going to get us into so much trouble.

We could both lose our hard-fought positions at the hospital. But right now, I'm not sure I care.

CAMERON

As our lips massage each other's, I feel Chelsea's fingers press against my shirt. Instead of her trying to remove the fabric from my body as I anticipated, she's pushing away from me.

"Cameron, we can't do this," she mutters against my lips as though she doesn't want to break the connection.

Her pager still on her hip begins to beep.

"Yes, we can," I reply.

Chelsea checks the device before puffing out a breath. She pushes against me more forcefully. "No, Dr. Chase. We can't be in this position. That page is from Ava. This is how entwined the hospital is in mine... no, our... lives."

Slowly nodding my head, I gaze into her eyes. She's right. That clause in our contract makes any form of non-professional relationship between us difficult. We can't be doing this. "I apologize, Chelsea. That should never have happened."

"No, it shouldn't have," she whispers before moving away from me slightly. "Perhaps I should go."

"You don't have to. Finish your coffee, then I'll take you home."

"I think it's best if I call an Uber. Safer."

"Do you feel unsafe with me, Chelsea?"

"Oh no, Dr. Chase. That isn't what I meant. All I mean is that this thing between us…" she waves her hand back and forth, "… it can't happen. We had a fling before we knew we were working together. Now if anything does happen, it could jeopardize our positions."

"I know this, but you're so hard to resist."

A small smile pulls at her lips. "I know that feeling."

Chelsea nibbles at her lip, a gesture that drives me wild, and I can't resist. I slide my hand along her cheekbone before running my thumb across her lower lip.

Her eyes flutter at the sensation, and I inch closer until our lips are within reaching distance again. "Shit, I'm sorry," I mumble, pulling away from her.

"Geez. That needs to stop."

Shuffling over on the couch to gain distance between us, I offer her a sympathetic smile. "I'll do everything within my power to maintain my distance from now on, Chelsea." I run my fingers through my hair in frustration.

"It's best for both of us."

"You're right," I begin, pausing slightly to choose the correct words. "It's in both of our best interests not to give into our feelings for each other."

"Exactly."

"Whatever was between us at Matty and Sara's wedding needs to be put aside… for our jobs and our patients. It never ends well when two professionals embark on a relationship. How awkward would it be if we broke up?" I laugh.

"That's true. I pride myself on my professionalism. I feel that I've done a good job so far since you started at the hospital."

"Well, apart from a few times where you were like the ice queen," I quip before my lip twitches into a half-smile.

"Ice queen... hardly." She laughs. "I wasn't the one being a complete butthead during the first few weeks."

A chuckle escapes me. Did she really just call me a butthead? "I did it for a good reason," I reply.

"I realize that now," she whispers.

Whatever it is between us is still there, fighting against our common sense, but we're doing our best to keep it at a simmer.

Part of me wishes that the situation was different, that Chelsea and I would be tangled in the bedsheets right now as I bring her to ecstasy, but it can't be.

Risking your job for a fling isn't worth it.

But this isn't just a fling, either.

Shaking the thought from my head, I decide to change the topic. "How about we discuss the plan for the intern who will be joining us next week."

"Intern," Chelsea groans.

Puffing a laugh, I nod. "Yes, he's only with me for the week. Just to give him a taste of the surgical life."

"A week shouldn't be so bad." She nods.

"We were all once an intern. That's what you need to remember. Like what you probably had to do, they rotate through the hospital's different areas before applying for their resident program. He'll need to remain supervised throughout the entire week as he has not yet sat in on his board exams."

"Of course," Chelsea replies as she drinks the remaining coffee in her cup.

"Would you like another?" I ask as I down the last of mine. "I'm making myself another."

"Sure," she answers.

An hour later, Chelsea stifles a yawn. We've spoken about all aspects of work and our lives over the last hour. It's as though the kiss between us never happened, and that's just as it should be.

But I still wish I could kiss her again.

"How about I take you home?" I suggest.

"I think that would be a smart move."

She stands and moves toward the kitchen. I collect the coffee cups and move to the sink, placing them down.

Leaning against the counter, I offer Chelsea a pursed smile before asking, "Have you got everything?"

"Sure do." She pats her bag.

Swiping my keys from the counter, I straighten up and walk toward the front door.

"Cameron," Chelsea whispers.

Turning around, she's right behind me. She stands on her toes and throws her arms around my neck.

For a brief moment, I'm frozen, unsure what to do, but before I know it, my arms slide around her back, and I hold her to me. Her hair smells like coconut and lime, a smell that will linger in my memory for eternity.

"Thank you," she whispers.

"For what?" I reply.

"For allowing me to do this. I needed just one more hug from you." She pulls away before side-stepping me and walking to the front door.

Puffing out a breath, I calm myself down before following Chelsea out to the car, stopping to lock the door.

This is such a fucked situation. I want her, and I'm sure she wants me, but there's a huge obstacle stopping us.

The ache from earlier has returned and won't let up.

Balling my hand into a fist, I punch it into my other hand before twisting and locking the house.

Unlocking the car, we both slide into our seats before she punches in her address into the GPS.

The ride to her place is quiet. Both of us tired after a long and somewhat emotional day.

Pulling up outside her apartment, we sit for a few moments, unsure of what to say.

"Thanks for tonight, Cameron," Chelsea whispers. "As well as the ride."

"It's my pleasure."

"I'll see you at work."

"Sure will." I grin.

Chelsea unbuckles her seatbelt but still doesn't leave the car. I have the feeling there's more she wants to say but is resisting.

That's understandable since I feel the same way.

She puffs out a breath.

"Chelsea, is everything all right?"

"Yes... umm, no. I don't know, Cameron."

"Oh," I mutter.

"Okay, I'm just going to come out and say this." She takes a deep breath. "Are you seeing anyone else?"

"What? No," I reply.

"Sure?"

"Yes, Chelsea. There's no one else. In all honesty, if we didn't work together, or if that stupid clause in our contracts didn't exist, I'd be asking you on a date. But it can't be."

She looks down to her clasped hands in her lap. "I understand."

"But I think after our conversation tonight, we'll be a strong surgical team and have an exceptional professional relationship."

She twists her head to look at me. "That sounds great, Cameron. Good night."

Chelsea pops the car door and exits the vehicle. I watch as she walks to her front door. She turns and offers a wave before walking inside.

For a few moments longer, I sit in my car, processing what has happened tonight. It's the best of a bad situation.

We work well together, and we don't want anything to interfere with that.

I need to constantly remind myself that my priority is making Chief, and nothing can come in the way of that process.

CHAPTER
15

CHELSEA

A warmth spreads across my stomach, waking me from a deep sleep. The kind of sleep that you get after expending as much energy as you possibly can the night before.

Stretching my arms above my head, I stretch before rolling over, hoping for another five minutes. However, the warmth floats across my back this time and moves down to my ass.

Prying my eyes open, I realize it's still dark and wonder why I'm being woken at this hour.

"Mmm," a sound murmurs next to me.

A smile spreads across my face as I realize it's Cameron.

"What time is it?" I croak before licking my dry lips.

A groan escapes him as I feel the mattress move in what I assume is him rolling over.

"Four forty-five," he whispers.

"Why so early?" I complain.

But then it dawns on me. We have a shift today, a shift that starts in less than an hour.

"Shit. I need to get up," I cry, jumping from the bed. I'm

grateful that there's only moonlight shining in the bedroom window as I'm stark naked.

"Not yet. I plan on bringing you to the highest of the highs before we go to work today."

"Hmm," I mumble. "But we'll be late."

"What about the shower then?" he asks.

Cameron sweeps me into his arms, his thumb caressing the top of my thigh. He flicks on the light switch to the bathroom before placing me down on a soft mat in the middle of the floor.

He runs the shower, the steam filling the room. Cameron steps in first, the water cascading over his sexy body. Stepping under the stream, I lean my head back and let the water run over my hair.

Sensing that Cameron has closed the gap between us, my eyes flutter open. Taking a step toward me, Cameron places his lips on mine. Instinctively, I kiss him back.

His hand slides down my leg to my knee, and he slowly lifts it, bringing us closer together. His cock hardens between us.

In the blink of an eye, he pushes me against the cold tile wall as his kisses trail down my neck. Cameron effortlessly lifts me. His hands firmly gripped onto my ass.

But I push him back before things get too heated, my fingers finding his and gently prying his hand from my leg.

"We don't have time."

"Yes, we do," he replies, his lips twitching before he lowers me a little onto his cock.

Wrapping my arms around his neck, I nuzzle into him as I rock my hips in time with his.

As my climax nears, my lips find his, and I close my eyes tightly as we burst into a million pieces.

The incessant buzz in the background annoys me as I come back down to earth.

My eyes flick open, and I instantly realize I'm lying in my bed.

Looking left and right, I'm in my bed, alone. There's no shower running. I pat my body under the covers, and I'm fully dressed.

No, it can't be.

It can't have been a damn dream. It was as real as real can get. I can even feel where Cameron's hands were on my ass. My lips are tingling from where his were pressed against mine. My breathing is labored, and the remnants of the euphoria of an orgasm lingers low in my belly.

Is it possible to even have a full-blown orgasm while you sleep?

Would this be the equivalent of a teenage boy's wet dream?

How embarrassing.

The buzz of my alarm starts up again, and I groan as I extend my hand to swipe at the screen.

Reluctantly getting up, I quickly shower and dress before walking to the kitchen to switch on my coffee machine. As the coffee is being made, I lean against the counter, my head resting on my hand as I think about my incredibly real dream.

Auto-pilot takes over as I have a quick breakfast before walking out the door to get in my car.

But I shake myself from this daydream when my car isn't parked in its usual spot.

Shit.

The memory of last night floods to my mind—the car breaking down, going back to Cameron's, the kiss before pushing him away.

I wanted him more than anything last night, but I still said no. We need to think about our positions at the hospital.

That kiss must have left me so turned on that I went home and dreamed about what would've happened had I said yes.

Pulling my cell from my bag, I order an Uber before looking

up at the ominous clouds above. Rain, damn. Knowing my good umbrella is still in my car, I run back up to my apartment to grab a spare and make it back down just in time to see the Uber pulling up at the curb.

Jumping into the car, I confirm my destination with the driver before sitting back and watching the world pass by as he drives me to the hospital.

My mind is a scattered mess, and I know it can't be this morning. I need to scrub in with Cameron to do several surgeries today, and that needs a clear head.

Once arriving at the hospital, I change into scrubs before noticing that Ava is talking to someone in the doorway. She's being flirty with a cheeky hair toss and twirl every now and then. I don't recognize the man. A doctor I'm assuming, by the stethoscope around his neck and white lab coat, but he's older than her, graying hair with matching salt and pepper beard. He's handsome and definitely Ava's type. She likes older men.

It's not surprising I haven't seen his face before. It seems I basically only know the surgical ones. He could be from another department.

Ava waves goodbye before joining me in the room. "Hey," she beams.

"Hey," I reply. "Someone's happy today."

"Oh, you have no idea," she gushes. "I had like the best fucking night ever last night."

"Did you now?" I answer, my brow raising at one side.

If only she knew what my night involved.

"I went to the bar after work. I was a bit down after Mrs. Gray coded last night. We worked on her for an hour, but we couldn't save her."

"I'm sorry about that, Ava. Losing them is so hard."

"Tell me about it. So, I went to the bar down the street, you know, to drink away my sorrows. That's where I met Mark."

"Mark?" I question.

"Hmm, Mark," she repeats as her lips twist into a grin.

"Mark? Who's Mark?" I ask. I don't think I've ever had her mention that name before.

"Oh, no one," she replies, shaking her head slightly, her lips twitching.

"You do look happy, though, Ava."

"Thanks, Chels. I'll share more details when I can."

"Of course. I'm not prying."

Ava's off in dream land too. A great pair we'll make today, although I'm a lot more clear-minded since I arrived at the hospital.

Nerves tingle low in my belly at the thought of seeing Cameron. He'll never know about my dream, of course, unless I tell him, which I won't. But I remember every single thing he did to me in that shower in my dreams, and it's hard not to feel turned on by it.

Remember your discussion last night? Professional all the way, Chelsea.

"How was your night? Your car was here late... did you do an extra shift again?" Ava asks, breaking my thought.

"No, the damn thing broke down. I had to get a ride home."

"A ride?" She smirks. "From whom?"

"Umm, no one that you'd know. It was just an Uber," I lie. My voice wobbles slightly.

"What's up today? You seem... off. You're not getting sick, are you?" Ava asks.

"No, nothing like that. I, ah, stayed up for a while after I got home last night. You know what it's like when you want to binge a TV show?" I chortle.

"Yeah, but you can't resist."

"Come on. We better get going, or we'll be late for rounds."

Ava groans at my reminder but quickly throws on her

comfortable shoes and lab coat as I tightly twist my hair into a bun and secure it in place.

As we leave the locker room and head to the ward, Cameron is standing at the nurses' station collecting the folders we need for our cases today.

"Good morning, Dr. Chase." Ava grins as she scoops her hair into a low ponytail. It doesn't go unnoticed that she flirts with Cameron and several other doctors in the building. It's generally a playful flirt, as though it is her way of getting a better case or being the first to fill Dr. Chase in on newly admitted cases. But this morning's flirtation with Mark was a serious wants-to-get-in-his-pants type of flirting.

"Dr. Chase," I mutter before standing next to him.

There's an unease within me, which is ridiculous. Unless Cameron can read minds, he doesn't know about my dream. It's me making the situation more than it should be.

"Morning," he replies with a smile.

Cameron hands us each some thick folders. His fingers brush against my outstretched palm causing me to suck in a breath. It's as though it is the same thing I felt in my dream—a jolt of electricity and a calm wash over me. It's as though Cameron hears me as he gazes into my eyes. My cheeks warm from his intense look, and I quickly take a step back from him and busy myself with the folders.

Cameron asks Ava to go and meet with her patient before pulling me aside.

"Can I have a quick word?" he asks.

"Sure," I reply.

Even though we're on the other side of the hallway to the nurses' station, each time I look toward the nurses' station, the two nurses sitting at the desk quickly flick their head away as though they're trying to listen in on us.

Cameron pushes open the storeroom door and invites me

inside. This is doing nothing for the inevitable rumor that will be around the ward shortly.

But he doesn't seem to care.

He lightly pushes the door closed behind us. My knees begin to go weak as the images from my dream flash before my eyes again.

"Did you manage to get an Uber here this morning without any trouble?" he asks.

"Yes, fine. Perfect timing."

"Great." He pats my arm. That gentle gesture is such a turn-on. My eyes drift to his hand on my coat. No, he can't be doing this. He can't be turning me on here, even if it's unintentional.

"This, Cameron... this... touching, hiding in storerooms... I thought we were keeping things professional."

"We are... I am... I'm checking on your well-being," he retorts.

"I appreciate that, but we could've done that in the hallway."

"True, but I didn't want the nurses to hear. I apologize if I've made you uncomfortable. It won't happen again."

Pulling my lips tight, I nod my reply.

Perhaps Cameron is finding it hard to think of us as only professionals too.

He pulls the door open. "After you."

As we step into the hallway, I notice Elizabeth Atkins standing at the nurses' station. I inwardly groan. Some of the interns call her the grouch, and I can understand why. It's as though because she's ranked higher than us, she feels it's her right to treat us like shit.

"Dr. Chase," she announces rather loudly, causing several nurses and another doctor to spin around to look at us. I will my cheeks not to flair at this moment.

"Dr. Atkins," Cameron replies in a much more normal tone.

Elizabeth takes several steps toward us. Her high heels add several inches to her height, so she's taller than me.

"Dr. Chase... I shouldn't need to remind you. You speak to your residents as a group in an open area, you don't need to hide away in a closet."

"Elizabeth—" Cameron starts, but she cuts him off.

"It can lead to rumors and suggestions."

"I was trying to discuss a patient's treatment with Dr. Mitchell, Elizabeth. His wife likes to eavesdrop and I thought it would be best," Cameron lies.

"Well, take it to a staff room or a stairwell away from the ward. We don't hide away in storerooms in this hospital. If I see anything again, I'll be forced to report it to Dr. Walker," she gruffs out.

"Of course," he answers.

"And you, Dr. Mitchell. Don't you have a patient to see?"

"Yes, Dr. Atkins," I reply before rushing off.

Glancing over my shoulder, I notice Elizabeth is still talking to Cameron before she fixes his collar.

A tinge of jealousy washes over me.

Keeping our relationship professional will be hard since we're so compatible, but I never thought the green-eyed monster would rear its ugly head.

Maybe this is going to be a hell of a lot harder than I thought.

CAMERON

Walking over to the operating table, I hold my hands up in front of me before closing my eyes and rolling my neck left to right and back again.

It's my little ritual before I start my surgery. Some surgeons will say a prayer, some walk backward into the OR, but I like to feel limber before I embark on what's an unknown timeframe for a surgery. It could be simple and out in under an hour, or there could be complications, and I could be there half the day.

Chelsea stands opposite me, her hands mirroring mine before closing her eyes and tilting her head twice to the left before repeating it on the right and rolling her shoulders. It's only been in the last week that I've noticed this little ritual of hers. I can't complain. Seeing her neck exposed like that reminds me of our night together after the wedding.

It's been over a week now since I helped Chelsea out the night her car broke down, and we decided that we'd be professional. At first, it was awkward, but I feel that we have settled into a nice rhythm now, but that doesn't stop me from admiring her from afar.

I've been desperate to stop my thoughts of Chelsea in that way, but the harder I fight, the more I seem to think of her.

Making the callous mistake of speaking to Chelsea in the storeroom earlier, Elizabeth's warning of reporting me to Dr. Walker has me wanting to be a model doctor—speak to her in public areas, avoid touching—things a normal resident-supervisor would do.

Surely, I can manage to do that. After all, it's my job on the line.

But I can't be thinking any of this now. I need a clear mind, even though I feel I can do this simple hernia operation in my sleep.

Less than an hour later, I offer Chelsea the chance to do the small-incision sutures near his belly button.

Chelsea makes the first suture perfectly, yet she struggles a little with the second.

"Could you show me, Dr. Chase?" she asks.

Nodding my head, I reach out to grasp her hands and gently guide her through the motions of the suture. She doesn't tense up at my touch—it's as though we are one, our hands perfectly in sync.

But it doesn't last long. Once the last suture is tied off, we both step back from the table and allow the nurses and anesthesiologist to complete their jobs as we make our way to clean up.

"Good surgery, Dr. Mitchell," I mutter as I remove my cap and dispose of it.

"Thank you for your help, Dr. Chase," she replies.

"That's what I'm here for, to help when you need it."

"Well done, Dr. Mitchell," a voice booms from behind us before another echoes the compliment.

Spinning around, I notice two of my colleagues, Cosmo

Falzon, a plastic surgeon, and Marcus Baxter, a fellow general surgeon, standing in the doorway.

"She did very well," I agree with the men.

We both leave the operating room and head back to our lockers, an uncomfortable silence replacing the usual banter between us. Grabbing the water bottle from my locker, I take a big drink before pushing the door closed and looking straight at Chelsea. "Have I upset you?"

"What?" she screeches.

"Have I upset you?" I repeat.

"No. Not at all. Do I seem upset?" she asks.

"I don't think so. But something feels different."

"I did get spooked by Dr. Atkins' warning earlier. I appreciate you checking on my well-being, but perhaps a quick text would've been easier."

"Point taken. Now would you care to get a coffee before our next surgery?" I ask.

"Now, would that be inappropriate? I'm struggling to understand what may and may not be appropriate anymore." Chelsea runs her hand up the opposite arm before throwing her palms in the air.

"How about I make one in the staff room then? We can hang out in there together and discuss our next surgery."

"Sounds good," she replies, a smile pulling at the corner of her mouth.

We move to the staff room and find Daniel in there chatting to Ava. She's leaning forward in her seat as though she's listening intently to whatever he has to say.

Daniel is a very knowledgeable man who started at this hospital as an intern. He's also dabbled in many specialties before he settled in trauma.

I've been advised that Ava is looking for another specialty as she doesn't think general surgery is enough for her. I'm completely fine with that, of course, and my guess is that's what she's speaking to Daniel about.

But as we enter to room, their conversation finishes.

"Don't stop on our behalf," I offer as I place a coffee cup under the machine.

A pager begins to beep.

"It's fine," Daniel begins, "I've got to get down to the ER, anyway."

Turning around to face him, I notice him whisper something to Ava before she begins to nod furiously.

"Good luck, Daniel," I call as he walks to the door.

"Thanks, man," he replies.

Chelsea sits down next to Ava. I offer to make her a coffee too, which she happily accepts.

Placing the cups down on the glass-top table in front of the chairs, I join the women and decide to discuss our next surgery.

"This afternoon's surgery, I was wondering if you'd both like to scrub in?"

Ava turns to Chelsea, and her eyes widen in excitement. "Yes, Dr. Chase. That would be fantastic."

"Thank you, Dr. Chase," Chelsea adds.

"How long before we have to be in the OR, Dr. Chase?" Ava asks.

"An hour and a half," I reply.

"Great. I'll be back by then." Ava grins before downing her coffee.

"And where are you going?" Chelsea asks. Her tone is cheeky.

"Umm, I want to check on a patient," Ava responds. I can't help but notice her cheeks are tinged pink. "But I'll be back quickly."

Ava runs out the door, and I look toward Chelsea, who shifts uncomfortably in her seat.

"Alone again." I laugh.

"Seems that way."

"You don't need to feel uncomfortable around me."

"I don't. I just don't want people to assume something is happening when it's not."

She doesn't want to have a rumor spread about her life, and she's concerned for her position here at the hospital. I understand this completely as I feel the same.

"I understand that, Chelsea. Perhaps if you're that uncomfortable speaking together at the hospital, then we could go to a bar or even go to my place. Think of it as a meeting."

"I'm not sure that will help at all if we go to the bar. Many of our staff members head there," Chelsea replies.

"What about my place then?"

"Umm," she hesitates.

It annoys me that she feels she can't have any male friends at the hospital in case someone misinterprets it as something romantic.

"We could meet once a week. Of course, we can't discuss emergency cases for obvious reasons, but we definitely can about our scheduled surgeries."

"Ava could come, too," Chelsea adds.

"Of course," I reply, not wanting to spill the beans to Chelsea on Ava's plans. That's not my place.

"Sounds good, Cameron."

"First one after shift tonight? I can give you a ride there and home?"

"That'd be lovely."

A rush of excitement washes over me at her agreement.

It's purely professional, Cameron, I remind myself.

Maybe this is my solution to being unable to speak to Chelsea privately at the hospital, or perhaps it's my way to spend some quality time with the woman who drives me wild.

Either way, I'm looking forward to being close to her again.

CHAPTER 17

CHELSEA

Fluffing a cushion on my couch, I check that it's perfect before collecting my running shoes off the floor and run to throw them under my bed.

I'm not usually this fussy when I have visitors, but today's visitor isn't just anyone. It's Cameron, and it's his first time coming to my apartment.

The arrangement that we meet to discuss upcoming surgeries has been great, and I feel in these last few weeks of additional simulation lab work and Cameron's knowledge from our meetings, I'm a better surgeon for it.

Cameron advised me a couple of days ago that this week's meeting would have to be somewhere else as he was having his house fumigated today.

It was a no-brainer for me to suggest my place. It's nowhere near as luxurious as Cameron's, but it's comfortable, and I've bought the same coffee pods as Cameron has. After all, they are the best I've tasted.

The first night, it was great having Ava there with us. It was almost a buffer between Cameron and me. Purely a work thing, nothing inappropriate.

But Ava is no longer supervised by Dr. Chase, not since she was approved to join the obstetrics program and found a new supervising doctor, Dr. Mark Fisher. So, it's just Dr. Chase and me.

Lately, I've noticed some tension between Cameron and me. Nothing bad but a sense of longingness. It's a look here, a brush on the arm there. I can still feel the tingle from when we touched hours later. I'm trying my hardest to fight this, but maybe I can't anymore.

Today, he'll be standing inside my apartment. Of course, I'm excited to learn about these upcoming procedures as I've never seen these types of surgery done before, but I'm also a little nervous as I want this day to be happier for both of us, especially since last night was very tough when we lost a patient on the table.

Perhaps I shouldn't have offered to make lunch for us today. Or maybe it's my sneaky way of getting 'the way to a man's heart is through his stomach' in.

Only I'm not a very good cook. Sure, I can make toast and boil an egg, but even then, I've been known to let the pot go dry on occasion. I followed Mom's recipe on this pasta sauce as precisely as I could, and it doesn't taste half bad if I do say so myself.

Quickly glancing up at my wall clock, I notice that Cameron should be here in five minutes, so I head over to the kitchen and pop the cork on the bottle of red wine I purchased earlier before checking on my pasta sauce.

Cameron is wonderful at everything he touches. Of course, he's an amazing surgeon and hands-on doctor, and he definitely knows how to make a woman scream in delight, but he's also a fantastic cook. He's made us some incredible meals for our meetings.

A knock sounds at the door, and I jump. Pasta sauce on the spoon splatters against the counter.

"Damn," I groan, grabbing a towel and wiping up my mess.

Double-checking that I don't have any pasta sauce on myself, I run my hand over my hair and down my ponytail before smoothing my skirt. I wasn't sure if a skirt was suitable, but I want to look nice, even if we're simply having a meeting.

Walking to the door, I look through my peephole, making sure it is, in fact, Cameron.

The intercom on the building door has been out of action for a while now, and as such, the door is always open. The super continues to tell the tenants that he'll arrange to have it fixed, and he's placed a security guard on the door after hours, but I still can't help feeling a little vulnerable, especially being the first apartment after the stairs.

Cameron's side profile is just as handsome as his front-on, and I quickly unchain the door and pull it open. I shake the handsome thought from my head, desperately trying to replace it with a professional thought.

My heart beats quicker as he turns his head to me, his face beaming.

"Hello," he greets with one of his hands is behind his back.

"Hello," I reply.

It's only been fourteen hours since I last saw him. He dropped me home last night after my Uber canceled several times. But there's a nervous excitement buzzing around me today, a hope that we may give into our feelings.

Both Sara and Matthew have hinted numerous times about us getting together. I'm tired of being asked now but also wishing that it will one day come true.

Cameron brings his arm back to the front with a large bunch

of flowers in his hand. "These are for you."

Gasping, I take the bouquet from him. I've never received flowers before from anyone. "They are gorgeous," I whisper as I take in the bouquet of yellow, pink, orange, and purple flowers. "They're so vibrant. Thank you."

"You're welcome."

My gaze is fixated on the flowers in my hand. It's such a thoughtful gesture from Cameron but not exactly professional.

"Something smells nice," Cameron says, breaking my daze.

Laughing, I stand to the side. "Sorry, please come in."

"Thanks." He chuckles.

"Welcome to my shoe box of an apartment," I quip as I close the door behind us.

"It's lovely."

"It's nothing like your place. But it's big enough for just me." Shrugging my shoulders, I walk over to the kitchen to find something to put the flowers in. I don't own any vases.

After finding a tall pot, I fill it with water and place the flowers inside.

"A pot?" Cameron questions before a chuckle escapes him.

"Don't judge. I don't own a vase, and truth be told, I don't really use this pot, either."

Cameron roars with laughter before walking over to the kitchen. "You're so cute, Chelsea."

My mouth drops slightly at his statement.

"Did you call me cute?" I ask.

"I did. Is that all right?"

"I guess so. Not exactly professional, though."

"True. In that case, I apologize."

"Don't, it's fine." I laugh.

The timer sounds on my phone, and I stretch across the counter to grab my device and turn it off.

"What's that for?" Cameron asks.

"Telling me that it's nearing time to cook the pasta to go with the sauce for lunch."

"Yum," Cameron mutters. "May I try some? Pasta is my guilty pleasure," he asks, taking a step closer to me.

"Of course."

Leading Cameron to the cooktop, I dip the spoon into the sauce and bring out a small amount for him to try.

Blowing on it, he tastes the sauce, and I watch on nervously.

"Hmm, that's good," he hums as his head bobs up and down.

"Oh, thank God." I puff out the breath I was holding, breathing a sigh of relief.

"You don't have anything to worry about. That's some awesome sauce right there."

My cheeks warm at his compliment. I only hope he isn't saying it so that he doesn't offend me. Although from my time with Cameron, he's pretty straightforward when it comes to things he likes and doesn't.

A long beep sounds from my bedroom, followed by another ringtone in Cameron's pocket.

"Shit," he mumbles.

"Is that your pager?" I ask, knowing the tone from my bedroom is from mine.

"Yeah. But I'm not on-call... are you?" he asks.

"Nope."

Cameron stands up before fumbling in his pocket for his device. I race into my bedroom to collect mine from my nightstand.

The message on the device says Code 99. I wrack my brain to remember what that means. I think it's a large casualty incident. In other words, they need as much staff to get to the hospital as soon as possible.

As I return to the living room, I notice Cameron has both his cell and the pager in his hand.

"An out-of-control bus has collided with a cable car. Several cars were involved as well as pedestrians. It seems our hospital is taking a lot of the casualties."

"Shit," I mumble.

"Have you been involved in a large casualty situation before?" he asks.

"Not really. I've seen it, but the last time I was only an intern and was sent to help in triage."

"This will be a baptism of fire for you, then. I hope your pasta sauce will keep."

"It'll be fine. I'll turn it off and get changed."

Cameron's cell begins to ring as I run off to my room to throw on some casual clothes. I'll grab a fresh set of scrubs at the hospital.

This is the life of a doctor.

You can't ever predict when someone will need you.

CAMERON

Stepping into the ER, I take in the scene before me. People are being rushed around on stretchers, while others with less life-threatening conditions wait in the hallways. This department is normally quite busy, but this is the next level. The wails and screams from patients and their families make it hard to think straight, let alone hear anything over the PA.

"I'm here," Chelsea puffs beside me, her voice trailing off. "Wow," she mumbles.

As I shift my gaze to her, I instantly notice her eyes have grown large.

"It's a lot to take in," I sympathize. These situations are extremely daunting to witness.

I gave Chelsea a ride to the hospital, given her car is still out of action. I honestly couldn't care less who saw us arrive together. This is a serious emergency, and my resident and I got to the hospital as fast as we could. Surely, no one will have time for idle gossip today.

Being in Chelsea's apartment gave me goosebumps. I was

tempted to tell her that my feelings for her haven't gone away, and I'd like to give us a shot, even if it is in secret. But then the pagers went off, and any hope I had of telling her disappeared.

I'm absolutely infatuated with this woman, and I can't tell anyone about it, let alone take her to a nice restaurant for a meal or even to a movie. A simple date is all I ask.

While driving in, my dad called me after hearing about the large-scale accident. It was uncomfortable for Chelsea to have to listen to the conversation and not say a word.

Dad was concerned that the hospital can't handle such large-volume casualties and offered to come in. I declined his offer. I think he's forgotten that it was expanded just after he left and is more than able to handle the large volume. The hospital has called asking for his advice, though. While he's technically retired now, Dad's expertise has been called on several times for more complicated surgeries, but it's usually over the phone.

"While you were changing, Dr. Atkins briefed me on their procedure. They are clearing out acute patients or moving patients as quickly as possible to the wards. We'll then have to assess each patient's injury and then move them on to whichever department they need," I advise Chelsea.

"Check," she replies.

"We could be busy for quite some time, I think. You might be asked to assist any surgeon or even go to triage. Just run with it."

Chelsea nods as she continues to look around at all the different areas in the ER.

Ava runs past us, following her new supervisor, Dr. Mark Fisher, an OB-GYN. They are rarely called for these incidents unless there are pregnant women involved.

"Oh my God," Chelsea gasps as she brings her hand to rest on her stomach at the realization. I know exactly how she feels. It's just as bad when it involves children.

"Dr. Chase... over here, please," a nurse calls from one of the resuscitation bays.

"Ready?" I ask Chelsea.

"As I'll ever be."

Walking into resuscitation, we're met with a male patient with an abdominal injury wrapped in gauze and bandages.

"What do we have here?" I ask.

"Male, fifty-one, was on the bus. He was pushed against a rail which has become embedded in his abdomen. He was cut free, and paramedics stabilized him at the scene."

"Right," I reply, as ways of removing this foreign object from this man's stomach begin to run through my head.

After putting on my surgical gloves and the nurses giving me his vitals, I begin to look at the injury, explaining to Chelsea how I plan to tend to it.

Once we decide that he's stable enough to move to the OR, I inform one of the nurses to call ahead to let them know we're on our way.

As we begin to push the stretcher to the doorway, a man in his early twenties staggers into the room, an open wound bleeding on his head and onto his off-white polo shirt.

"Where are you taking my father?" he cries. His voice is slightly slurred, and he rubs at his temple opposite to his wound.

"He needs to get to surgery quickly," I reply.

"He's not going to die, is he?" he asks as another stream of blood runs down his face. "Why are there like fifteen people in here?"

Looking around, there's only Chelsea, myself, and two nurses as well as the patient in the bed.

"Have you been seen to yet?" one of the nurses asks him.

"I'm wa… waiting," he stutters.

"You've got an obvious head trauma. I'll call someone to take you back to your bed." I pick up the receiver, but Chelsea stops me.

"It's fine. How about I take you to be seen?" Chelsea calmly suggests, taking a step toward the man. "Your father is in good hands."

Grasping her arm, I whisper, "I think he needs neuro. Call someone, don't you take him."

She gives me a small smile but dismisses my warning, shaking her arm from my grip.

"But you didn't answer my question. Is he going to die? My mother is never going to talk to me again. He has early-onset dementia. I wasn't meant to take him for a bus ride, but he loves them. I didn't think he could hurt," the younger man wails.

"You did what you thought was right," Chelsea responds. I'm impressed by her cool and calm demeanor.

In a flash, this guy has grabbed Chelsea and spun her around, he wraps his arm tightly around her neck. It all happened too fast that I couldn't stop it even if I tried.

Seeing Chelsea like this has my blood running cold. But it's quickly replaced by the rage of anger that's beginning to build within me.

"Let me go," she cries, scratching at his arm around her neck.

"What are you doing?" I ask, raising my voice as I ball my hand into a fist. "How is this going to help your father?"

"Fix him... fix him now," he demands.

Chelsea's face is crimson as tears fall down her cheeks.

"We can't fix him here," I roar.

The nurses startle at my outburst before continuing to manually pump air into the patient's lungs to keep him stable. He's already been disconnected from the machines, ready to be transferred.

Keeping our patients stable and safe is always our priority.

However, keeping our staff safe is number one.

I've been threatened before, punched, and we once had a shooter come into the ER. But this time is different. Never before has anything happened to someone, I have deep feelings for.

The ER continues as normal around us. With so many other capable bodies around, they aren't stopping to help Chelsea. Damn protocol.

"You need to let go of my resident for me to do that. She's going to assist in the surgery." I lower my voice. Remaining calm is everything in this situation, but I'm not sure how much longer I can hold out.

Security arrives behind the man, and he spins around to look at the two guards, pulling Chelsea with him. Her foot catches on a cart stocked with gauze, gloves, and bandages and knocks it to the floor. The crash of metal on the lined cement floor echoes through the ER.

The guards have their hands on their gun holster.

It's an absolute last resort if this situation can't be resolved.

It better be resolved.

This is my girl.

My heart aches seeing Chelsea like this. I should be the one to rescue her, but I have no idea how, without putting her and myself in danger.

"Let her go," one of the security guys says firmly.

"Get them to fix my dad," he says before a sob escapes him. His speech seems to slur more as the minutes tick on. He could have a severe concussion.

"What don't you understand? This doctor needs to be in surgery to fix him. You're making it worse," the other guard explains.

His blood has now dripped onto Chelsea's beautiful face as she digs her fingers into his skin to try to pry him off her.

With his back to me, I take a step toward them. These types of situations don't call for heroics, but this isn't any emergency. This guy has his arm around my girl's neck.

"Let her go," my voice booms over the noise in the ER.

But he ignores me.

"Cameron," Chelsea cries before beginning to cough.

One of the security guards grabs him when he's distracted by Chelsea.

"Fuck," the guy cries before letting go of Chelsea's neck and pushing her against another cart.

Chelsea flops to the floor, her hands wrapped around her neck.

"Chels," I cry as I drop to my knees to check she's all right. "Take some deep breaths."

She does as I ask as I rub her back. The color in her face returns to normal as fast as it turned red. On inspecting her neck, a small red mark has appeared across her throat.

Security drags the man from the room as he screams, "Sorry" over and over. His apology means nothing. He could have injured Chelsea severely.

"Doctor?" one of the nurses calls.

"Ah, yes," I reply before standing.

Chelsea stands with me.

"We better get this man to surgery," she croaks.

"No, you're getting checked over. I'll take this patient to surgery. After your check, you can watch from the gallery."

"But Ca... I mean, Dr. Chase. I'm fine, really."

How can she be fine? A man just held her against her will. *Heck, even I'm still shaking.*

"Doctor," the nurse repeats, her tone short and snappy.

I'm torn between wanting to protect Chelsea and making sure she's fine and doing my duty as a doctor and saving this man's life.

"We'll take him now. Can you see that she's checked over?" I answer the nurse.

"Yes," she replies, handing the manual ventilator over to another nurse.

Leaning into Chelsea, I whisper, "Please get checked out and cleaned up. I'll see you later."

Almost leaning in to kiss her cheek, I stop myself. Now isn't the time for anything like that.

As we move the stretcher toward the elevators, I glance back at Chelsea being taken to a room to be checked over and breathe a sigh of relief.

If this situation has taught me anything, it's that my feelings for Chelsea are so much stronger than I thought they were.

Surely, there has to be some way around this non-fraternization rule.

CHELSEA

Ripping the blood pressure cuff off my arm, I swing my legs to the side in an attempt to leave the room. I've been here for more than an hour now, and I am furious that I've missed a surgery that I'm not likely to see again for some time. They are keeping me to monitor for signs of a concussion after I hit my head against the metal cart. I feel fine besides a slight headache and tenderness around my neck.

"I need in on that surgery," I grumble to myself as I push the blanket to the end of the bed.

It's my stupid fault that this situation happened in the first place. I was trying to calm the man so that we could get the patient into surgery. I should've recognized the signs that his son had severe head trauma, which occasionally brings violent outbursts. Only I made it worse. I put myself in danger, and I'm sure I'll be receiving a lecture from not only Cameron but from my Chief Resident.

As scary as the incident was, I don't hold any grudge against the man who grabbed me. I've been told that not only did he have head trauma, he also has a mental disability which would've made it difficult for him to process everything.

But there were several moments where I wondered if I'd make it through. I'm sure I saw some of my life flash before my eyes, parts that I've not yet experienced, and Cameron was a part of those events. If anything, what happened today made me realize that life is short, and you need to validate your feelings before it's too late.

Bella, one of the nurses who has kept me here against my will, rushes in to stop me from getting out of the bed.

"Chelsea, stay put. We've told you... you can't leave yet." She places her hands on my shoulders to try and gently lay me back down, but I'm desperate to get up and feel useful again. My hands should be upstairs helping Cameron save lives.

"This bed could be used for someone who was seriously injured in the accident. I'm fine, Bella," I protest.

"Stay," Bella demands. Her tone shocks me. She's normally so sweet and friendly.

"But Cam... I mean, Dr. Chase needs me in surgery with him," I plead.

"I'm sure he's quite capable without you there. You're only a resident, remember?" She chuckles as I roll my eyes and puff in frustration. "Have you got a thing for your supervisor, Chelsea?" she whispers as she leans in. Her plump red lips twist into a smirk.

"What, are you serious?" I reply, trying to stop myself from blushing.

"I wouldn't blame you. I think around eighty percent of the nursing staff in this hospital think Cameron is mighty fine, including me." She looks at her ruby nails.

"But you're married, Bella. You shouldn't be thinking like that," I protest. A pang of jealousy washes over me at her comment. I don't want anyone else thinking that way about

Cameron... *my Cameron.*

"Honey, it's always a look-but-no-touch situation. It's like a marriage law or something. I'm sure Jamal does it, too." She laughs, referring to her husband. "Now lay back. Dr. Atkins will be in shortly. She wants to speak with you."

Inwardly groaning, I do as I'm asked and wait for Dr. Atkins' inevitable lecture on safety protocol. My headache pounds against my skull in the spot that hit the cart, and it's more noticeable than it was five minutes ago, although given the conversation I've just had with Bella, perhaps that's the reason why I'm tensing up.

"Bella, do you think I could have a painkiller? This headache has picked up."

"I'll check for you, honey."

A half-hour later and still no medicine in sight, Dr. Atkins walks into my room and pulls the blue curtain behind her. It's not as though that's going to stop anyone from listening to the lecture I'm about to receive.

"Hello," Dr. Atkins starts. "How are you feeling?"

"I'm fine. A slight headache and my neck's a little tender, but it's nothing major. A couple of Tylenol, and I'll be ready to go."

Bracing myself for her words of disappointment, I clasp my hands together in my lap.

"Sure, we can arrange that, and then we'll send you home to rest for the remainder of the day."

"What? No. Really, Dr. Atkins, I'm fine. I'm sure if you ask Cam... I mean Dr. Chase, he'll tell you that he requires my help in surgery."

You need to stop calling him Cameron, Chelsea.

"Cameron's fine up there. He's the one who asked me to send you home to rest."

He what!

"He *wants* me to go home?" I repeat.

"Given Cameron will be in surgery for some time, and it's against hospital policy for anyone who's been injured on the job to even be in the operating room, he thought it'd be better if you go home."

"Oh," I mumble. "Umm... of course."

"Is there something here that I should know about?" she asks, tilting her head slightly.

"Sorry?"

"Something... between you and Dr. Chase? I'm not the only one who's noticed little things between you. I've heard you almost call him Cameron on several occasions, and you do seem very close, plus I did see he gave you a ride to the hospital today."

"My car is in the shop. An Uber would've taken too long, and he was in my neighborhood when we got the call. He's my supervisor, Dr. Atkins. We call each other by our first names every so often. There's nothing more between us."

She nods her head. "I'd hope so. We both know the rules. This is your second official warning about the situation, though, Chelsea. One more, and you'll get a new supervising doctor."

My eyes widen slightly at what she says. Official warning.

I didn't think she had that kind of authority.

Her smile starts out as kind, but within seconds, she slightly narrows her eyes at me. There's something about this woman that doesn't sit well with me.

"What you did today, to try and calm down the family member, that was both brave and reckless. I won't lecture you on this, I'm sure most of us would've done the same. But if this ever happens again, try to stay out of their reach. Next time you may not be so lucky and could end up with something like this."

Dr. Atkins lifts the sleeve of her coat and shows me a long scar up her arm. My eyes flit between her and her now-healed injury.

"Many years ago, I did something similar to what you did

today. I didn't realize he had a scalpel, and he slashed me. So, all I'm trying to say is you need to be a little more careful and read the signs for danger."

"Yes, Dr. Atkins. It won't happen again."

"Good. We'll see you bright and early tomorrow morning. Of course, if your headache worsens or you start to feel different in any way, call us or get here as soon as you can."

Nodding my reply, I watch as she leaves the room before breathing a sigh of relief. I half-expected her to bellow at me, perhaps lose my surgery privileges for a week, or be reprimanded in some other way.

Maybe Cameron stood up for me.

But he now wants to send you home.

Damn well knowing that I don't have any form of transportation to get home.

After Bella finally brings in some tablets for me, I ask if I can leave then head up to the locker room to fetch my belongings.

Walking into the brightly lit room, I punch the code into my lock before popping open the door. Grabbing my bag, I throw it over my shoulder before closing my locker again. A noise at the doorway has me spinning around.

"Hey," Cameron whispers as he leans against the doorframe. "I saw you come in here. Are you all right?" Cameron folds his arms across his chest. He looks so sexy standing there in his blue scrubs. His surgical cap sits tight on his head, forcing the ends of his hair to stick out. It looks quite cute.

"I'm fine. What are you doing here? I'm heading home since someone said that he doesn't need my services today," I grumble.

Yeah, I'm sulking about being sent home. I could've easily stayed and completed some boring paperwork, but instead, I'm being forced home to sit and do nothing in the middle of an extremely busy time.

"I've stepped out for a moment while vascular does their magic." He nods before shifting slightly. "Chels..." he mutters as he pushes himself off the door, "... it's for the best that you go home. It is partly because of protocol but also because I want you to be safe."

"I am, Cam. He's under security guard now, and my headache is slowly easing. I'd have been fine. I could've done anything. Been useful in some way."

"I understand that, but they have strict protocols here. I had full intention of having you assist with the surgery. It would've been amazing for you to see it, but I couldn't have you not at your best in there today. I'd have been constantly worried about you. Oh, that reminds me, I nearly stumbled earlier in front of Elizabeth."

"Oh," I mumble, worried by what he means about stumbling.

"I've sorted it out, and I think she's none the wiser, but if today's shown me anything, it's that us working together is becoming more and more difficult."

"Difficult?" I repeat, the word catching in my throat. "I thought we made a good team, Cameron."

What's so difficult about being a supervising doctor to a resident? Because that's all we are.

"Difficult is the wrong word. We do, Chelsea. We're a great team. But it's the first time I've ever put a fellow doctor before a patient. You consumed my every thought as we headed to the operating room. As we were prepping, I asked for someone to check on how you were going. They then relayed that message to Elizabeth instead of finding out directly from ER. She spoke to me just before I started the surgery."

His every thought?

Why is he thinking of me?

"Shit, was it bad?"

"She said she appreciated my concern for my resident, and

she'd find out how you were."

Guilt racks my body, knowing that Cameron wasn't focused on his patient, but instead, he was worried for me.

Nodding as Cameron closes the gap between us, a tear slides down my cheek. He reaches out for my face, his thumb skimming over the droplet on my skin.

My eyes close as I savor his reaction to my tears. I'd love nothing more than to hug him right now, give in to my feelings for him. But it can't be.

Perhaps whatever this is between Cameron and me is getting out of control, as though our emotions are running the show.

Is it time for me to bow out gracefully and step away from the hospital? The thought scares me. It's never dawned on me before how much I'd miss Cameron if we weren't working with each other anymore.

But I would. I'd miss him terribly.

My feelings for this man run much deeper than I ever knew possible.

"Cam," I utter, my voice barely audible.

"Head home. I'll call you later."

Cameron places a hastened kiss on my cheek before turning on his heel and leaving the locker room.

My cheek tingles at the sensation. I can't believe he just did that.

He stops dead in his tracks at the door of the locker room.

"Elizabeth," he starts.

My blood runs cold as I hear her name.

"Cameron. I believe they are ready for you again."

"Yes. On my way," he utters before rushing off.

Dr. Atkins sticks her head in the locker room door, and her eyes widen as she sees me.

"Didn't I tell you to go home and rest, Chelsea?"

"Yes, I had to collect my things."

"Chelsea," she begins as she takes a few steps toward me. My heartbeat quickens. "Just a friendly word of advice... don't get too close... with your supervisor. Rumors are already rife about you both, and it'll be detrimental for your career if it gets into the wrong hands."

"I'm not sure what you mean, Dr. Atkins," I mumble before gulping down a breath.

"I know you do, Chelsea. Just be careful is all I'm saying."

With a sly grin on her face, Dr. Atkins leaves the locker room as I stand glued to the spot, trying to process what just happened.

She must have seen Cameron kiss my cheek.

But had she heard our whole conversation? Not that we were talking out of school. Or were we?

My mind races as I even begin to wonder if she knows about our surgery meetings. This woman seems to know everyone's business as though she's gathering the information for some grand evil plan.

Taking several deep breaths to calm myself, I fetch my drink bottle from my bag before downing almost the entire contents.

It's best that I get out of here now. After all that's happened today, I have to clear my mind of not only the hospital and the rumor mill but also Cameron.

I'm so confused by the kiss.

CHAPTER 20

CAMERON

Heading into the staff room, I make myself a strong coffee before walking over to the couches. They're not the most comfortable of chairs, but right now, they will be more than adequate after being on my feet for many hours.

As desperate as I am to check on Chelsea, I need a few minutes to myself to process the events of today. Not only did we miss out on our surgical meeting, the one day each week where I can spend time alone with Chelsea—even if it's in a platonic way—but my girl was held against her will, and I had several surgeries that required delicate work.

My girl—she's not really my girl, but I wish she were.

Placing my coffee cup down, I flop onto the faux leather low couch and instantly kick my shoes off. My little toe feels sore to the touch, and I pull my sock from my foot and discover a small blister has formed.

"Great," I groan as I inspect the severity of the injury. These shoes aren't new and are well worn in, so I can't understand why a blister would have formed.

"Can I help at all?" a female voice comes from the doorway.

Internally groaning as I look up, Elizabeth standing there, her white jacket slung over her arm.

"I'm fine," I reply. "Heading home for the day?"

"No, I'm doing a double. I was going to come in and heat up some food for myself. Mind if I join you?"

Yes, I do mind, I don't want you here, I think.

But I need to remember to remain polite. I don't know what she actually saw between Chelsea and me earlier today.

"Sure. I'll put my shoes back on," I offer, knowing what they can be like after wearing them for such a long time.

"Please," she scoffs. "I've smelled much worse today." She lets out a chuckle before lightly touching my arm as she walks past. My skin crawls at her touch.

Elizabeth is a nice enough woman—attractive, but she's not my type. There's nothing more than a strictly professional relationship between us, but it's becoming more and more apparent to me that she feels something more than that toward me. I need to discourage her feelings and fast before it has an impact on my job.

Once she's warmed her meal, she chooses to sit next to me instead of the other seats in the small staff area.

"Long day," she comments.

"Very," I reply as I take a long sip of my coffee.

"Heading home soon?" she asks.

"I was thinking of it. It seems the on-call surgeons can handle the night shift now. I'd like to head home and grab a few hours sleep so I can enjoy my day off tomorrow."

"Sounds like a good plan," she answers. "It's a shame we won't be working together for a few days."

"Guess that's the life of shift work. Can't work with the same people all the time," I reply, trying to shut down the conversation.

A sudden shift in the air between us has me concerned. Elizabeth brushes a finger against the material of my pants.

Looking down to see what she's doing, she leans toward me, her lips pouted for a kiss. Instantly standing from my seat, I move away from the woman. Sure, I knew she was flirting with me, but I never thought she'd try to kiss me, especially on hospital property.

"Woah, what was that?" I ask.

"I only wanted to see what your lips taste like," she replies, her lips pulling to one side.

"Sorry, Elizabeth, but that's never going to happen between us."

There, it's been said.

Straight to the point.

Surely, she gets the hint now.

From what I've heard from a couple of other male surgeons I've gotten to know recently, Elizabeth uses her sexuality to get what she wants. Whether it be operating room one, or a shift change, she'll use her *assets* to get her there.

The smirk slowly vanishes from her face as her eyes narrow at me. "What's between you and Chelsea?" she blurts out.

"What?" I scoff. "There's nothing. She has amazing potential as a surgeon, and I'm trying to nurture that."

"I call bullshit on that, Cameron."

"Elizabeth, there's nothing happening. I'm not in a relationship, and I don't want to be in a relationship. I'm happily single, and I'm well aware of the hospital's policy about fraternization. Something that I think you may have almost breached."

"Say what you want to say, but if there's really nothing there, then why wouldn't you want to have a little fun with me? Off-premises, of course. I'd let you do anything to me," she purrs as she undoes one of her buttons.

Is she sleep-deprived?

On some form of medication?

I've never seen Elizabeth act out in such a way before, but this must be what the other surgeons meant.

"Elizabeth, I've clearly said I'm not interested. Please stop. This is making me feel very uncomfortable about our working relationship."

She huffs before doing up her button again. "I never thought I'd be turned down like this. Most other doctors are more than happy to have a romp with me either at their home or in the on-call room."

My mouth drops open at her admission.

Collecting my shoes and coffee, I wish Elizabeth a good night before heading to the locker room to grab my bag. I can't help but glance over my shoulder several times to make sure she hasn't followed me.

Elizabeth's behavior has me concerned about my non-relationship with Chelsea. She's obviously suspicious about what's going on. Perhaps she did see me stupidly place a kiss on Chelsea's cheek earlier today. But it was a comforting kiss, nothing more.

I'm playing with fire here, and I'm not sure what to do about it. The easy solution would be to ask Chelsea to find a new supervisor. Remove the temptation. But my feelings for her are real. I've never felt such a deep connection with anyone before. Plus, I haven't seen skills like she has since, well, myself. We make a good team, and I want to help her see out her residency.

My stomach growls as I head to the elevator to go home. I decide to stop in the cafeteria to grab a snack before leaving. I've grown to like the protein bars from a certain vending machine.

The area is dark but not void of light. The cafeteria closes around nine in the evening, but the area is always open for the vending machines. It's mainly the staff who uses them after hours.

As I walk over, I fiddle in my bag for coins prior to noticing two people whispering in front of the machine before tapping on some buttons.

Angry with myself that I don't have the correct change, I pull several dollar bills from my bag's pocket before waiting for them to finish.

That's when Ava and her supervisor turn around.

"Hey, Dr. Chase." She grins.

"Hello, Ava. Nice to see you. Enjoying obstetrics?" I ask.

"It's fantastic. Dr. Fisher here is an amazing OB-GYN."

"That's very sweet of you to say, Ava," he replies. "Mark Fisher. We haven't been formally introduced."

"Cameron Chase."

"Your loss was my gain with this one." Ava beams up at her supervisor. The look in her eyes reminding me of the way Chelsea occasionally looks at me. Admiration for her supervisor, or maybe something more.

"I'm glad you're making a good team."

"Dr. Chase, I've been meaning to come see you. Be careful of Dr. Atkins, she's got a thing for you—"

"That's fine. Thanks for letting me know, Ava," I interrupt.

This isn't new information anymore.

"I overheard her speaking to Dr. Wendy in our staff room last week. Like she has it bad and won't stop until she gets you."

Dr. Fisher lets out a chuckle. "Ava, you shouldn't meddle. I'm sure Dr. Chase can handle himself."

"Yes, I can, but again, thank you for your concern. I've had the hospital policy drilled into me like I'm sure we all have." I laugh. "Listen, Chelsea may need you to call her at some point tonight. She was held against her will in the ER earlier today."

"Holy shit," Ava gasps.

"Was that the young doctor with the man with the bleeding head?" Dr. Fisher asks.

"Yes."

"It was when I asked you to rush back to obstetrics for the files for Mrs. Almer with the twins," he informs Ava.

"I can't believe no one told me. Mark, you should've told me before." She lightly slaps the doctor on the chest. "Is she okay?"

My brows furrow at their closeness.

"She'll be fine. Call her, though," I answer.

Ava nods continuously before Dr. Fisher places his hand on her forearm.

"Let's get back, Ava. We have several women in labor tonight."

"Bye, Dr. Chase," Ava calls as they walk toward the elevator. "Thanks for letting me know."

Standing in front of the machine, I search for the protein bar as a clap sounds throughout the cafeteria followed by Ava giggling.

What the hell was that? If I didn't know any better, I could've sworn that was an ass slap.

Shaking the thought from my head, I collect my protein bar before heading to my car.

Digging my cell out, I flip it in my hand, debating on whether I should text Chelsea this late at night. As I arrive at my vehicle, I bite the bullet and shoot a quick text to her anyway.

Me: *Are you still awake?*

A moment later, she replies.

Chelsea: *Yes, can't sleep.*
Me: *I'm coming over.*

The moment the word 'delivered' appears on my screen, a rush of energy floods my body. Throwing my belongings into the rear seat of my car, I rest my head against the cold metal of the door frame for a brief second trying to calm myself down.

Today's been a completely crazy day, and right now, I need to see Chelsea and make sure she's fine. I only hope she doesn't mind a visitor so late at night.

I'm desperate to hold her in my arms, place my lips on hers, and remain that way all night long. It was torture not being able to hug her today, which is why I kissed her cheek—the action that may have gotten us busted.

My only hope is that it won't cause us any further problems going forward.

CHELSEA

Rolling over again in bed, I punch at my pillow, hoping it will resolve my inability to fall asleep. I've never had problems falling asleep, even after some terrible shifts, but this time, it's more personal. I am worried about my professional relationship with Cameron and what will happen going forward.

My cell is switched to silent, and I'm determined to sleep this headache away, but my mind won't switch off. It's as though my brain is thinking at warp speed.

At first, I was annoyed at myself for being stupid and allowing myself to fall into what could've been a dangerous situation. After that, I kept thinking about what Dr. Atkins said to me and how Cameron was acting slightly off when I last saw him.

He kissed my cheek. What do I make of that?

But my hopes are raised when I receive Cameron's text.

After telling him I'm wide awake, I hold my cell and watch the three dots dance across the screen.

Cameron: *I'm coming over.*

At this time of the night?

Worry floods through me as I begin to think of reasons why he's coming over so late.

Is he coming to tell me that he shouldn't have kissed me?

Does he want me to find a new supervising doctor?

Has something happened at the hospital, and he needs to talk it out?

Maybe he's just coming over to help me search online for a new car.

Perhaps he's just desperate to see me and wants to take the kiss on my cheek further. A laugh escapes me at my silly thought.

"You're acting as though you are madly in love with him, Chelsea?" I warn myself.

Am I?

Can you be in love when you're unable to have a relationship?

Throwing my covers back, I slide out of my bed before flicking the switch on my nightstand light. With Cameron coming over after a long shift, I figure I'll get up and fire up the coffee machine. I'm sure we can both do with a nice strong coffee even though I know it won't aid my sleep.

Being sent home from work to rest was the worst thing that could've happened to me today. I love keeping busy, so to be told to do nothing was a challenge. Lucky for me, I found a series on Netflix to watch, and I binged quite a few episodes. It helped me forget about the situation I've placed myself in and the warning I got from Elizabeth and, of course, Cameron. But the moment I switched the television off, the thoughts returned with a vengeance.

The silence in my apartment is near deafening, so I tap my cell to play some music. One of my favorite songs begins, and usually, I'd turn it up but given the time of night, I opt against it. I couldn't bear to upset any of my neighbors at this time of night.

While singing along to a mix of good songs, I switch on the

coffee machine before straightening up the living room. It's tidy from earlier today, but I did have a throw blanket out while I was watching the television earlier.

As I walk back from my bedroom, I glance at myself in the mirror. The pink tinge around my neck is nowhere near as predominant as it was, thank goodness. It's still tender, and perhaps a faint bruise will form in the coming days, but I'm glad it's not as bad as I expected it to be. To be honest, I thought it would turn black and blue.

Before I know it, a tap sounds at the door. I knew it wouldn't take Cameron long to get here at this time of night. A cold shiver spreads throughout my body, followed by warmth.

How can my body be a mix of nerves and excitement, especially when I really don't know why he's here? I always get a rush of joy when Cameron is around, so that's not a surprise, but I'm feeling anxious about what the kiss means for our professional relationship.

Cringing as I look down at my old, yet comfortable, nightgown I'm wearing, I give a quick shrug of my shoulders before looking through the peep hole to check it is Cameron.

Unlatching my door, I pull it open. Cameron is standing there, leaning against the door frame, his white shirt has the top button undone, and the sleeves are rolled to his elbow. His hair is disheveled, but it definitely adds to his level of sexiness.

This isn't helping.

"Hi."

"Hey. Sorry, it's so late," he replies, his tone low.

"That's fine. I was awake. Come in." I offer him a small smile but don't get one in return.

As he walks by me, a waft of woodsy scent invades my senses. I can't say that it isn't a turn-on.

"I made some coffee if you'd like some," I offer.

"Yes, perfect. That'd be great."

After inviting Cameron to sit on the couch, I make our coffees and bring them over to the small table before sitting down next to him.

My heart is racing a mile a minute, and as much as I will it to slow down, it does absolutely nothing to help.

Taking a deep breath, I let a question fly from my mouth, one that I'm desperate for the answer to. "Cameron, why did you kiss my cheek earlier?"

"I... I'm... I'm not sure, really. Maybe I wanted to comfort you."

"Are you here to tell me to find a new supervising doctor?" I blurt out.

He releases his grip on the coffee cup he'd just clasped before twisting in his seat to face me. "What? What brought this on?"

"I thought it was what you were coming here to tell me. Dr. Atkins gave me a warning about us being close today, and I thought she must have seen you kiss me in the locker room."

"Not at all. I couldn't bear to see you working with another doctor. I've had a run-in with Elizabeth today, too. Sure, I questioned our professionalism, but after all that's happened today, it's made me realize something, something important."

"What's that?" I whisper.

"This thing..." he points between us, "... I'm not sure I can fight it anymore. I want to be with you." His voice is barely a whisper at the end.

Be with me? I've been waiting a long time to hear him say that.

Without giving me a chance to respond, Cameron shifts forward and gently places his lips on mine. My repressed feelings have returned, and I quickly find myself kissing Cameron back.

Something that feels so good is going to get us into so much trouble.

We could both lose our jobs.

But right now, I'm not sure I care.

Cameron pulls back from me, his eyes studying mine as though asking if it's the right thing to do. My lips twitch into a smile. Relief washes over me, knowing I don't have to suppress my emotions anymore. Several tears spring from my eyes and run down my cheeks. The sexual energy between us is rapidly growing, and I'm not sure if I can hold back much longer.

"You have no idea how much I needed to hear you say that, Cam."

But this brings a new set of problems.

His strong arms wrap around me as he pulls me to him. This is what I've needed all day, a firm cuddle to reassure me. He releases his hold of me before turning and taking a long sip of his coffee. I have no idea how he's drinking it so fast as it's much too hot for my lips.

"How are you?" he asks, his coffee cup sitting on his lips.

"I'm fine. Well physically. Mentally, I'm a little tormented, but I'm sure I'll feel better after a good night's sleep."

I'm hoping you'll stay and with me all night.

"I'm sure you will." He drinks the rest of his coffee.

After placing the cup down, he rests his arms on his legs before running his hands through his hair. "I do have several concerns about our situation. As much as I want to be with you, call you mine, I'm still concerned about life at work and what it means for us," he begins.

Gazing into his piercing blue eyes, I suck in a breath before puffing it out slowly. "What concerns?" I mumble.

"The warning from Elizabeth was one thing, but that was before she tried to come on to me—"

Cutting him off, I can feel the blood vessels in my neck growing the angrier I get. "She what?" I screech.

"Don't fret about it. It was absolutely nothing, and I put her in her place, but I think that we're going to have to be extremely careful around work. Elizabeth is very suspicious, and according to a few other doctors, she may be dangerous when it comes to rumors."

"That's a worry, Cam."

It's more than that. It could have a huge impact on both our lives, but I trust Cameron and his judgment, and if he says he's handled it, then so be it.

A warmth spreads over my face and down my body as he leans toward me.

"Forget everything tonight. We'll deal with any concerns tomorrow. Tonight is about you and me." He places his lips on mine. The soft kisses are just what I want and need right now.

Reality hits.

What we're doing is wrong!

But I simply do not care anymore.

I feel as though my heart is fighting against my head as my headache pounds against my skull.

Suddenly, Cameron stops, pulling away from me. *Is he thinking the same as I am?* Lightly touching my lip, I suck in a deep breath and try my hardest to stop myself from kissing Cameron again.

You shouldn't be doing this. Think of your job.

"I'm so sorry, Chelsea. I shouldn't have kissed you... twice," he mumbles.

"It's fine," I reply, my lips pulling to one side. "I wanted you to. I want you to keep going. We've been through this before. You kiss me, then we agree that it shouldn't have happened, and then there's this sexual chemistry between us that doesn't let up. Maybe we need to give in to it and see where this goes."

I need to see where we can go.

I can't stand this lust between us anymore.

CHAPTER 22

CAMERON

This woman before me is practically begging me to kiss her again, and I'm hesitating.

What the fuck is wrong with you, Cameron?

Chelsea stands and pulls her nightgown over her head, revealing her gorgeous body and a pair of white panties. A sultry smile pulls at her lips.

My cock hardens against the zipper of my pants, but I try to remain calm.

"This is serious, Chelsea. My God, I'm drawn to you. I crave you. So much more than I have ever felt for a woman, but we both know what Dr. Walker is like. One hint that there's something going on between us, and we'll be out on our asses. Me, whatever, I can get another job, but for you, this will affect your residency."

She nods before sitting down again on the couch.

Chelsea looks down at her lap, her head bobbing slowly. I know she agrees with me, and we both know it's true. She uses her nightgown to cover her breasts, and I desperately want to grasp her wrists and place them on her lap. Those luscious tits shouldn't be covered up.

"But maybe I can't stay away," she whispers.

"And I don't want you to, but this situation—"

"I know," she replies, her head sinks lower.

"Fuck," I grunt as I jump from my seat. I begin pacing across the living room floor. "What a fucked- up situation to be in. I finally find a woman I like, and, of course, she's a resident." The tone of my voice is gruff, and I shock myself. I never get frustrated like this.

"Maybe you should go," Chelsea offers, lifting her head. "We're both tired. Maybe we can discuss this tomorrow." She waves her hand between us.

"But what's this?"

Chelsea stands and takes a few steps toward me. Lightly biting on her lower lip, she wraps her arms around my waist before placing her cheek against my chest. Her warmth envelops me, and I'm struggling to control myself.

"What about if we had some sort of arrangement? We can't have a relationship, but what if we helped each other scratch an itch from time to time?" she suggests.

"You want to be my booty call?" I ask, puffing out a laugh.

"Um, no. Forget that idea. I don't want to be known as a booty call."

She places her lips against my shirt, her kiss floating over my heart.

My dick strains against my pants. He doesn't seem to be getting the memo on how Chelsea and I can't be doing this.

"Maybe you should get dressed again. The sight of you like that is..." I groan at the end of my sentence, unable to finish it.

"Perhaps I want to take more off, though," she teases as her fingers work on my belt.

"Chelsea," I warn.

Taking a step away from me, she places her hands on her hips. "You're not like most men, are you, Cameron?"

"What do you mean?"

"Well, from my small amount of experience with men, most get to this point of a woman standing in front of them without a top on, and there's no stopping them. But here you are, and you're suggesting I get dressed again?"

"There's good reason for it."

"I know, our jobs." She runs her fingers through her hair before turning away from me and walking to the glass door.

"I think that's as good a reason as any."

"I'm all for keeping my job. I love it." Chelsea turns around and steps toward me again. "But there's something here... between us. I thought it was just a wedding fling, but my feelings toward you have only gotten stronger as time has gone on, even though we were meant to be fighting it."

"Lust?" I ask, confused by what she's trying to say.

"It's more than that. Much more. I can't get enough of you. You consume my thoughts, and I do everything I can just to be around you, even when you were a complete dick to me all those weeks ago at the hospital."

"There was..." I start.

"I know, good reason. There's something pulling me to you... a need, a want." She takes another step closer. Her eyes fixate on mine—she's hungry, lustful. "You make me drop any inhibitions I have, and I feel as sexy as hell when I'm around you."

She runs her hands up and down her body, her thumbs brushing against the waistband of her panties.

"Chelsea," I mumble, trying to restrain myself. My cock has other ideas and is straining against my zipper.

It's every man's fantasy to watch the woman you dream of doing a strip tease in front of you.

She's so confident and sexy as she stands there, hands on her hips. I'm mere seconds away from closing the distance between us and carrying her to her bedroom.

"You're making this so hard, Chelsea."

"That's the hope, Cameron." She laughs.

"If we do this tonight, then we still face the problem of tomorrow and every day going forward concerning our situation."

"I understand that," she replies. "But can't we forget about all of that tonight and just enjoy this... us?"

My need for her overtakes any kind of rational thought I have.

Taking three steps to close the distance between us, Chelsea's eyes light up as I reach her and place a kiss on her soft lips. The kisses quickly turn feverish as her hands run over the buttons of my shirt, desperately trying to undo them as fast as her fingers will work.

With our lips still connected, I help her with my top buttons and shimmy my shirt off my shoulders before scooping her into my arms.

A moan escapes her mouth as she throws her arm around my neck, her warm, soft tits pressing against the hardness of my chest. Memories of our night together after the wedding flood back to mind.

My hands run up and down her back before sliding down to her ass. As I cup her well-proportioned tight butt and gently lift her, she squeals in delight, the sound a mixture of shock and excitement.

"Don't drop me, Dr. Chase." She giggles.

"Never."

As she wraps her legs around my hips, I begin to kiss her neck, slowly working my way from behind her ear to her collarbone.

"Bedroom?" I mumble.

"Through there," she replies, flicking her head back toward an open door.

Walking us into the darkened room, Chelsea suddenly claps her hands once behind my head, startling me. A lamp switches on in the corner, adding an ambiance to the room.

Chelsea unwraps her legs from around me and slides to the floor. Taking a step back from me, she stands against the edge of her bed before hooking her thumbs into the waistband of her panties and sliding them down her legs. My cock jumps to attention at the sight of this gorgeous woman.

"You're too dressed, Cameron," she whispers as she looks up at me through her lashes.

Taking a step toward her, she reaches out for my belt and quickly releases the tab before sliding it out of the loops of my pants, the leather strap joining Chelsea's panties on the floor.

She carefully sits on the edge of her bed as her fingers work their magic on the button and zipper of my pants. Gently sliding them down my legs, I step out of them before kicking them to the side.

"That's a bit better," she murmurs as her lips pull to one side.

Reaching for her face, I slide my hands along her cheekbone before cupping her ear, my thumbs running over the soft cartilage and her ear piercings. My lips meet hers, and our kisses turn frantic. I need this woman, and I need her now.

Gently pushing her back into the mattress, I slide my boxers down my legs before kicking them to the side as Chelsea slides back up the bed.

Kneeling on the mattress, I crawl up and over her before taking her mouth with mine again.

She widens her legs, and I settle between them before teasing her slightly by running my cock up and down her pussy. Chelsea moans at the sensation, the noise making my cock as hard as it can possibly be.

Guiding my cock to her entrance, I gently nudge her before burying myself inside of her. Chelsea gasps at the sensation as the warmth of her pussy has a moan escaping from me.

Stilling for a brief moment, a smile involuntarily spreads across my face as I look down at this beautiful woman underneath me. I know this could lead us into trouble, but I'm switching off any negative thoughts in my head. What I do within our own four walls should have nothing to do with our jobs. We can remain professional at the hospital.

This feels good, no, right.

Any issues we may run into going forward, we'll handle when and if it happens. We owe it to ourselves to pursue our feelings, at least for tonight.

Tonight is about us and us alone.

CHELSEA

After refilling my water bottle in the staff room, I take a big drink from my flask. Four hours today in one surgery, and I'm feeling dehydrated and my legs are aching. Perhaps it's exhaustion from what we got up to last night.

The surgery was more difficult than we envisioned. Each time Cameron would remove a little more of the patient's damaged spleen, he'd start bleeding again, and we'd spend quite a bit of time cauterizing the vessels. It was definitely the most challenging surgery this week so far.

Standing in front of the large whiteboard near our staff room, I look at all the operations scheduled for tomorrow and notice Cameron only has one surgery in the middle of the afternoon.

My brows knit together.

That can't be right.

Dena, one of the new interns, walks by before turning back and standing next to me. I twist my head and give her a polite smile. She's a sweet intern but does get a little in your face from time to time. She'd get along so well with Ava as they both love

153

idle gossip.

"It must be so awesome to see your name on the board, Dr. Mitchell." She beams.

"Yes, it is."

"Oh, but you're only on there with Dr. Chase once tomorrow. That can't be right."

"That's what I was just thinking, Dena."

"Maybe it's because Dr. Chase turned down Dr. Atkins. She's apparently got it *real* bad for him."

"What?" I unintentionally boom.

Dena's eyes widen, and she purses her lips together. "Sorry, Dr. Mitchell. I shouldn't gossip, but I heard it from another intern, Marcel."

Good going, Chelsea, let's make it obvious that you're jealous by some stupid rumor. It's only been two weeks of being officially together, and I'm already acting like some bitter schoolgirl.

Turning away, I begin my search for Cameron. Luckily, I don't have to look for very long when I find him in the locker room.

"Cam," I whisper as I walk right up beside him.

He closes his locker before facing me, his lips pulling into a smirk. Cameron looks left and right before placing a hasty kiss on my cheek.

"Hey," he replies.

"What happened to not doing that here?" I mutter.

"Couldn't help it. Your legs all right now?" he asks.

"Yeah, they're fine," I answer as I tuck a few fly-away hairs behind my ear. "Did you know you're only scheduled for one surgery tomorrow?"

"One?" he repeats "That can't be right. I'm sure I had at least two. One morning and one afternoon."

"Well, only the afternoon one is up there now."

"It's fine, Chelsea. I probably got bumped for an emergency. It happens."

"I understand, but we wouldn't know the emergencies yet."

"True."

"Could it be that she knows about us and is jealous?"

"She can't possibly know."

"Then what?" I ask.

Cameron looks at me and shrugs his shoulders before pursing his lips together.

"Hmm... all right. Come on, we'll go have a look at the board."

Following him back down the corridor, we both stand in front of the board and try to work out what's happened.

"Elizabeth," he mutters before pointing to where his name was scheduled on the board. "She's taken my place."

"I'm amazed that she's wanting to do the surgery... I mean, for starters, she can't wear her heels in there," I whisper into Cameron's ear.

We both start laughing before someone stands on the other side of me.

Twisting my head, I instantly see the red-heeled shoes of Dr. Atkins.

"Dr. Aktins," Cameron begins. "I was just checking my surgeries for tomorrow. Looks like you've taken one of my patients."

"Yes, well, I need surgery time, and after speaking to Donna today, she told me she'd feel more comfortable with a female surgeon."

"Donna?" Cameron asks.

"The patient. Donna Bates. Surely, you know patients' names, Cameron." She laughs. That evil cackle making the hairs on the back of my neck stand up.

"Mrs. Bates didn't seem to have an issue with me this morning," Cameron replies. He balls his hand into a fist at his side. I desperately want to grasp it and calm him down.

"Dr. Chase. We'd better go and check on our patients," I

mention, anything to get him away from this woman.

How can one surgeon so blatantly steal another surgeon's patient?

"Yes, of course," he mumbles. "I'll be speaking to the chief about this, Elizabeth."

"Maxim won't do anything about it, Cameron." She grins before turning and walking away. Her heels clicking against the solid flooring.

"That bitch," he groans. "I've consulted with Mrs. Bates for the past month. She's never mentioned any issue."

"Forget it," I encourage.

Walking back to the locker room, I check to see no one else is in there. Cameron sits on the small bench, and I next to him.

"Cam, there's a rumor that you turned Elizabeth down last week."

"What? How did... what?"

"One of the interns told me, who heard it from another."

"There's no way anyone could've known about that unless Elizabeth told them."

"So, it's true?" I squeak, my eyes widen slightly.

"Sort of. She hit on me... again. She's been doing it for a while now. She doesn't seem to get the message, though."

This time, my fists ball at my sides. If she were here right now, I'd swing one of them into her jaw. *That bitch, trying to get it on with my man.*

"Calm down, Chelsea," Cameron soothes.

Slowly releasing my hands, the tension begins to leave my body. "I am," I reply.

"Maybe she's taken my patient as a punishment for me telling her no. That sounds ridiculous." Cameron laughs.

Nodding my head, I agree. "It does, but everything about her is ridiculous. She's trying to fuck with your head. Probably best to stay clear of her."

I really don't want to come across as the jealous girlfriend, but I feel that giving him that small piece of advice is beneficial for him and us as a couple. She's really playing up to being a scorned woman.

Cameron definitely has a lot of shit to deal with at this hospital since starting here. He's taken most of it in his stride, but today was the first time I've seen him become angry about something. Cameron prides himself on being a great doctor and having a good bedside manner, so to have Elizabeth say a patient was uncomfortable, that would've cut deep.

My jealousy will need to be kept in check, though. Jealousy has never been a factor in my life, but I can't stand the thought of someone trying to hook up with my boyfriend. We're still in our early days, though, so surely, there's some room for improvement on my behalf.

"Let's go home," I whisper, a smile pulling on my lips.

"Sounds good. Maybe we can discuss the car situation, too."

Two residents walk into the locker room, and I move away from Cameron a little. We don't want to unnecessarily be seen close together.

Many things about our relationship are proving to be difficult at the hospital, like finding a reason not to join other staff members for a drink after work because I've already made plans with Cameron. Wanting to ask who's staying at who's house tonight, but not being able to get Cameron in private. Little things that start adding up.

But we won't let these obstacles get in the way of us. I won't let my jealousy interfere with my work. Cameron and I are made for each other, and we'll make the absolute best out of this situation.

CHAPTER 24

CAMERON

Watching Chelsea sleep as the early morning light streams in brings a smile to my face. She looks so peaceful, and it's calming, knowing that neither of us has to rush around to get ready for work today. We're going to spend the entire day together. I'm going to take her on our first official date, even if it's been a month since we started dating.

The sun woke me around an hour ago, and since then, I've been lying here thinking of where to take this beautiful woman today on our date. I'm toying with the idea of either driving up to Mount Tamalpais or taking her to Muir Beach Overlook. I must admit that I'm leaning more toward Mount Tam as Muir Beach can get so busy with tourists, and I definitely want to spend quality alone time with Chelsea today.

My body begins to crave caffeine, and I gently slide from the bed, trying not to wake her.

"Don't leave," she groans, reaching out to the side of the bed I slept on.

"Only making coffee," I whisper.

Chelsea rolls onto her stomach before pulling the covers up around her neck.

After using the bathroom and switching on the coffee machine, I grab my cell and begin to order picnic items for today which we'll collect on our way out. There's something about store-bought food compared to food you've made yourself that adds a little to the romance, I think, and that's definitely what I want to show Chelsea today.

Once it's all ordered, I open the car website we'd discussed several days earlier at the hospital before fixing the coffees and heading back to bed, placing her cup on the nightstand.

It only takes a moment for her to catch the waft of coffee before she's rolling onto her back and stretching her arms above her head. The sheet covering her moves slightly, revealing her soft yet perky breasts.

Placing my cup next to hers, I lean down and place my lips on hers before my hands skim over her chest.

"Hmm, morning," she hums against my lips as I gently roll her nipple between my thumb and forefinger.

"Morning," I reply.

As much as I'd love to continue this and explore every inch of her gorgeous body, I know we have much more to do today than stay in bed.

"Oh," she pouts when I remove my hand.

"Plenty of time for that later on. Today, I'm going to take you on a nice drive."

"A drive?" she repeats.

"A date. Our first official date. You don't have anywhere else to go, do you?"

"No. But what happens if someone sees us?" she asks.

"We're going somewhere remote. I highly doubt we'll be seen."

"Where to?" she asks, sitting up in bed. She pulls the sheet with her, tucking it under her arms to cover herself.

"It's a surprise, but I suggest you wear long pants and bring a jacket."

She screws up her nose in confusion as I take a sip of my coffee. As cute as she is, she won't be getting any hints out of me.

Crawling back into bed beside her, I show her my cell, still open on the car website.

"What's this?" she asks.

"Remember how we were talking about you buying a new car the other day, and I told you I'd happily help?"

"Oh, yeah."

"So, I thought we could have a look at some online, get a feel for what you're after."

She takes the device from me and scrolls through the page. A few oohs and ahhs tumble from her mouth.

"This is such a good idea. I only need something small. Pink or blue would be my preferred colors." She chuckles. "But I don't exactly have much money to play with."

"Money's no problem. We need to get you something that's safe and will get you from point A to point B without any hassles."

"Agreed, but within a small budget," Chelsea adds.

"Chels, I'm happy to chip in."

"I couldn't ask that of you."

"You're not," I reply. "I'm offering. The money is there, and I'd rather you spend it on something that will last you ten years than not spending it and my worrying about you each time you jump in another bomb. If you want to think of it as a loan, then do so." A chuckle escapes me.

"You're too kind, Cam. How about we see what's in my price range first, and then we'll talk money?"

Almost an hour later, Chelsea finds a car that she really likes and has agreed to my loan offer. The Audi's are definitely a safe and reliable car, plus it makes me feel so much better than her driving something that's already ten years old.

"I'll pay every cent back... with interest," she reiterates.

"I know how you can thank me... but that will have to take place tonight. Come on. Up and shower. We have somewhere to be, and I need to head home first for some clean clothes."

After emailing the Audi car dealer, where I helped my parents purchase their latest car, I wait for Chelsea to shower and dress before heading to my place. I figure it's easier for me to shower and dress at my place rather than putting yesterday's clothes back on.

"Your cell is dinging," Chelsea calls from my bedroom.

"It's probably the emails. I'm not on-call today."

She brings my device to me before leaning against the counter and watching.

"Car's all yours, sweetheart." I grin.

"Yay," she squeals before running over to me and placing a very passionate kiss on my lips.

"Ahh," I groan. "If we didn't have somewhere to be, you'd be naked and up against that wall right now."

Chelsea giggles and her face flushes before she steps out of the bathroom.

A few minutes later, I follow her, and she watches as I get dressed.

"You know I had a dream about that happening once?" she mumbles.

"A dream?"

"Yeah, in the shower. Both of us. I have to admit I thought about it all day at work."

Walking toward her, my cock is straining against my boxers at the thought of her sexual dream of us. Pushing her flat against the mattress, I hungrily kiss her and grind my cock against her jeans.

"Argh," she moans into my mouth. "Cameron, stop before I come."

A smirk spreads on my face, and I move away from her. Her face is tinged pink as she dabs at the corners of her lips.

"I know it's not exactly beach weather today, but where would we go that's within driving distance, and we'd need jackets?" she asks, somewhat rhetorically.

"You'll see soon enough. I've got a small table and chairs we can take. We also have to pick up some picnic items and then put down the deposit for your car before we can leave. Once that's done, we're out of here for the day."

"Table and chairs?" she repeats as she cocks her head to the side. "I'm not normally one for surprises, Cam, but this is really exciting. I could get used to this."

"You should be wined and dined. Be romanced. You deserve that and so much more. I plan on doing this each time we have days off together."

"Can women wine and dine men? If so, then maybe I could surprise you with a day out, too. I have the perfect idea for the first one," she teases.

"I enjoy surprises, so that'd be fun. I don't see why women can't plan dates for men." I beam. "Ready to go?"

"Sure am."

We pack the trunk of my car with the table and chairs before picking up the picnic items on our way to the car dealership. After paying for Chelsea's new teal blue A3, we're told it'll be ready for pick up in a week.

Grasping her hand as we leave the dealership, she squeals in delight.

"Thank you so much, Cam. I promise I'll pay you back."

"My pleasure, gorgeous. I was always planning on offering the money."

"That's very kind of you."

"My resident needs something safe to drive... and now she's my girlfriend."

"Girlfriend... I like the sound of that." She twists her head as a sweet smile spreads across her face.

"How about we have our fun day now?"

Chelsea excitedly nods her reply.

We jump back in my car and begin our trip to Mount Tamalpais. There's one lookout in particular that I absolutely adore and can't wait to show Chelsea.

Switching the radio on, I begin to tap to the rhythm of the music as Chelsea hums along. Normally, I'd be happy to sing to any song that plays, but I wouldn't want to subject Chelsea to my tone-deaf voice.

After a short trip, we drive past a sign that points toward the lookout. Glancing at Chelsea, I instantly see her face light up.

"Are we going where I think we are?" she asks, her question ending with a little squeal. "This makes sense about needing a table and chairs now."

"Maybe. We'll be there before you know it," I reassure her.

"As you can probably tell... I'm impatient." She laughs.

"Really? I couldn't tell at all." I feign shock at her comment before a chuckle escapes me.

Turning the car into a parking lot, I quickly realize that my plan of a pretty picnic here may not be the ideal location. The parking lot is much fuller than I expected, and there's no real place to set up our table and chairs.

"There are more people here than I thought would be," Chelsea mumbles as she looks out the window.

"Hmm, there is. Do you mind if we drive a little more? I know one more place that's much more secluded, and it's just as pretty."

"You're planning this day. Take me wherever you want."

As she realizes what she's said, she giggles before biting her lip. I can't resist leaning over to her and brushing my lips against hers.

"I'd take you here and now if there wasn't anyone around."

"I'd like that," she whispers before running a finger down the side of my face and across my beard.

The way the soft sunlight is hitting her face and hair makes Chelsea look angelic. My heart pounds knowing that this woman is finally mine. I'm so glad we've decided to give us a real go. I've never felt so strong for someone. Dare I say it. Love her?

Love. That's a word I wasn't sure I'd ever use. I was sure I was destined to a life of being chained to the hospital because of no social life, but Chelsea's changed all that for the better.

Argh, this has gone from a fun day out to wishing we had stayed home in bed all day, doing anything and everything to each other.

But sex in a public place isn't my thing, so we'll need to control our feelings until we can let them loose later tonight back at my place.

We need to be more than sex, though. I want to show Chelsea how much I care for her and tell her how much she means to me.

These past weeks have been almost torture in fighting these feelings. Now I can let them out to Chelsea, and we can see where things lead.

Puffing out a breath of sexual frustration, I leave the lookout and drive on to our picnic location for the day. If this one is taken too, then all my plans for the day have failed, and my cock may get some much-needed relief sooner than anticipated when we head home.

I'm determined to find somewhere to picnic today, though, even if we have to find a small alcove. This mountain area is so peaceful and why it's my favorite. I love nothing more than coming here and sitting in my car, allowing the noise of the day to float away. It's my way of relaxation. Well, it was before

Chelsea came along and allowed me to discuss my day with her.

Now I get to share my slice of tranquility with the woman I'm in love with. Perhaps today is the right time to tell her those three little words too.

CHAPTER
25

CHELSEA

Cameron places his plastic wine glass, half-filled with soda, back on the table before reaching out for my hand. We've set up our picnic away from as many people as possible, not because we're hiding since today wasn't about that, but because we want to be alone and spend that much-needed time together.

Our picnic lunch was simple but absolutely delicious. It was so huge, I couldn't eat it all. I think Cameron struggled too. It took a ham and cheese with slaw sandwich to the next level. I've never tasted anything like it. I'll definitely be going back to that shop to try each of their subs.

His thumb skims across my knuckles as he sits back on the chair, crossing his legs over at his ankles. We're surrounded by nothing but trees and rock formations as the sounds of birds chirping fill the air.

"I should've bought a bottle of wine with us," Cameron tuts.

"This is perfect."

Today's been amazing. Sure, we've spent many times alone,

but not like this. This time there's no tension between us. We're relaxed and open about our feelings, even if the niggle of the hospital plays in the back of our minds.

It's a little cooler than I was expecting, so I'm glad I brought my jacket, but I'm starting to wish I had worn warmer pants.

Discreetly trying to rub my hand up and down my leg for a little warmth, Cameron flicks his head toward me. "Are you cold?"

"Not really. I should've chosen warmer pants, though."

"I've got a blanket in the car if you'd like that."

"Don't fuss, I'm fine," I reply, waving my free hand at him.

Cameron quickly shakes his head at my dismissal. "Maybe I should've brought a picnic blanket, so we could've cuddled together and kept each other warm. Although, I'm not sure my old ass could get up from the ground."

"Hardly old. You're more fit than some twenty-somethings we work with."

"From time to time, I do feel my age, especially during winter."

"Your forties are the new thirties, didn't you know?" I chuckle before adding, "Cam, this day has been amazing, and I can't thank you enough."

"Come here." Cameron gently pulls on our connected hands. I stand and walk around the table to where he's sitting, wrapping my free arm around his neck.

Letting go of our hands, Cameron guides me to sit across his lap. I wrap my arms around his neck as he nuzzles into mine.

"The view here is amazing," I mutter to Cameron.

"Not as good as the one I'm looking at, sweetheart," he replies.

My heart skips a beat at his comment. The connection I have with Cameron is so strong. I'm the moth to his flame. Men like this don't exist in the real world. Usually, they are actors in movies playing a part. I feel so blessed to have found someone who can make me feel like a princess but also keeps me grounded.

The added bonus is that he's taught me so much since he has become my supervisor, and we definitely haven't let our relationship interfere with work.

"Where'd you go?" he asks, placing a kiss on the top of my arm.

"Thinking how lucky I am to have found a man like you," I gush, twisting my neck so I'm facing him.

"The feeling is mutual. But I'm the lucky one."

Leaning in, I place my lips on Cameron's, his facial hair tickling my face much more than usual.

Pulling away, I giggle before lightly touching my face.

"What's wrong?" he asks.

"Someone needs to trim his beard, I think." I laugh.

"Ah, yeah, it's a few days overdue."

"I don't mind it, really."

"I know where you like it most," he whispers as his hand skims across my thigh before tickling between my legs.

"Hmm," I moan before leaning down to kiss him again. I'm not sure how he feels about sex in public, but right now, he could strip me bare and take me on the hood of his car, and I wouldn't care who saw.

Breaking our kiss, I readjust my position on his legs before deciding that I need to walk for a moment to calm myself down.

Shaking my hands as I puff several times, I look back at Cameron silently laughing at my arousal.

"Quiet you… you did this to me," I playfully grumble.

"And I'd do it again and again. I love how I can turn you on so easily."

"I'm not sure I want to do anything in public, though. I'm all for our little rebellion with going on a date, but I'm not sure I want to be breaking the law."

"Me neither, sweetheart. We'll keep that for our beds."

Hell yeah, I inwardly cheer.

"Good."

"Want to head home?" he asks, his eyes twinkling in the early afternoon sun.

"Not yet. I mean, yeah, I want to, but I also don't want to head back to reality just yet."

"I completely understand that."

It feels as though we're in our own little slice of heaven here. There's no traffic, and our cells are in the car. It's just us, nature, and most importantly, being together.

After all the time that we've spent together at our weekly meetings, I was sure Cameron would've grown tired of me by now. But instead, he's willing to break the clause in our contract and have a relationship with me, which could have repercussions.

"You know, I was thinking earlier..." Cameron begins. "About you... me... us." He stands and walks over to me. "Chels, I've never felt this strongly about someone as I do about you."

"Me, too. It's kinda blown my mind. Even with the amount of time we spend together, I find myself missing you when we're apart."

He rubs his hands up and down my arms. "That's exactly how I feel."

"When we agreed that night to keep our relationship professional, I'd often think of you much more than that. My feelings for you grew, even though we weren't together. I didn't even know that was possible, to fall for someone when you aren't officially together."

"I used to think it was all in my head, that I was imagining these feelings, but I wasn't. I was the feeling the exact same."

"When that guy held you against your will, I wanted to rip him limb from limb for hurting you. It was then I realized that I can't fight my feelings anymore."

I don't know how to respond to that, although I feel the same. It put things into perspective.

Cameron puffs a breath as he pulls me to him. Wrapping my arms around his middle, I rest my head against his muscular chest. His heart thumps against his ribcage as though it's trying to escape.

Why is he so nervous?

The single thought increases my heart rate. What could he need to say that's causing him to feel anxious?

Pulling me back from his chest, Cameron brushes his lips against mine before a slow grin spreads across his face.

"I think I'm fal..."

At that exact moment, two loud cars drive by, blocking me from hearing the rest of Cameron's sentence. It's as though they are revving their engines as much as they possibly can.

Dammit. There's no way I could make out the words on his lips.

"Fuck," I see him mouth with a grimace.

As the cars disappear into the distance, Cameron scruffs his face before his chin dips to his chest.

Cameron's disappointed by the event that just unfolded. But I can't help laughing at the untimely nature of the only cars we've seen for a good couple of hours. I calm myself before asking him to repeat it.

"No. Maybe some other time."

"Please?"

"Chels, maybe it was a sign that it's too soon for me to say what I was going to."

My breath hitches in my chest at the suggestion of what he was planning on saying.

"Bad timing, yes. A sign, no. If it's what I think it is... that's how I feel, too."

Cameron lifts his gaze, our eyes connecting. His eyes are different in this moment, somewhat softer. These are the eyes of a man who's declaring his love, and I'm more than ready to hear those words.

"I think I'm falling in love with you."

My heart feels as though it's going to burst through my chest.

"I've fallen for you as well, Cam. I love you."

As our smiles grow at the same rate, Cameron lowers his lips to mine. In this kiss, full of sweetness and passion, a thousand thoughts rush through my mind, all completely condensed in a single moment.

Any insecure feelings I had about us are long gone. My heart is full, and I never want that to change. If I could climb to the peak of this mountain and scream my love right now, I would.

Pulling myself away from Cameron, I raise on my toes and wrap my arms around his neck and nuzzle in.

"I was worried you weren't ready to say it," he whispers.

"I don't think I'd have said it yesterday, but after yesterday and being here today, it has made me realize how much I do love you and how much I want a future with you."

My body stills after the words leave my mouth.

A future. How do you plan a future with someone when you're single, according to every person you know?

While it's going to be a challenge for us, I'm sure we'll find a solution to our situation together. We have to.

CHAPTER 26

CAMERON

Three Months Later...

My ideal day off is a Sunday spent in bed with Chelsea. However, today, we both have to attend a brunch at Matthew and Sara's place, separately, of course.

Chelsea rolls over in bed to face me, the light blanket covering her chest slips as she moves, exposing her perky tits.

Gently massaging her breast, she doesn't seem as into it as I was hoping she'd be.

"What's wrong?" I ask.

"Nothing. Nothing's wrong... I'm actually enjoying what you're doing."

I don't believe that for a second.

"Your face tells me another story, sweetheart."

She lets out a deep sigh. "I just think it's sucks that we can't show up at Matthew and Sara's together today. Like, we've been together for quite a while now, Cam. I want to be able at least tell our family about our relationship."

This isn't a new conversation. It's been ongoing for a few weeks now, and I'm beginning to tire of it. We seem to go around and around this topic but never find a solution. I can't understand why she wants to begin telling people about us. I'm enjoying being in our little bubble, just the two of us.

It's not as though it's becoming hard to hide our relationship at work. If anything, it's quite easy. We both switch into doctor mode, and we remain busy throughout our shift. There's never a lull where we're itching to jump each other's bones. We save that for home.

Puffing in frustration, I remove my hand from her breast and cover her back up.

Chelsea watches what I do before sucking in a breath. "I'm sorry," she mutters.

"We've spoken about this, Chels. We can't tell my family as my father knows people who work at the hospital. As happy as Mom and he would be for us, all it would take is a slip of the tongue that I'm your supervisor, and all hell will break lose."

"I realize that, Cameron," she whispers.

"You're always saying that your mom will shout from the rooftop that you're with someone. That will hardly help our situation either, and then there's Sara and Matthew."

"What about them? She's my cousin, and he's your best friend. They don't have any connection to the hospital. Neither of them would do us any wrong," she protests.

"But all it takes is a slip of the tongue. What if they accidentally mention us to anyone at all? If Sara mentions it to her dad, and he tells your mom..." Rolling onto my back, I grasp at my unruly hair in frustration. "There's so much at stake."

"I agree. But where does that leave us." Chelsea runs her finger along my arm.

"We keep doing what we've been doing. If we don't say anything, then no one's any the wiser."

"Don't you understand my frustration at this, though, Cam? It's like we have a dirty little secret that we need to hide. We're both consenting adults who have been together for months now. We both love each other." Chelsea runs her free hand through her hair. "I don't know, Cam. Would the solution be for me to find another hospital to work at?"

What? What the hell is she thinking about? Giving up a job because we can't be seen together by anyone at the hospital? Why don't I understand why she feels the need to tell people?

"What? God no. Do you not like working with me anymore?"

"It's not like that at all, Cam. I love working with you. I love being with you. I'd just like to be able to introduce you to my parents as my boyfriend. It's difficult to keep you out of conversations. Perhaps if I told them, they'd stop trying to set me up with every Tom, Dick, and Harry in San Francisco."

"Sweetheart, I'd love to introduce you to my family, too, but it's too risky."

There has to be a solution. Chelsea is my forever, but I really can't see a way past this clause in the work contracts.

"Anyway, come on, enough with this for now. We have to start getting ready to head to Matthew and Sara's."

Chelsea scoffs at me. "Of course, sweep it under the rug again."

"Excuse me?" I grumble.

"You heard me. You prefer to bury your head in the sand about us rather than have us go public. We aren't a fling, Cam. We're very serious about each other. Unless... you're embarrassed to be with me?"

"I'm not burying anything, and I'm definitely not embarrassed to be with you. I'm not sure how to proceed."

"Our relationship isn't a surgery that you have to strategically plan out and come up with a course of action alone. We're a team. Both of us need to agree about what happens. Otherwise, maybe we have to agree to disagree and go... our separate ways." Her breath hitches on the final words.

Does she want to end things?

"Is that what you want?" I quietly ask as I turn my head to face her.

"Not at all... but it's beginning to become clear that we don't see eye to eye on this." A tear rolls down her cheek.

"Neither do I. Can we please talk about this later?"

"Fine. I'm going to go home and change there, especially since we have to arrive separately, anyway."

"You don't—" I begin as she throws back the covers interrupting me.

"Yes, I do."

Chelsea dresses in the clothes she wore here last night before collecting her belongings.

"See you there," she sniffles before placing a hastened kiss on my lips.

Chelsea sees herself out as I sit on the edge of my bed and rest my head in my palms. What the actual fuck just happened here?

Have we broken up? It sure as hell feels like it was some form of breakup.

My heart grows heavy as the realization sets in. Never in my wildest dreams did I see this coming. Chelsea is everything to me, and I'm not sure if I'll function without her in my life.

Even if this relationship breaks up, my love for Chelsea will never wain. I'd rather remain single for the rest of my days than try to find someone half as good as she is for me.

But I need to fight for her. Show her that even if we need to hide our relationship for a while longer, it will all be worth it in the end. I had plans to ask her to be my wife, not right away, but someday soon. The hospital wouldn't be able to do shit if we were married. I know for a fact that Maxim Walker is married to a doctor at the hospital.

After dragging my sorry ass off the bed, I get myself showered and dressed before heading over to my friend's place. Plastering a smile on my face is much harder than I thought it would be. This isn't even the first time that Chelsea and I have had brunch at their place, so why does today feel so different?

Pulling up outside their house, I notice Chelsea's car is already here. Grabbing the bottle of red that I brought with me, I exit my car before taking several deep breaths. Each one burns as it expels from my body, almost to the point of tears.

This hurts not knowing if Chelsea and I will make it past today.

But I must remain strong because, according to Matthew and Sara, nothing is new or different with me, and they must remain under that illusion.

Chelsea and I will have a long, possibly hard chat later on today, but for now, it's all smiles and faking happy.

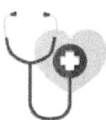

Placing my fork down on my plate, I pick up the napkin and dab the corners of my mouth. The eggs Sara made were absolutely divine but a little messy.

"So..." Sara begins. "We have some exciting news to share."

Glancing across the table, I watch my best friend grasp his wife's hand and place a loving kiss across her knuckles.

"We're having a baby," Sara cries. As wide as her grin is, tears begin to fall down her cheeks.

"Congratulations," Chelsea squeals as she stands to hug her cousin.

"Congratulations, dude," I exclaim as I stand with my hand outstretched to shake Matthew's. But instead, he pulls me in for a man-hug.

"I'm shitting myself, man, but we're fucking excited,"

Matthew whispers in my ear.

"You'll do awesome," I reply.

As we all calm down, we sit back in our chairs. I take several sips of my water.

"So, it's only around six weeks in, but we had to tell you guys, given you're both doctors. We'd figure that you may clue on to a symptom or something and accidentally blab it in front of someone before that safe twelve-week mark. We couldn't have that happen," Sara explains.

"Sara's family are known gossipers," Matthew adds.

"No, we're not. We keep secrets well. Good secrets, don't we, Sar." Chelsea throws a look at me before turning her attention to her cousin.

Was that a swipe at me?

Gulping down my water, I begin to cough and splutter as it's gone down the wrong way.

Matthew pats on my back as he laughs at my misfortune.

Thanks, bud. Won't rely on you if I'm dying.

Standing from the table, I excuse myself and make my way to the bathroom to compose myself. By the time I close the door, the coughing has stopped, but I'm slightly breathless.

Resting my hands on the basin, I stare at my reddened face in the mirror.

Fuck, this situation is crap. Maybe I should give in to her request, but it defeats the purpose of why we need to keep it quiet. The hospital. Our work. That's why.

In a parallel universe, Chelsea and I would be able to share our happy news with our nearest and dearest, but this is the real world, and we're hiding it. All because of a stupid clause in our contracts.

Maybe the solution is simple. Have Matthew look over my employment contract, see if there's a way around this clause. If there is, then wonderful. If not, do I give up a job of a lifetime for the woman I love? Or do we accept that time has been called on our relationship and move on, even if it hurts like hell?

Fuck, the stupid non-fraternization rule.

CHAPTER 27

CHELSEA

Wrapping my arms around my cousin, I pull her close and close my eyes as we enjoy a sweet embrace. We don't normally hug goodbye like this. Usually, it's a quick kiss on the cheek. What she doesn't realize is that I need this hug a lot more than she knows.

Cameron is also saying goodbye to Matthew out on the front step. He glances in my direction, offering me a small smile before turning and leaving.

As Sara rubs my back, likely in confusion about why we're hugging for so long, a tear slips down my cheeks, and I madly try to discreetly wipe it away.

But I can't fool my cousin. Sara pulls back from me, searching my face for an answer as to what might be upsetting me.

"Chels?"

"I'm fine." I laugh. "I've missed you. That's all."

"It was less than a month ago that I saw you. No, it's something else."

"Really, Sar, I'm good. Maybe it's that time of the month."

My cousin raises an eyebrow at my comment before pulling me back inside her front entrance.

"Chels... come on. Something is definitely up. You don't get emotional. I can't pinpoint it, but you're so different than usual. Oh my God, did Cameron say something to you today to upset you? Normally, you two get along so well."

"No, it's nothing he said. We had a disagreement about something last week."

"What type of disagreement?" she asks.

"At work. I accidentally said to Ava, within Cameron's earshot, that we're both having brunch here today. Well, of course, Ava laughed and asked if we were dating. Cameron got furious as our employment contracts at the hospital clearly state there are to be no relationships between staff."

"As if they can police that," Sara scoffs.

"They can, and they have. My old supervisor was rumored to have done it, but I don't know for sure."

"The one you loved?"

"Yeah. Cameron doesn't want the rumor mill to go into overdrive when there's nothing between us."

I've just lied to my cousin. Of course, there's more between us than a professional relationship. We're in love, but the downfall is he's unwilling to share that we've been a couple for almost as long as Matthew and Sara have been married.

"Don't let it get you down," Sara soothes.

"It's hard not to."

If only she knew the full extent. My heart is breaking. It was quite hard watching Matthew and Sara sit next to each other, his hand placed on her knee, or them sharing a sweet kiss as the other left the table—things a normal couple would do. Up until this morning, I considered Cameron and me to be a normal couple when we're alone, but the more I think about it, the more I realize we are far from normal. We're a lot more along the lines of a Romeo and Juliet, loving each other in secret because all hell would break loose if we were found out.

"Is there something there? Do you feel something?" she quietly asks. "I saw you look at him as I was carrying out our meals. There's sadness there, gorgeous. Did you contact him after the wedding?" she asks before her eyes light up. "Did that bastard turn you down?"

Sara doesn't know the full extent of what happened between Cameron and me at their wedding. She knows we made out once, but nothing more. I'd have shared with her earlier, but they were honeymooning for over a month, and by the time they got back, Cameron and I had decided to have a relationship in secret. I wouldn't want to risk Cameron never speaking to me again if I told my cousin now.

Maybe that was the first error I made—agreeing to the secrecy. At first, it was fun doing something a little naughty and the fear of getting caught, but the further you fall for someone, the less exciting it is to remain a secret.

If I had said no straight up, I wouldn't have fallen in love with him and be in this mess now.

"I never contacted him, Sara," I reply, ignoring the rest of her questions. I don't want to elaborate any further as the mere thought will send me into a downward spiral of tears, and I've already cried more than my fair share today.

Sara cocks her head as she narrows her eyes. She knows something is going on. "Hmm... well, I don't know what's going on, but there *is* something. Call it pregnancy intuition."

Laughing at my cousin's surprising sixth sense—she's never been this clued in before—I cup her face with my hands before placing a quick peck on her nose, something we always used to do as kids.

"Bye, Sar," I whisper as I turn to walk out the front door.

"See, even that... you never do that unless something's up.

Argh, Chels, just know I'm here for you."

"Thank you," I mouth as I head down the steps.

"Bye," I offer both Matthew and Cameron as I walk by them. My lips are pursed together like I do when I need to give a half-hearted smile. Luckily for me, I already said a proper goodbye to Matthew earlier, so I can avoid any awkwardness between Cameron and me. It's not as though we're forced into the kiss-kiss-hug-hug situation, after all. Matthew and Sara are none the wiser about us.

"See ya, Chels," Matthew calls as I walk over to my car.

Glancing over my shoulder, Cameron raises his hand before flicking it to one side, his standard wave. Instead of a return gesture, I slide into my car. While we haven't yet made any definite plans to talk about our issues, I know it's happening at some point today, and I'll head home to await his call.

Maybe I shouldn't have snapped at him like I did this morning, but this situation has been irking me for some weeks now. I want to openly enjoy my boyfriend's company, not having to hide at home or find secluded places.

The silence in the car has me on edge, so I switch on the radio and turn the volume up a little louder than I'd normally have it.

"How Deep is Your Love" by the Bee Gees blasts through the speakers. Admittedly, I don't know all the words, so I don't sing along as I usually do, but I listen to the lyrics intently as I drive. The line leading into the chorus of "and it's me you need to show," has my breath hitching. A lone tear falls down my cheek as I pull up outside my apartment.

After switching off the engine, I madly wipe at my face as several more tears fall. It's so true. Cameron is the one who needs to show me how deep his love for me is. I think he knows how much I love him, purely based on me wanting to tell people about us. But now I'm questioning if I'm anything more than some girl he likes to have sex with.

Does he really love me?

But I don't even know what will come of our situation. For all know, I'm hyping this up to be much bigger than I thought.

Overthinking situations is one of my downfalls.

Straightening myself up, I collect my belongings and exit my car before racing into my apartment, desperate not to see any of my neighbors.

My cell rings as I unlock my door, and I fumble with the device, trying to wedge it between my ear and shoulder.

"Hello?" I answer, not even checking who the caller ID is.

"Hello, Chelsea," my mom's voice greets me in a slightly worried tone.

"Mom," I puff. "How are you? Sorry I haven't called. I've been—"

"Busy with work," she interrupts me. "I know. I know."

"Well, it's true. My days are hectic, and my shifts are all over the place. You wouldn't want me ringing you at two in the morning after a shift, would you?" I groan.

"Don't sass me, young lady. I'm still your mother, and if you called at two in the morning, I'd always answer your call," she grumbles. I hate it when her voice takes on this tone.

Guilt washes over me. I shouldn't have spoken to her like that. It's my fault that I haven't called her lately.

"Sorry, Mom. You've caught me in a grumpy mood."

"Well, don't take that out on me." My shoulders slump as I push open the door to my apartment. "Anyway, the reason for my call is that both your dad and I miss you. We were hoping you'd come over for dinner tonight?"

"Umm," I begin as I close the door behind me. I drop my keys and bag onto the kitchen counter and walk over to the couch.

Today is definitely not the day to be sharing a meal with my parents, the two people who know me best in the whole world. Well, except Cameron. It's hard to keep a huge secret from them.

"Chelsea Alexandra Mitchell, don't you dare *umm* me. Are you working tonight?"

"No, I'm not, but—"

"Then, it's settled, dinner at our place. Come over any time after five, and we'll eat around seven. Dad's excited to see your new car, although we're a little confused as to how you were able to afford that on your own."

"Finance, Mom, and yes... I'll see you at five," I reply, cringing at my white lie.

"Great. See you then." How Mom's mood can go from cranky to overly happy in point two of a second is beyond me.

We end the call, and I throw the device down on the couch. Why tonight of all nights? I love my parents with all my heart, but given that they don't know anything that's going on with me now, it's going to be difficult for me to pretend that everything is fine when it may not be.

Laying back against the soft cushion, I close my eyes as I take several deep, cleansing breaths. Typically, this is something that can instantly calm me, but right now, nothing seems to be working, and I feel as though I'm a ticking bomb of nerves ready to explode.

My ring tone begins to chime again, and I glance at the device, hoping not to see my mother's name on the screen.

Cameron.

Fuck.

I'm not ready for this.

Scooping up my device, I take a deep breath before swiping across.

"Hi, Cameron," I quietly answer.

"Hey, Chels, I've just gotten home. You think we can talk?" he asks.

I'm not ready for this, but it needs to happen.

"Umm, yeah. I guess."

"Would you like me to come to you or you to come here? Either way, I don't mind."

My mind races at the scenarios. If I go to him, I can leave if I can't handle the situation, but if he comes here, I can kick him out.

Stop thinking negatively, Chelsea.

"Chels?" he calls down the phone.

"Sorry... umm, I'll come to you."

"No problem. I'll see you when you get here."

Pulling the cell away from my ear, I stare at my device as Cameron ends the call, the screen going back to the standard background picture.

As the screen goes to black, I roll the phone in my hands several times before taking a deep breath. This conversation we're going to have in a mere half-hour will make or break us. I'm hoping I can get Cameron to see my perspective on our situation, and we can move forward from this.

But why do I get the feeling that Cameron's stubborn streak will win out?

CHAPTER 28

CAMERON

My running shoes squeak against the wooden floor as I pace back and forth in my kitchen. The ticks of the wall clock somehow appear to be growing louder yet further apart.

It's only been five minutes since Chelsea said she was coming over. She wouldn't have made it here in that time even if she had magically flown here. But here I am, counting down the seconds until she arrives.

It was beyond awkward at Matthew and Sara's this morning. She couldn't even look at me, and I didn't think that me making small talk with her would make things any easier. Unfortunately, Matthew noticed our lack of talking and asked me about it. What could I say besides I felt she was being cold toward me. It was a half-truth.

Deciding I need to distract myself for even a short time, I decide to do some laundry, not that I have a lot of things, but it's always best to keep on top of it.

After collecting the few dirty items in the bathroom, I head to the laundry room and throw the clothes in the machine before gathering the other items from a nearby basket.

As I remove my shirt from the basket, I notice a pair of Chelsea's socks have somehow gotten caught up amongst my clothing. A small smile appears on my lips as I throw them in with my things. I'll hand them back to her once they are washed.

Turning on the machine, I head back to the kitchen to check the time again. *Three fucking minutes.* So much for a distraction.

Deciding some fresh air would be good, I open the rear doors and allow the cool air to waft throughout the house. Mrs. Manzic, whose house backs up to mine, has her rear doors open along with her kitchen window. Whatever she's got cooking smells amazing.

But my mind is definitely not on food right now. As I allow the fragrant air to infiltrate my lungs, a calm washes over me, or it's possibly a chill from the cool midday air. Either way, I need to put my straight-to-the-point hat on and have a frank discussion with the woman I love.

I don't want anything to change between us. I like us just as we are. I need to calmly explain to Chelsea what the likely scenario of others finding out about us is. She's an intelligent woman and knows that it would be dire for both our careers.

Switching on the television, a documentary has already begun and catches my eye. Good, perhaps this will keep my mind occupied for the next ten or so minutes.

It works well, and before I know it, my front doorbell rings.

Leaving the television on, I run over to the door and pull it open. Chelsea's changed from what she was wearing earlier and now has on her favorite jeans and a light sweater.

"Hi," she quietly says, trying to avoid eye contact with me.

"Hey," I reply. An unintentional smile has spread across my face. Chelsea does this to me each time I see her. "Come in."

Walking into the living room, I offer her a seat on the couch. "Would you like a drink?"

"I'm fine, thank you." Her dull tone makes my heart ache. "I only came here to talk."

This time yesterday, we did an amazing surgery together and saved a teenage boy's life. Last night we celebrated with a glass of wine and many hours of making love. But a little over twelve hours later, a cold front has blown in between us, and neither of us knows what's ahead in this relationship.

"Chels, you can't even look at me. What's going on with us?" I blurt out before running my hands through my hair in frustration. I'm desperate for answers. I sit down on the couch, allowing some space between us. Usually, I love nothing more than having her cuddle into me, but right now, I feel as though that may never happen again.

"This is how you want to start it?" she fiercely says. She peels her bag off her shoulder and places it on the floor. "Okay, fine. I want to know exactly why you don't want to tell anyone about us."

"Chelsea, we've been over this. Surely, you can understand that I'm thinking of both of us and our jobs."

"What happened to not giving a shit about what the hospital will think? We can go on dates around the city as long as they are in secluded places. You want nothing more than to be with me, but we can't tell our closest friends and family about us. To me, that says you *do* care what others think and makes me question your feelings for me." She's on the brink of tears as she takes in a deep breath.

"My feelings... come on, Chels. I love you. I can't say it any clearer. Dates are one thing. Yes, they are in remote locations, but for a good reason. You're my everything, Chelsea, but it's our family and close friends' interlocking networks that I'm concerned about. It could affect our jobs." I run my hand through my hair in frustration.

Why can't she understand I'm doing this for her, for me, for us.

"Jobs..." she rolls her eyes. "Your job shouldn't dictate your life. It's not that important."

"That's where we differ... my job is everything to me."

The second the words leave my mouth, I wish I could retract them. Yes, my job is my life, but so is Chelsea.

Chelsea scoffs. "So, let me get this straight. You're worried about the *possibility* of someone *maybe* saying something to someone they *may* know at the hospital? Because if that's the case, do you realize how stupid that sounds?" she snaps.

"Stupid... hardly. More like an actual possibility. Not to mention that my father knows Dr. Walker, remember?"

"Okay, so your family is out. What about mine? I'd love nothing more than to introduce you to Mom and Dad. I know they'd both love you... as I do." Her voice trails off as she ends her sentence.

"I don't think us loving each other is in question here, is it?"

She looks at her hands in her lap as she shakes her head in reply. "No. Not at all."

"Chels, answer this. If we were to tell people about our relationship, and it did get out, accidentally, of course, and then the hospital finds out, what would you do if you lost your job?"

"I guess I'd apply to other hospitals in the area," she murmurs.

"I can tell you now, it'd be near impossible to get anything, especially at this time of year," I reply.

It's true. Even with a glowing reference, she'd find it difficult to get into another program now.

"I really don't know, Cam, but what I do know is that I'd do whatever it takes to stay with you." A sob escapes her.

"And me, you. Which is why I don't understand why you want to tell people." I extend my arms and lean toward her. I'm desperate to comfort her, but she moves away.

Tears well as the blue in Chelsea's eyes grow brighter by the second. "Because I... I..." her voice trails off, not able to finish the sentence.

Chelsea clears her throat before wiping at her eyes and sits up a little straighter.

"Ava and I were talking the other day. She's openly dating her supervisor. Sure, they aren't shouting it from the rooftops, possibly because he's still technically married, but a few people at the hospital know, and her family knows. Being in love with someone shouldn't be a secret. It's a rare thing to find and should be enjoyed."

"Chels, we aren't Ava and Mark. Being so open about their relationship is extremely risky. Ava would struggle to find a residency at another hospital if they were caught. Mark would be fine to start a private practice, though. That's where we differ in our specialties. I rely on the hospital, and their policy is very serious about relationships. Dr. Walker is a harsh man and always looking for someone to make an example out of."

"But I don't know of anyone who was fired over this rule, not in recent history, anyway."

"Yes, you do. I shouldn't be telling you this, and it remains between us, but your previous supervisor, Dr. Arthur was caught having an affair with her resident."

Chelsea scoffs. "That's only a rumor."

She furrows her brows as I nod. "It's true. Apparently, she ended up pregnant."

"Holy shit," Chelsea gasps, her eyes widening at the information. "It was true."

"Between us, yeah?" I repeat.

"Of course, Cam. I can't believe Dr. Arthur and Paul were together. But I guess it does explain a few things then."

Shrugging my shoulders at her revelation, I desperately try to get her to see sense. "So, there's that, which is why I don't want us to get caught."

"I understand all of that, Cam, but can't we even ask Matty to have a look over the contract? Maybe there's a loophole we can find."

"I thought about it, but I think it would open us up to too many questions. Let's face it, Chels, we have to remain incognito for the foreseeable future."

Chelsea's eyes fall to her clasped hands in her lap, her thumbs roll around each other, but she remains silent, not even a flinch in response to my statement.

"Do you think you can continue with our relationship being a secret?" I tentatively ask, scared of what her answer may be.

I'm watching as her chest rises and falls and her thumbs spin faster and faster around themselves. Her mouth opens as though she's going to say something, but her breath hitches before tears run down her cheeks and drop onto her jeans.

"Chelsea?" I repeat as my eyes dampen.

"Cameron, I'm..." she begins, but the rest of the sentence is inaudible.

"I didn't catch that."

She intakes a deep breath. "Cameron, I'm not sure I can continue with us if we can't be open with at least our immediate family."

"And you know I can't do that." Blinking my eyes, a tear rolls down my cheek.

"Well, I guess that's all we need to discuss then," she mutters as she collects her bag and stands from the couch.

"It doesn't have to be this way, Chelsea. We were so good for so many months." Rising from the couch, I try to block Chelsea from leaving. I'm attempting to remain strong, but this is one of the hardest things I've ever experienced.

"Perhaps it went on for a few months too long then. We fell for each other, knowing this relationship was doomed as long as we both work at the same hospital. I was once told that surgeons

191

struggle to have relationships as they are married to their job. I think it's accurate."

"It's... You... This..." The words stammer from my mouth.

Chelsea looks up at me, her blue eyes rimmed red. Both of us unsure what the next move is.

Bringing my hands to her face, I quickly sliding them along her cheekbones before bringing her lips to mine in a desperate attempt to have her reconsider.

Chelsea's arms flail at her sides before she pushes me back.

"Cameron, stop."

"I'm sorry. I need to show you how much I love you." A sob escapes my chest.

"It won't help. I love you, too, but we can't go on like this. If you'd like me to find another supervisor, I'll do that first thing on Tuesday."

"No, I don't want you to do that. We can remain professional. We always have."

"Fine." Her lips part as though she wants to add something, but she quickly closes them again, steps around my coffee table, and walks to the front door.

Unable to watch her leave, I listen as her footsteps soften. The door unlocks and creaks as it opens.

"This was never about love, Cam. I'll always love you."

The door softly clicks before I can even reply. Spinning around, I race to the front door in the slight chance that she changed her mind, but she's gone.

My girl is gone.

She's no longer my girl.

Not once did I see this happening between us.

Walking back to the kitchen, I grab a beer from the refrigerator and remove the top before walking over to the couch and flopping down.

I feel like I'm in a trance, and none of this is real.

Only, it is.

I need to work out how the hell I'm going to get the love of my life back, and I'll go through hell or high water to do so. You can't throw away your one true love.

CHAPTER 29

CHELSEA

Struggling to see the lock of my door through my tears, I finally get the key in and flick it open before pushing on the door. It swings back much harder and faster than I anticipated, knocking against the wall. A loud bang sounds before the shatter of glass.

Rushing into the apartment, I close the door behind me before stepping carefully over the shattered picture frame. The picture of Cameron, Matthew, Sara, and me from their wedding day was one of the few photographs I'd framed and hung on the wall.

"Shit," I cry as I bend down to scoop the photograph off the floor.

Not only is all of the glass fragmented into a hundred pieces, but the frame is permanently damaged.

Maybe this is a sign. In the same way the picture frame shattered beyond repair, our relationship has met the same fate today.

After fetching the trash can, I kneel amongst the glass slivers and begin to pick up each piece carefully. One pointed piece catches the side of my finger, nicking the skin.

"Dammit," I cry before dumping those pieces into the trash.

Tears stream down my face, but it's definitely not from the small cut on my finger. My heart is broken, so much more broken than I ever knew could be possible, and I'm unsure how you move on from this.

Of course, I could text Cameron and admit to making a terrible mistake and proclaiming how much I love him, but that doesn't solve the problem we have before us.

Standing up, I fetch a Band-Aid for my finger before using the dustpan to sweep up the rest of the glass. Taking the photograph, I prop it up against my fruit bowl on the kitchen counter before changing my mind. I don't want that reminder in front of me at this point.

Maybe as time goes on, the pain will ease, and I'll be strong enough to display the photograph again. The happy memories of a short relationship will be welcome. But until that time, I'll place it in my nightstand drawer.

My cell begins to ring in my bag, but I ignore it. I'm really not in any mood to speak to anyone right now.

But what if it's Cam? Especially if it is Cameron. I think we have both said exactly what we needed to say, and I want these next two days off work to process what's happened so we can move forward professionally. After all, we need to continue working as a functional team at the hospital.

Quickly glancing at the clock in the kitchen, I have less than an hour to be at my parents' house. It's definitely the last place I want to go tonight. They'll pick up that something isn't right with me straight away, but I also know if I don't attend, then I'm likely to have them on my doorstep, which will only make things that much harder.

As I get ready to leave, my cell rings several more times, and the message chime dings again. Gathering up my courage, I quickly pull it from my bag, constantly telling myself that a quick look to see who it is doesn't mean anything.

One call from Mom and Dad and a text to remind me to arrive around five. One text from Sara to see how I am and to ask me a random question about pregnancy cravings, and three missed calls from Cameron. There's also a text from him, but I'm not brave enough to look at that right now.

After replying to Sara and laughing at her so-called craving for peanut butter, I grab my things and head over to Mom and Dad's.

Standing on the front stoop, I raise my hand to knock before lowering it again. I'm not sure why I suddenly went to knock on their door as I always let myself in. My mind clearly isn't thinking straight right now.

"Darling," Mom sings as I walk through the door.

She races over and pulls me into a bear hug, holding onto me for slightly longer than normal. Truth be told, it's very welcome today.

Mom lets go before holding me at arm's length. "You look tired, Chelsea. I worry about you working those long hours all the time."

"I'm fine. Really. Didn't sleep very well last night."

"Well, no alcohol for you tonight then, miss," she orders.

Rolling my eyes in jest, my dad laughs as he walks up to me and places a kiss on my cheek before pulling me to him for a hug. "My Chelsea," he whispers.

"My pa," I reply.

I've got such a special relationship with my dad. He's the kindest man you'll ever know, well, besides Cameron. They always say a girl will likely choose someone like their dad, and for me, that is one hundred percent correct.

Dad then releases me before holding me at arm's length. "How are you, sweetheart? Are you *really* all right?"

"Of course. Never better," I lie, plastering a cheesy smile on my face.

"I wish I could believe it," he whispers before letting me go. "Come, darling, I have a new cider for you to try, and then we need to go and have a look at this new car of yours. I love a good Audi."

"Alan, for once, listen to me. I just said no alcohol," Mom chastises.

"It's cider, for Pete's sake," Dad replies before turning to me with a cheeky grin.

Their banter is pure entertainment. They have a wonderful relationship, one I was hoping to replicate one day. It's not often that you marry your high school sweetheart and stay together for thirty-five years.

After showing Dad my new car and allowing both him and Mom to drive it, I help Mom with the finishing touches of dinner before we all sit down to have an earlier than anticipated meal. Mom thinks it's best for me to have an early night. I have to admit, I appreciate her kind gesture. I think I need sleep to envelop me tonight.

"So, how's the hospital?" Dad asks before shoveling a forkful of pasta carbonara into his mouth.

Swallowing the remnants of mine, I answer, "It's great. Always very interesting."

"I bet it would be," Mom adds.

"Many difficult surgeries?" Dad asks with a mouthful of pasta.

"Alan... please," Mom scolds. My mom is a stickler for good table manners, and that means we don't wear hats while we eat, no elbows on the table, and definitely no speaking with our mouth full of food.

"Sorry, Hen," he mumbles before taking a drink of his cider.

"I've assisted on quite a few surgeries lately and learned many new techniques."

"Do you see yourself continuing with general surgery? I mean, I thought you wanted to be a trauma surgeon," Mom questions.

"I've thought about several specialties. I enjoy general. Dr. Chase, my supervisor, has helped me see how good it is. It's not all appendixes and hernia repairs."

"This Dr. Chase sounds like a good fellow." Dad's words catch me off guard, and I begin to cough, a breath of air going down the wrong way.

"Get her some water, Alan," Mom calls as she quickly stands and walks to where I'm sitting, frantically patting me on the back.

Calming myself down, I stop my mother from the pats that have now turned into much harder slaps. "I'm fine, Mom," I croak.

Dad walks back in and places the glass of water in front of me.

"Thank you," I mouth.

Once we all settle back into our meal, the topic of conversation changes—much to my relief—and we begin to discuss the vacations my parents have planned for the next six months.

"Vegas is my number one," Dad grins.

"I'm interested to see Alabama and Texas, I think," Mom adds.

Gazing at my mother, my lips pull into a smirk. "Mom, you don't think Alabama is going to be exactly like you see in the movie, *Sweet Home Alabama*, do you?"

"Of course not," she snides. "Well, not all of it, anyway."

Both Dad and I laugh at her reply. She loves that movie with a passion, so it's no surprise she wants to visit there. Although I believe Pigeon Creek is a fictional town, so I may have to tell Dad that on the sly.

"So, how's the dating scene?" Mom bluntly asks.

Slowly lowering my glass, I glance sideways at my mother.

My heart begins to ache again as I try to stop myself from getting upset.

"Henrietta," Dad warns, using Mom's full name.

She startles at Dad's booming voice.

"I'm sorry, but I'm curious," she mumbles.

"It's non-existent, all right. I'm much too busy with work."

"Fair enough. Although you know Mrs. Bountheim from my Tai Chai class, her son, Marcel, is also studying to become a doctor and has applied for an intern position at your hospital."

"Mom, don't set me up. He's an intern. What is he, twenty-four?"

"What does age matter when you have that in common?" she remarks.

"The hospital doesn't allow relationships anyway, so it's pointless," I sadly reply. If only she knew, she wouldn't be bringing this up at all.

"Hen, drop it. You're making Chels uncomfortable."

"Thanks, Dad."

"It doesn't have to lead anywhere, but maybe it'd be nice for him to know someone there."

"I'll keep a look out for him, I guess," I answer, hoping my reply is enough to have her give up on the topic.

A short while later, after finishing our mini cheesecakes Mom made from scratch, a yawn catches me off guard, and I can barely cover my mouth in time.

"Sorry."

"Don't be. Perhaps it's time to head home. Can't have you driving tired."

Looking at the time, it's barely eight at night, but I'm emotionally and physically drained.

"Yes, I think I'll head off."

Collecting my belongings, I hug my parents and promise that I'll try harder to come and see them more often, especially before their upcoming trip.

After arriving home and getting into my comfortable pajamas, I make myself an herbal tea that promises to help make sleep much easier for you before snuggling under my blanket on the couch.

Switching on Netflix, I decide to watch the next episode in the series Cameron and I was watching. But only five minutes in, and I quickly switch it to *Friends*, hoping the more upbeat theme will clear my mind.

It doesn't help, though. My eyes drift to the spot on the wall where the only photo we've ever taken together once hung. Sadness overcomes me, and as I slowly release my breath, my emotions begin to run wild as tears slip down my cheeks, and I sob out loud.

Placing my tea down, I grab several tissues before fetching my cell from my bag.

Madly scrolling through, a sudden urge to see what Cameron's text to me earlier said.

> **Cameron:** *Chelsea, if there were another way, we'd be doing it. But there's not. My love for you will always be there. Real love should never be painful unless you're parting ways. The pain I'm experiencing now is like nothing I've ever known. I'm always here for you as your supervisor and a friend. Take care, sweetheart.*

Clutching my device, another burst of sobs escapes my mouth.

I can't handle this.

Will this pain ever subside?

Know you did what's right for you, Chelsea.

Even if it was right, why does it feel like I've thrown away the best thing that's ever happened to me?

CAMERON

Three Weeks Later...

Walking through the corridor, I quickly stop to tie my shoelace. In my rush this morning to get to work, I must have forgotten to double tie it. It's small errors like this that I've been making ever since Chelsea and I split up.

It's definitely been far from a walk in the park, especially working together, but we've both given it our all when it comes to maintaining normalcy around the hospital. No one is any the wiser.

As I pull the lace tight, I collect my clipboard and stand upright, only to be met with Elizabeth Atkins walking toward me with her new intern, Marcel. According to other doctors in the hospital, Elizabeth has never agreed to supervise an intern before, which leads me to believe that she has something over him, or he's exceptionally gifted at brown-nosing.

"Cameron. Have you met my new doctor, Marcel Bountheim? Marcel, this is Dr. Chase. One of our star surgeons."

"Yes, we've met. Nice to see you, Dr. Chase," he answers rather bluntly while looking me up and down.

Who does this kid think he is?

"Marcel," I reply with a sharp nod. I don't have time for this kind of crap with Elizabeth and definitely don't have time for an intern who thinks his shit doesn't stink.

Elizabeth lets out a sharp chuckle. Completely fake, of course, but one she often uses around here. "Forgive my student," she begins before leaning toward me. "I think he's got a thing for your resident and sees you as a threat."

Fuck. Here we go again. Elizabeth's weekly attempt to get some sort of reaction from me about my now non-existent relationship with Chelsea. I'm not sure why she continues to do this. It's beginning to make her look like even more of a troublemaker than she's already perceived to be.

Not wanting to give Elizabeth any ammunition, I keep my reaction to myself before curtly nodding at her suggestion. "Well, I'm sure your intern understands the hospital policy of no fraternization between staff."

"I'm well aware, Dr. Chase. But Dr. Atkins here has told me about the ways around the rule, and with any luck, Dr. Mitchell will fall for my charm in no time. Our mothers are friends, after all." He runs his hand through his hair as though to look cool. In reality, he looks like a fuckwit with way too much product in his hair.

Grasping my clipboard a little tighter, I'm conflicted by wanting to laugh at his ridiculous comment and angered by his disrespect for *my* girlfriend.

Ex-girlfriend, Cameron.

This has been one of the more challenging parts of when Chelsea and I were together, and, of course, since we broke up, helplessly watching on as she's flirted with or asked on a date. Even after several weeks now, I still care deeply about her.

Who are you kidding? You still love her.

"I'd be careful about openly admitting to wanting to court someone, Dr. Bountheim," I warn, hoping to rid myself of these two annoyances.

"Court?" he scoffs. "What are we, in the eighteenth century? These days, you date, and if those dates go well, then it leads to more... fun things."

"Exactly right, Marcel. Sex is fantastic, especially when it's forbidden," Elizabeth agrees as she reaches out to lightly brush my arm, her fake chuckle making an appearance again before she eyes me up and down.

Fuck. Both of them are like two peas in a pod, or perhaps she's groomed him this way. I wouldn't put it past her. She angers me, so much more than any other person I've met. It could be because she hits a nerve each time she mentions Chelsea, but her personality is one I wouldn't associate with either. Unfortunately for me, you can't pick who you work with.

Elizabeth has been very subtle in her ways of flirting with me. A suggestive wink here and brush of the arm there. Her obvious eye-fuck just then is a new one, though. Not once have I ever given her any reason to think there's even a smidgen of a chance between us.

Even if I weren't mourning the end of my relationship with Chelsea, there's no way I'd even consider seeing Elizabeth. Her Jekyll and Hyde persona isn't to my liking.

Needing to leave this conversation now, I excuse myself and begin to walk by them.

"Dr. Chase," Elizabeth calls.

Twisting my head to listen, I don't turn to face her.

"Please don't say anything to Chelsea about Marcel's intentions."

Unless I feel obliged to say something to her, I'm trying to refrain from discussing anything with Chelsea other than patients and surgeries, so that shouldn't be a problem.

An easy breakup is definitely not the description I'd give ours, but it's been as good as it can be. She's on my mind all the time, and there's not a day that's gone by that I don't wish we could reunite.

Chelsea, on the other hand, seems fine about it. She's always cheery, and if you didn't know what had happened, you'd never guess that anything was wrong with her. It's completely business as usual. Although for me, I notice her tensing when we're close and the unfortunate discomfort when we need to be on the same side of the operating table.

I wish it weren't that way.

The thought has crossed my mind that she's suppressing her feelings, but it's no longer my place to question her about her emotions.

Deciding not to reply to Elizabeth's request, I walk off to the ward and set about doing my rounds of patients who had surgery yesterday. I usually entrust Chelsea with this job, but the three patients I'm checking in on today are ones I want to do myself. The surgeries were far from easy.

Feeling relieved that the beginning of their recovery has started off on the right foot, I place their files into the tray at the nurses' station before heading down to grab a coffee from the cafeteria. I'm still annoyed and angered by Elizabeth and her new toy. Perhaps the caffeine will help rid me of the thoughts of what happened only a short time ago.

I'm unsure why I feel so unsettled since seeing Elizabeth and her sidekick. His suggestion of what he'd like to do with Chelsea definitely has gotten my back up, and it's going to take more than a single coffee to calm me down.

Sitting at a table in the cafeteria, I slowly drink my double espresso as I watch the hustle and bustle of the hospital before me. It may only be a fifteen-minute break, but it's much needed right now if only to clear my head.

As I place the paper cup down on the table, I notice Chelsea walk in with her friend, Ava. Ava waves at me, but Chelsea only offers a small smile before joining the line to order.

This lack of conversation between us is beginning to drive me mad, and it also makes for a tension-filled atmosphere inside the operating room.

I consider calling her over to me, any excuse to talk to her, but I decide against it. What would the point be? I know that I'll be face to face with her in the next half-hour, anyway. The less awkwardness between us, the better, I think.

But it shouldn't be like this.

Drinking the last of my coffee, I decide against getting another. I wouldn't want a caffeine rush to cloud any judgments I'll need to make in my next surgery.

As I think of getting up and leaving, I notice Elizabeth and Marcel walk in and make a beeline for where Chelsea and Ava are standing, waiting for their drinks. Marcel has his arm behind his back. It's clear I'm within hearing distance of the girls, and I'm beginning to think this is a deliberate move to piss me off some more.

Watching on, I wonder what plan they have hatched now.

Marcel walks over to Chelsea with a swagger only the most arrogant person would have.

"Chels," he begins, which, of course, sends a chill down my spine. No one calls her that except her nearest and dearest.

I was once one of them.

Chelsea doesn't turn around, though, too engaged in a conversation with Ava.

"Chels," he repeats, much louder this time, and she spins around. Ava's face contorts as she sees who's standing there.

"Hi, Marcel," Chelsea answers, her eyes darting around the room.

"Chelsea, I like you."

"Umm, that's... nice?" she replies, her voice raising a few decibels.

"Go on a date with me?" Marcel asks.

What?

His bold, overconfident smile is enough to make anyone sick.

This little asshole is being extremely gutsy in his moves.

But I know Chelsea, and she's got a good head on her shoulders. She knows that this is a public area, and she wouldn't do anything to jeopardize her position here.

"Sure," she replies, waving her hand to dismiss him.

My ears are deceiving me.

She can't have just agreed to date this guy.

The words are like a kick to the gut.

"Awesome, I'll text you," Marcel replies before walking out of the cafeteria, Elizabeth right behind him.

Why is Elizabeth encouraging this? There's something about this situation that has me on edge.

It's jealousy, surely.

Ava excitedly rubs Chelsea's arm as she stands there stunned.

As Chelsea turns back to face Ava, she notices I'm watching what's just unfolded before me and gives me a slight shrug.

What does that mean? Is that a fuck you? I'll date someone who's willing to tell others we're together or an attempt to make me jealous?

Of course, I'm jealous. Extremely envious, but I'm also seriously concerned.

They know the rules. All of them do. Why would they risk their positions?

Then it dawns on me—my suspicions about Elizabeth. She's always had a grudge against Chelsea. My feeling is that it's because we work so well together and have great chemistry. Perhaps this is Elizabeth's way of getting Chelsea into trouble with the hospital's senior staff and a bid to get her dismissed.

That would make perfect sense.

If only I could prove it in some way.

But how?

CHELSEA

Excitement bubbles through me at the thought of being asked out by Marcel. I mean, seriously, he's not my type. At all. He's got more grease in his hair than there is in a car, plus he's younger than me. But it's exhilarating to be asked out on a date, and for it to happen in front of Cameron was simply perfect.

Am I out to make him jealous? Maybe.

Perhaps it's the initial thrill of having someone show some interest in you.

Things have been difficult between Cameron and me over the last few weeks. Of course, I slap on a happy face and get on with the job, but most nights, I find I'm curling up on the couch, crying over a picture of us.

I never thought I'd be that girl who would still be mourning a broken relationship weeks later, but this wasn't any old relationship. I thought that this was my forever. But now it's over, and I need to move on. If Marcel can help me move on from Cameron, then that's great.

"I can't believe he asked you out here... in front of everyone,"

Ava grimaces.

"I think it was cute, publicly declaring that he likes me."

"Have you forgotten where we are, though?"

"I know. But you and Dr. Fisher don't hide your relationship away."

"True, but we aren't all over each other at work, and he definitely wouldn't be that bold in the cafeteria."

"Do you think I should go out with him?" I ask quietly.

"Honestly, no. He's not for you. He is a sleazy-looking intern. Plus, he's so far up Dr. Atkins' ass that it's a real concern. But if you want to, then it's your call. Dates are a way to get to know someone without any real commitment." Ava shrugs.

When did Ava get so wise? But she's right. One little date won't kill me.

Will it?

Perhaps that's what was wrong between Cameron and me. We didn't date, so we never got to find out our true selves.

Don't lie to yourself, Chelsea. You know the real Cameron and are in love with him.

Hushing my inner voice, I turn my attention back to Ava.

"You know, I always thought you'd get with Cameron. You two are like a perfect match, and you could be a serious power couple as surgeons. Like Marie and Pierre Curie." Her voice is low so Cameron can't hear us talk from where he's sitting.

"I don't think they were surgeons, Ava." I laugh. "No, my relationship with Cameron is strictly professional."

"Umm, I know. I meant a power duo. It's a shame. I'm good at picking matches with people."

"Maybe you're in the wrong line of work, then." A chuckle escapes me as Ava playfully slaps my arm.

"Just be careful, Chelsea... these walls talk."

"I will. I will," I reassure my friend.

Cameron standing and collecting his cup catches my eye. Our

eyes lock for a split second, but I quickly break the connection. His shoulders slump as he walks to the trash and throws his cup in before leaving the cafeteria.

While part of me feels bad this happened in front of him, another part of me is glad that it did. I want to show him that I'm moving on and deserve someone who isn't shy to tell the world how he feels.

Ava and I are called to collect our coffees, and I quickly realize that I now have around five minutes to down it before needing to head to the operating room.

Saying my goodbye to Ava, I decide to take the stairs as the line for the elevator is way too long.

On the second flight of stairs, I notice someone is coming down and move to the side to let them pass. Only it's not just anyone, it is Dr. Atkins.

Shit. I don't have time for her crap today.

"Dr. Mitchell," she sings before plastering her phony smile on her face.

"Hello, Dr. Atkins," I reply as I take another step up. Hopefully, if she sees that I'm still moving, she'll realize I don't have time to talk.

"I'm so happy for you and Marcel. You're a great match."

"He's only asked me out. We haven't made any plans. I'm sorry I must go."

Walking up two more stairs, she calls out, "Of course. I hope you have a successful surgery. Enjoy being Cameron's resident..." There's more to her sentence, but I am too far away to hear.

Craning my neck to look at her, I furrow my brows before continuing on. If Cameron taught me anything, it's not to allow myself to fall for anything Elizabeth Atkins is saying.

Her comments play through my mind as I get myself ready for surgery. Cameron is already in the room as I scrub in.

"Glad you could join us, Dr. Mitchell," he grumbles.

"Sorry I'm late," I reply.

"Perhaps less talking in the cafeteria and more concentration on your job would be beneficial."

"Yes, Dr. Chase."

Like many other surgeries in recent weeks, the surgery is a complete success. However, it was me watching Cameron operate while I hold an instrument instead of him showing me his techniques and allowing me to help. My guess it's his pathetic way of punishing me.

Cameron leaves the room first, and I decide to follow him.

"Will I ever get a chance to assist you again?" I ask.

"I'm sure you will. Today was... difficult, and needed my level of expertise," he replies as he removes his gown and cap.

Following his lead, I remove mine too, throwing them into the nearby cart.

"I..." I start, but he turns to me, his eyes tight and worried.

"Chelsea, obviously, I overheard what happened today. I'm going to remind you of the non-fraternization rule at this hospital. I feel it's my duty as your supervisor to reiterate that point."

I scoff at his comment. "I'm very aware of that damn rule."

"Well, then, I'm concerned that not only was he so bold, but you were too quick to accept."

My eyes narrow. "You have no need for concern. I'm a big girl and can look after myself."

"I do not doubt that, but please be careful. I feel there's more going on here than just being asked on a date."

My brows furrow at what Cameron says. "What do you mean?"

"I have no proof, only a feeling."

"Your feelings are pretty on point."

We're interrupted by the anesthetist and a nurse leaving the room. For the several minutes they are with us, Cameron and I act as though nothing is wrong.

But something may be. I'm interested to know what Cameron's thoughts are on this situation, especially after Elizabeth's snide remark in the stairwell.

They finally leave, and I move closer to Cameron.

"Please… continue with your hunch."

"It really may be nothing, but I have a feeling Elizabeth is still trying to get between us."

"There's no… us, Cameron."

"Figuratively speaking, of course. I think she holds a grudge against you because we have… I mean had, no, it still has… a good working relationship. She's hit on me several times."

Hearing she's done that stabs at my heart. Even after this short time, it still hurts knowing that someone else wants what you once had and still love.

"Oh," I whisper, unable to extend my sentence.

"I still care for you, Chelsea. I really do. I'm concerned that Elizabeth might be wanting to rid you from the hospital."

"What?" I screech.

Her words flood back through my head. *Enjoy being his resident.* Was that a threat?

"Again, it's only a hunch."

"I think you may be on to something, though. I ran into her in the stairwell. She made out as though she was excited for Marcel and me going on a date, but I told her it was nothing really. She then told me to have a successful surgery and to enjoy being your resident. She said something else, too, but she whispered it. The more I think about it, the more I realize that her tone was slightly threatening."

"Hmm… okay. I think we have to tread very carefully here."

"We…" I shake my head at Cameron's choice of word. "*We* don't have to. I'll handle this on my own."

"Chels, I've dealt with people like this before. Ones who have no hesitation in stepping on everyone who gets in the way of what they most desperately want."

"As I said, Cameron, *we* don't have to."

"Dammit, Chelsea," he loudly whispers. "I want to help you. Let me help you."

His voice startles me as my eyes drop to the floor.

How can he possibly help me in this situation?

I'd planned on telling Marcel no, definitely no, when he asked me out. But I knew Cameron was within earshot, and I thought I'd try to make him a little jealous. Perhaps it was spiteful, and now it's backfired on me big time.

However, will allowing Cameron to help me out of the self-dug hole only bring my feelings for him to the surface again, ones I've been desperately trying to suppress?

"Listen," he begins. I raise my head to look at him. "Speaking inside the hospital has its dangers. You never know who's around the corner. We have a while until the next scheduled surgery. Meet me at my car, the usual spot, and we can talk in there."

"Okay," I mumble.

Cameron leaves the room, and I stand for several moments, trying to process everything. My head pounds with this new information and the enormity of the situation I've found myself in.

Calm down. It's only temporary. You can rectify this simply by telling Marcel no. Right?

Maybe it's not that simple.

Walking into the parking lot, a rush of nerves hit me as I spot Cameron's car.

Memories flash across my mind at our happier times, including the night that started it all when my old car broke down.

Taking a deep breath, I try my hardest to control my emotions.

He's offered to help me in a sticky situation. I can't read further into it.

Tapping on the passenger window, he startles before reaching over and popping the door open.

"Sorry," I mutter.

"It's fine. I was checking emails."

Sliding into the car, I close the door behind me. Never in my wildest dreams did I think I'd be sitting next to Cameron in his car again.

"So," I begin.

"So," he repeats.

Pursing my lips together, I puff a laugh. We seem to do this a lot.

"I do want to help you, Chelsea. I honestly think that Elizabeth is trying to set you up to fall. She's got a thing for me."

"Really?" I ask.

Cameron nods. "I never wanted to tell you as I was worried it would upset you. Elizabeth would do anything to make trouble for me for turning her down but also to get you out of the picture. Having you fired for that stupid non-fraternization rule sounds exactly like something she'd do."

"So, let me get this straight. Dr. Atkins has a thing for you and wants me out of the picture to get to you. She knew about us?" I ask, confused by what he's telling me.

"No. She was suspicious about us but never knew for sure."

"Right. I don't see how any of this is helping get me out of a situation I stupidly put myself in."

"Why did you agree?"

Thinking quickly, I give Cameron a generic reply. "I have my reasons."

He doesn't need to know that I wanted to show him what he's

missing out on.

"I may know a way, but it means putting us both in the firing line."

"You know I don't really want to date Marcel, don't you?" I mumble. My filter has failed me. Instead, I've blurted out something that should've only been thought.

"You don't?" he asks and twists his head to face me.

"No. My mother knows his mother, and they've been trying to set us up. He's too young for me," I answer without adding, *he's not you*.

Cameron quiets for a moment, absorbing my words. "Parents and their meddling, hey."

Shaking my head of this heaviness I'm feeling, I decide to go back to the topic at hand, the one we should be discussing. "The more I think about this, Cameron, the more I don't want to involve you. I made this mess, and I'll clean it up."

Popping the car door open, Cameron tries to stop me. "Chelsea, please."

"Thank you, Cam."

Before he can reply, I close the car door and hurry back to the hospital. I'm mortified that I told him my feelings for him are still there, in not so many words.

But right now, I need to focus on avoiding Elizabeth Atkins. If I stay off her radar, maybe she'll find someone new to pick on.

CHELSEA

One Week Later...

After placing a freshly made coffee on my glass table, I relax back into my couch. There's nothing but silence in my home, and after the busy night I had last night, I'm more than happy to do nothing right now.

It's the middle of the afternoon and my day off. I spent the morning with my parents before they left for a short trip to Sacramento to visit some of my dad's friends for a few days. Mom must have told me a hundred times how to water her flowers and where to put any mail that may arrive. It's as though she didn't think I knew how to look after a house.

After picking up some takeout for lunch and ordering extra for dinner, I've come home to just sit. I've freed myself of my bra's tight restrictions, the shoes are off, and my comfortable fluffy socks are on. I really don't want to be doing anything right now.

Sure, there are possibly a hundred things I could be doing

instead of sitting on the couch, but right now, I plan on sipping my hot drink and listen to the nearby wall clock tick the seconds away behind my closed eyes.

Unfortunately, it doesn't last long before the clock's rhythmical noise starts to aggravate me, and I need a little human noise in my apartment. I switch on Netflix, hoping to watch a television show or movie that doesn't require too much concentration.

The past week has been incredibly odd. Not only do Cameron and I seem to be getting along much better than before, and he's allowing me to be of more assistance in surgeries again, but I have successfully avoided Dr. Atkins for a whole week and only seen Marcel once and was quickly able to escape him.

Scrolling through Netflix, I'm unable to make my mind up about what I want to watch. Every television show or movie seems just too much for my brain to process right now until I come across *Friends*. A little humor and easy watching. Sounds perfect. I grab my favorite blanket and pull it over me, tucking it in around my legs as I always do.

Barely halfway through an episode, my cell chimes with the text tone.

"Argh," I groan before choosing to ignore it.

Chuckling as the character in *Friends* has a mishap with a spray tanning machine, the chime sounds again. The minute reminder to check my texts.

Grumbling as I throw the blanket off me and haul myself off the couch, I trudge over to the kitchen counter and scoop it up.

Marcel. Wonderful.

Marcel: *Chelsea, I was hoping you're home. Maybe we can go on that date tonight?*

Is he serious about giving me a few hours' notice for

something like a date? Even if I were half-interested in him, which I'm not, I'd definitely want to allow myself time to primp and preen myself.

Debating on what to reply, I type several messages before deleting them. It's either too formal, too polite, or a possible lead-on, and not the type of message I want to be giving Marcel. I want to avoid him.

> **Me:** *Hi, sorry I'm not home at the moment. Maybe we can talk about this another day?*

Lying is never the answer, but I feel boxed in.

> **Marcel:** *You sure?*

Huh? What a strange message to send.

> **Me:** *Yes. Another day, please.*

A knock sounds at my door, and my stomach drops. Who the hell is this? I'm not even wearing a bra.

Switching the television off, I walk over to the door and peer through the peephole. A cold rush washes over my entire body. Marcel is standing at my front door.

Fuck! I'll be making damn sure that maintenance gets this front door malfunction fixed as soon as I can.

Maybe I should've come up with a much better lie than I wasn't home. A headache or extremely tired would've been much better.

> **Marcel:** *I know you're home. I can hear your cell chiming.*

Slapping my hand across my mouth, I quickly turn the device to silent before pacing back and forth, my socks the perfect noise buffer.

He knows you're home. Just try and get rid of him.

Unlocking the door, I slowly open it, just to make sure my eyes weren't deceiving me through the peephole. They weren't. Marcel is standing there wearing a nice button-down shirt, jacket, and pants. Luckily, there are no flowers in sight. Hopefully, he just took a chance that I was home.

"Hi," I croak, trying to make my voice sound strained.

"Hey. Why'd you say you weren't home?" he asks. He actually looks a little hurt, which, in turn, makes me feel a bit bad.

"The truth is, Marcel, I'm so tired, and I have a slight headache." I open the door wider to speak to him face to face.

"Ah… headaches are my specialty. I can help you there. May I come in?" He runs his hand over his jacket pocket.

"If you don't mind, I'd prefer to be on my own right now."

Get the hint. I'm really not good at getting rid of people.

"Five minutes, that's all I ask."

"Five minutes," I agree as I step aside and let Marcel into my apartment.

The moment he steps foot over the threshold, I instantly regret letting him in. He's giving off this vibe, and it's one I don't like.

"Hmm… the coffee smells good." He grins as he leans against my kitchen counter after I close the apartment door.

"Sorry, I'm out of pods. I need to get some next time I am at the grocery store." I toss my cell on the couch.

"Shame. Online shopping makes life so much easier, Chels." His hand again runs deliberately over his jacket pocket.

What's with that? Maybe it's something he does when he's nervous.

Cringing as he uses my nickname, I decide to correct him. It's normally only my good friends and family who call me Chels. "Marcel, no one calls me Chels. Only my dad. It's a special nickname between us."

"Ah… sorry. I figured that since we're dating, it's acceptable to call you that."

"Marcel, we aren't dating. We haven't even started to date," I correct him. "You asked me out, and at the time, I agreed. However, after thinking about it and knowing what the hospital rules are, I figure we'd better be safe than sorry about this and choose not to start anything. We couldn't want to lose our jobs." A faux chuckle escapes me as I try to keep this light-hearted.

He should get the message now. I was direct while being courteous, and I stated the truth. Surely, you can't go wrong with that.

"Right," he starts as he straightens from the counter. "So, you led me on?"

"I did no such thing," I protest.

"You text me, call me, find me when I'm on a shift," he announces.

"I've never. Perhaps you're thinking of someone else?"

Marcel again runs his hand over the pocket of his jacket.

"What's in your pocket, Marcel?" I ask, my brows furrowing in confusion.

"My cell is vibrating. I should've put it in my pants pocket."

But I'm sure I did see him slide it into his pants before he came into the apartment.

Giving my head a quick shake, I suck in a breath.

This needs to end now.

He needs to leave.

"Marcel, this isn't helping my head at all. If you don't mind leaving—"

"But the five minutes aren't up yet," he replies as he takes a step toward me.

Taking a step back to keep the distance between us, I aim my body toward the door. Maybe I can slowly walk him there and then shove him out. I knew I should've listened to my gut feeling on this.

"I won't ask again, Marcel. Please leave." My voice is firm but wavers slightly on the last word.

"Then don't ask again."

Marcel takes several steps toward me and catches me off guard, sliding his hands around my waist and holding me there.

An audible gasp escapes me.

What the fuck is going on?

"I know you want this. Chelsea. You've wanted this since we first met." He runs his hand over my ass, holding me tight.

"You have your wires crossed, Marcel. I don't, definitely *don't*." A shiver runs over my body as I begin to feel a mixture of nerves and sickness at the situation. Never before has a man held me against my will.

Wriggling to try to break free from his constraint, he grips onto me even firmer. His lower arms are much stronger than I thought they'd be for someone who's barely taller than me.

"Marcel, you're hurting me," I grunt as I continue to wriggle.

"Well, stop squirming. It'll make it worse." An evil look flashes in his eyes before a grin creeps up the side of his face.

If I was scared before, now I'm petrified.

Marcel leans toward me, forcefully placing his lips on mine.

"Ahh," I mumble into his mouth. "Get off me."

He pulls back, the grin even bigger than before. "I knew your lips would taste as sweet as they look."

At the moment, his eyes are closed from enjoying our so-called kiss, so I push against him, and he releases me. I run toward the door, but he catches me again within a second. Squealing at the realization he's caught me again, I punch at his hands to let me go.

"Stop, Chelsea. It's only turning me on more." He grasps my hands before placing them on his crotch.

His words and actions are making me feel violently ill.

In desperation, I try to pull my hands away from his junk. I don't want to be touching him in any way, shape, or form.

A knock sounds at my door.

Whoever this could be, I'll kiss their feet for knocking right now.

"Who is it?" I call.

"Ah, it's Mr. Evans from down the hall," the voice calls back.

Mr. Evans? There's no Mr. Evans in the building that I know of.

Taking a deep breath, I open my mouth to scream for help. "Hel—"

But Marcel slaps his hand over my mouth. The rest of the word muffles against his skin.

The doorknob twists, and the painted wooden door swings open. Cameron is standing on the other side, a bottle of wine in his hands.

"Help," I mutter behind his hand.

Marcel instantly lets me go the second he sees Cameron. I drop to the floor as it all gets the better of me. Cameron races inside and drops to his knees to make sure I'm all right.

"Dr. Chase. Good to see you. Not sure why you're barging into my girlfriend's apartment, though. We were just ahh... fooling around."

"I was here to discuss a plan of action for our esophagectomy day after tomorrow."

"Do you always come over unannounced?" he asks. "As you can see, we were in the middle of something."

"Like hell we were. He had me trapped," I cry.

"You what?" Cameron exclaims as he helps me to my feet.

"It's all horseshit, Dr. Chase. Chelsea likes it rough."

"Get the fuck out of my apartment," I growl, throwing my hand toward the door.

Marcel holds his hands up in protest before his hand runs over his jacket again.

"Cameron, stop him. He's got something in his pocket."

Cameron looks confused but does as I ask. He grasps Marcel's arm before reaching into his jacket pocket and pulling out a second cell.

"What the fuck is this?" Cameron growls.

"My other cell. My personal one."

"I call bullshit on that," Cameron retorts.

Glancing at the screen, he shakes his head with a frustrated smile on his face before showing me the device's screen.

It's the recording app.

The asshole's recorded everything that we've said tonight.

"Why the fuck are you recording?" Cameron asks, shoving Marcel back toward the kitchen counter so he can't escape.

"Because it's my proof of a relationship with Chelsea."

My stomach twists. He was trying to set me up. How could he use what he recorded to his advantage?

"Hardly fucking proof, buddy. All it's proven is that you've forced yourself onto a woman."

"Haven't you heard of editing? I can make that recording sound like whatever I want." He smirks at me.

My stomach twists again as I struggle to keep my lunch down.

"Who put you up to this?" Cameron demands.

Marcel stutters at first as his smirk vanishes. He drops his head before looking up toward me. The look on Marcel's face tells me exactly who has before he even says the words.

"Elizabeth."

My blood runs cold, and I clasp my hand over my mouth.

Cameron was right. She does have something against me.

But what?

CHAPTER 33

CAMERON

Balling my hand into a fist, it's taking all I have not to throw a punch at this asshole right now. He's standing against the kitchen counter, bending into it as much as he possibly can to maintain a distance between us. My hands aren't on him or anywhere near him. If they were, I don't think I'd be able to control my actions.

Not only has he held Chelsea against her will, which I'll be insisting that she file charges for, but he's deliberately recording conversations for Elizabeth. He's much more than her little minion now. This is downright dirty, not to mention illegal.

The vendetta that Elizabeth has against Chelsea is beyond a joke and doesn't make sense. She claims to have a thing for me. So go after me, make big moves on me. I'm capable of knocking her back. But would you really go to such extremes to remove someone from a job because you like someone they work with? That's stalker-level right there.

As much as I want to throw Marcel out, this is so much more than someone who can't take a hint that someone's not interested. Whatever Elizabeth has taught him, he needs to understand that you can't do things like this in the workplace, and especially in a hospital. If he keeps his internship after all of this drama, then I'd be amazed and would reconsider working for such an establishment.

"Chelsea, I think it's time we call the police." My eyes don't leave the piece of shit. He's going to pay for what he's put Chelsea through.

Chelsea races over to the couch and collects her device.

"You really don't have to do that, Dr. Chase," Marcel mumbles as he watches Chelsea fumble with her cell. Her hands are still jittery.

"Not sure you have a right to say anything now," I grunt.

Chelsea drops the device on the floor before crying out in frustration. She scoops it up before shoving it to me. "You'll need to call. I can't process anything now. My nerves are shot."

How can I blame her? Who knows how far this worm would've gone if I hadn't shown up when I did?

Of course, I hadn't planned on talking to Chelsea about the surgery that we have scheduled in a few days. I took a chance on her being home and thought we'd discuss us over a bottle of red.

Over the past week, I've realized more and more how much I miss her. I'm craving her, and I'm willing to say fuck it all, I want to be with you. If telling people about our relationship is what it takes to get her back, then so be it. No matter what happens. I was also going to tell her that I've given a copy of my contract to Matthew to see if he can find a loophole in this stupid clause the hospital has set.

"Keep your cell, I'll use mine." I hand Chelsea Marcel's phone for safekeeping. I won't let my guard down around him. Who knows what other tricks he may have up his sleeve?

"Please, Dr. Chase. This will end my career before it even starts," Marcel pleads. My eyes leave my cell and move to this asshole in front of me. His hands are clasped together as though he's begging me.

"Perhaps you should've thought of your career before agreeing to whatever crazy notion Elizabeth had for you. Surely, someone would've warned you how toxic she is."

"They did, but I was blinded by the fact that Dr. Elizabeth Atkins had agreed to be my supervisor. That never happens. She hasn't taken on supervising duties for years now."

"And that didn't send out warning bells?" Cameron asks. Before Marcel can answer, Cameron continues, "Look, I understand we do things when we're young that aren't exactly a great idea, but what you've done is beyond that. You've held a woman against her will. That's a felony."

Tears roll down Marcel's face, but I have no sympathy for him, and neither does Chelsea, judging by her folded arms across her chest.

"I understand that," he sobs.

"Why, Marcel... why... what's the reason behind all this?" Chelsea stammers.

"Elizabeth wants you," he mutters.

"What?" Chelsea and I say in unison.

"When it came to hiring Dr. Chase, Elizabeth was the one who insisted on you joining Mercy. Apparently, she's admired you from afar for many years, both professionally and personally."

"So how does Chelsea fit into this?"

"Elizabeth's plan was to have you start, Dr. Chase, and immediately you two would be teamed up as this new power-duo of surgeons at the hospital. She hoped to get some rare cases into the hospital, and therefore, more money. Over time, she'd seduce you, putting you under her thumb for her to do whatever, whenever to you. It was this grand plan, but instead, Dr. Chase was given a resident to supervise, and Dr. Atkins has been furious ever since," Marcel replies, sniffling at the end of the sentence.

"So, she wants to get rid of me so she can put this power plan into place?" Chelsea asks.

"Yes."

"Doesn't she realize that Dr. Walker is in charge of who's paired with who, though?" I ask.

"She has that all figured out... now," Marcel answers.

Now? What does he mean by that?

"How do you know all this?" Chelsea asks.

"She told me. It was meant to remain pillow talk. It was part of our deal."

So, she's sleeping with him too.

What a piece of work she is, and then to go and groom an intern to behave the same way.

Not wanting to hear any more about this, I open the keypad to dial 911.

"Please, Dr. Chase. I'll delete the recording. I'll apply to other hospitals. Please don't call them," he pleads again.

Hesitating for a second, I consider doing as he asks, but he could also be playing me for a fool.

Instead of calling the police, I scroll through my texts and find Dr. Walker's number.

Me: *Doctor Walker. Serious situation between Dr. Atkins and her intern. Meeting requested urgently.*

Pressing send, I glance up at Marcel still grasping his hands at his chest.

"That text just went to Dr. Walker. I've requested a meeting about your behavior. I'll leave it up to Chelsea if she wants to place charges against you. Although, I think she should."

"D... Dr. Walker?" he repeats. "Why?"

"Because this hospital needs to know what the fuck is going

on. You can't have staff acting in such a way and expect no one to say anything. It's detrimental to the hospital's functionality."

He slowly nods as he looks to the floor.

"It's pointless getting him involved," Marcel murmurs, but I ignore his comment.

"You did this to yourself, Marcel," Chelsea whispers.

In the blink of an eye, Marcel grabs his cell from Chelsea's hand and begins to run to the open front door.

Spinning around, I take off after him, my cell slipping from my hands. Even though he's quick, I finally catch him after he runs past the door for the fire stairs.

"Let me go, you asshole," he cries and wriggles beneath me.

"You should've checked your surroundings better," I grunt as I struggle to hold him down.

Chelsea's neighbor opens her apartment door and stares at the commotion.

"Call the police," I yell as I struggle to contain Marcel's limbs.

Lifting my eyes to the neighbor, I can see she's unsure of what to do in this situation.

"He tried to assault Chelsea," I groan to her as Marcel continues to fight me.

"Oh my God," she cries before closing her apartment door.

Placing my arm across his back, I snatch the cell from his vice-like grasp and slide it along the floor back toward Chelsea.

She rushes out and grabs it before holding her cell to her ear.

After Chelsea asks for police assistance, she ends the call. "They'll be here shortly," she quietly says.

"Good," I groan, not sure how much longer I can hold Marcel down.

"Let me up," he cries.

"I'd only do that if you promise not to run, and I'm not sure I can trust you with that right now."

Chelsea's female neighbor opens her door again and walks

toward us, pulling her robe tight around her body. She drops a set of handcuffs near my hand, and my eyes fly up to her at the sight of them.

"They aren't what you're thinking." She chuckles. "My husband works in security. These are a spare pair he has here."

"Thank you."

The neighbor looks to Chelsea and smiles before walking back to her apartment.

Chelsea walks over to me and leans down. "Know how to put them on?"

"Not really, but it can't be too hard."

Between the two of us, we finally handcuff one of Marcel's wrists, and as we begin to do the second, the police arrive.

The next hour is a blur between watching them lead Marcel away and both Chelsea and me making our statements to the police. Chelsea hands over Marcel's device to them as well as evidence of what he had planned.

"We'll be in touch, Dr. Mitchell," the police officer says to Chelsea before leaving the apartment. "I'd be on to your super about fixing that broken lock on the front door, too." He hands her a business card.

Chelsea nods before closing the door after them. She spins around and rests against the painted wooden door.

"Woah, what an eventful afternoon," I joke before chuckling.

Chelsea narrows her eyes at me, telling me that now's not the time to joke about it.

"Sorry," I protest as I take a step toward her. "How are you?"

"I'm angry at myself."

"Angry?" I question.

She's not at fault.

"I shouldn't have let him in. I shouldn't have told him I'd go on a date with him in the first place." Tears begin to build in her eyes.

My cell chimes from the kitchen counter.

"Chels, you weren't to know that any of this would happen. But be glad to know that none of this will ever happen again." Taking a step closer again, I hesitate briefly before reaching out my arms and tentatively pulling her in for a hug.

She allows me to and slides her hands past my waist and to my back, holding me. Several sobs escape her as she buries her head into my chest.

"Shh," I soothe, my palm massaging her back.

My cell dings again.

Chelsea pulls back from me. "You should get that." She moves away from me and sits on the couch, bringing her legs up under herself.

Walking over to the counter, I scoop up my device and notice that it's a return message from Dr. Walker.

Dr. Walker: *Meeting scheduled for 9am tomorrow. Please be prompt, I have a busy day. Dr. Atkins has agreed to attend. Dr. Bountheim is currently unreachable.*

Puffing out a laugh, I say to myself in a whisper, "I wonder why."

"We have a meeting tomorrow morning," I relay to Chelsea.

She nods her head but doesn't say a word, only stares at the blank television screen.

"Chelsea?" I ask softly.

"Why did you come here today, Cameron? Don't get me wrong, I'm incredibly glad you did because God knows what he'd have done to me. But why are you here?"

The entire speech I had memorized earlier is no longer there, and I find myself stammering a reply to her, "B-Because of the surgery."

"That's crap because you said we'd talk about it tomorrow afternoon, and why bring wine?" She throws her hand toward the counter.

"Because I wanted to see you," I reply. It's a pathetic response, but it's all I have right now.

"You wanted to see me?" she repeats.

"I wanted to tell you that I've given a copy of my contract to Matty to look over. If there's a way for us to be together because of a loophole in that contract, then Matty will find it."

"You did what?" she asks.

"I thought this would make you happy. Show you that I still care deeply for you."

"I'd have much preferred you'd discussed that with me before telling my cousin's husband about us."

"He doesn't know."

"I'm not sure that's any better. He'd have to be at least a little suspicious."

"I asked him for discretion. Told him that it's a personal hospital matter."

She runs her hand across her head, smoothing her slightly messy hair and puffs out an audible breath. "Cameron, you know that I'm still in love with you, but I'm not sure that my heart can take the slight possibility that Matty will find a loophole. I don't want to hope for the best if it's a long shot."

"I understand that. I never intended on telling you what I'd done. I just wanted to reassure you that my love for you is just as strong as it was before."

Her lips flicker as though she wants to smile at what I say, but she doesn't.

Maybe it was stupid to think that she'd jump into my arms after telling her what I have done. Of course, it's a long shot, as Matthew said hospitals have strong legal teams. But I was sure I'd get more from her than an acknowledgment.

"Want to get some takeout for dinner?" I ask.

"I already got some for tonight. If you don't mind, I think I'll have a quiet night. But I will see you at the meeting tomorrow."

"Of course," I reply.

Walking to her apartment door, I look back at Chelsea as she switches on the television. I'd love nothing more than to cuddle into her right now, telling her that everything will work out.

But I don't know that. Hell, I don't even know what will happen at this meeting tomorrow. All I know is that my love for Chelsea is forever, and I need her to know that I'll do whatever it takes to get her back.

Even if it means giving up the job I desperately wanted.

CHELSEA

As Cameron closed my apartment door last night, my heart felt as though it was breaking all over again. Have I pushed him away for a second time? His face looked pained as I asked him to leave.

It's not as though I wanted him to leave, but I couldn't get swept up in a moment again, only to have my heart broken when Matthew is unable to find any way for Cameron and me to be together. I saved myself the heartbreak, or did I?

Simply being around Cameron again is tearing my heart to shreds, and I'm not sure how much more of this I can take.

How I wish I never stepped inside his car.

Unfortunately, that broken-heart feeling hasn't subsided at all overnight, and now I'm lying on my couch, wondering how much coffee it will take to get me through today.

After heating up some food for dinner last night, I sat on the couch, then lay down and haven't moved since. Even though this is the most comfortable couch ever, I rarely sleep here, as I don't enjoy sleeping upright. But I had no motivation to move last night.

Perhaps this feeling I'm fighting is from the ordeal yesterday or the fact that Cameron has just told me that he's trying to find some form of a loophole so we can be together. But even if I know the reason, it doesn't ease the pain.

Wriggling down on the couch, I switch the television on before bunching the blanket in my hands and pulling it up around my neck two minutes before I get up and make my coffee before showering. Surely, I can allow myself two minutes today.

My cell sounds just as my eyes flutter closed again.

"It's a sign that I need to get off the couch and wake myself up," I mumble.

Not quite remembering where I left my device last night, I finally find it on the floor.

Scooping it up, I check to see who it is. It's the one name that I should be trying to clear from my thoughts.

Cameron: *I hope you slept all right last night. I was worried about you all night. See you shortly.*

How do I reply to that?

Me: *I'm fine. Really. See you soon.*

Deciding that straight to the point is probably best, I shoot him the text before setting my coffee machine and heading to the shower.

Stepping into the cubicle, my body burns as the scolding water hits my back. I normally don't have the shower this hot, but it's somewhat soothing with all that's going on in my mind. However, it doesn't last more than a minute before the heat gets the better of me, and I twist the cold faucet a little more.

After a very quick shower, I dry myself and pull on my navy dress pants, cream blouse, and one-inch heels before heading out to the kitchen for a much-needed caffeine fix.

This meeting today is of a very serious nature, and I figure I better dress in more formal attire than wearing scrubs.

The coffee tastes like heaven as it helps wash down a single piece of toast before I race back to my bathroom to apply some light makeup and twist my hair into a neat bun low on my head.

Most days, it would take me twice as long to get ready, as I like to take my time with my breakfast—something Cameron taught me—but today's rush will have to do. I have no regrets in allowing myself an extra two minutes of calm this morning.

After grabbing my jacket and handbag, I head out to my car. The chill in the air has me wishing I'd put my jacket on before leaving my apartment. The drive to the hospital takes a little longer than I'd planned, but I'm grateful for some good music on the radio. It's definitely helped to stop me from getting too worked up about this meeting. As I'm nearing the hospital, an unfamiliar song blasts through my speakers and the nerves begin to creep back in.

"Facts, Chelsea. State facts only. Don't get emotional," I chant to myself as I turn the corner into the parking lot.

Pulling into one of my preferred spots, I switch the engine off, and instead of exiting the car and collecting my things as I normally do, I remain seated in the driver's seat and rest my head against the steering wheel.

Exhaling long breaths, I try to calm myself. I was confident I wouldn't be nervous about today, especially knowing that Cameron would be by my side, but a small part of me thinks that perhaps the nerves are there *because* Cameron will be next to me. Maybe I wouldn't be feeling this way if I knew he wouldn't be there.

But today isn't about Cameron, or me, or even us. Today is

about informing the hospital of what Elizabeth Atkins and her minion, Marcel, have been doing, and hopefully, we'll get some idea on how they plan to handle them both.

In my moment of clarity about the situation, my nerves ease considerably, and I pop open the car door and exit my vehicle before collecting my things from the rear seat.

Walking into the hospital, I head straight to the locker room to put my things away.

Walking from the elevator, I'm almost bowled over by Ava.

"Hey, chick," she beams. "Hope I didn't crease your blouse."

"It's fine," I reply. "Busy?"

"Flat out. It must have been a full moon last night. We had women giving birth left, right, and center. I've just come out of a complicated C-section. Mark was amazing." Her grin increases at the mention of his name. It seems like they are really happy together. "Why are you dressed so fancy? Scrubs not good enough for you anymore?" she teases.

"I have a meeting this morning."

"Sounds serious?" Ava replies, her smile slowly vanishing and her eyebrows knitting together.

"You have no idea."

"Spill... I have like fifteen minutes."

"Not here. Maybe we can catch up for a drink after a shift?" I ask.

"Sounds good... but since when do you go for a drink after your shift?" A small chuckle escapes her. "What have you done with my friend, Chelsea?" she asks, placing her hands on either side of my face and looking into my eyes.

"Ha ha," I reply.

"I was already going out with my cousin. You're welcome to join us. There's some juicy gossip I'd love to share. Maybe we can catch up tonight?"

"Sounds good. I finish around nine, hopefully," I answer.

"Me, too."

Ava runs off as I head to the locker room, my eyes darting left and right, trying to avoid seeing Cameron any earlier than I need to. I feel as though I'm attempting to avoid him more now than when we first broke up. After putting my items in my locker, I collect my freshly laundered lab coat and slide it on. Placing my cell and the police officer's card into my coat pocket, I head up to Dr. Walker's office.

Upon arrival, I see Cameron already there, sitting outside, his leg bouncing up and down. Giving Cameron is always so confident, it's an unusual sight to see him showing any nervous reaction.

"Hi," I whisper as I walk up to the bank of chairs he's sitting on.

"Hey," he replies. "The PA said he shouldn't be too long."

Looking up at Ava's cousin, Maryella, she's not her usual bubbly self. I can't help but notice she's on Facebook rather than doing whatever clerical work she should be. Ava said she loved her job and always made sure she did high-quality work. I shrug it off and turn my attention back to Cameron. It's not my place to say anything to her about her work ethic. Perhaps she's having a bad day. I only hope she's in a better mood later on.

The intercom buzzes, and she picks up the receiver before looking over at us. "Yes, I'll send them in. No, she's not here yet." Placing down the receiver, Maryella stands and walks around the desk. "He'll see you now."

"Thank you," both Cameron and I say in unison.

My nerves return at seeing Dr. Walker. His persona is very intimidating, and you'd never want to anger him. But I know what Cameron and I tell him today will surely show what the true Dr. Walker can be like, keeping his reputation alive.

After shaking his hand and taking a seat, we sit in silence as Dr. Walker signs paperwork in front of him. Looking over to

Cameron, I furrow my brows in which he slightly shrugs his shoulders in return. Normally, Dr. Atkins is a stickler for time, but she's now three minutes late.

"Perhaps Elizabeth is stuck in surgery. Should we proceed, and we can fill her in when she arrives. By the sound of your text last night, it sounded very serious, Cameron."

"It is, Dr. Walker." He nods before turning toward me. "Would you like to begin, Dr. Mitchell?"

Caught off guard by his question, my mouth drops to speak, but no words come out. I look to Dr. Walker tapping his pen against his desk, awaiting my answer.

My heart races, and I'm unable to find the words. Now I look like a complete idiot in front of the Chief.

Calm down and speak.

Cameron can obviously see that I'm struggling with knowing how to start this conversation.

"I'll begin," Cameron begins. "Last night, an incident occurred at Chelsea's apartment."

"An incident?" Dr. Walker repeats. "What do you mean?"

"Marcel Bountheim," I add.

"He's the intern Elizabeth was so desperate to supervise," Dr. Walker adds.

"Correct. Chelsea was being set up by him."

"Set up? How so?" he asks.

"She—" Cameron begins, but I stop him.

"Marcel wanted to date me. He came over yesterday afternoon to ask me again. I know full-well the rule about fraternization and told him that, too, but he persisted. He ended up grabbing me last night and forcing himself on me."

"Did he..." Dr. Walker questions, not finishing his sentence.

"No, he kissed me and held me against my will, but nothing more. I'm not sure how far he'd have gone, but I was glad that Dr. Chase showed up when he did."

"Cameron? You were there?" Dr. Walker asks.

"Yes, I was. Chelsea and I have a very complicated surgery and we agreed to discuss the procedure. We thought it'd be much better to do it at one of our homes rather than at a public place for confidentiality."

Well, there's a little white lie in there, but who am I to correct my supervising doctor.

"Of course. Completely agree," Dr. Walker nods.

"I heard a cry for help," Cameron continues. "Chelsea's door was unlocked, so I entered and saw Marcel holding her against her will."

"Did he hurt you, Chelsea? Did you call the police?"

"Yes, we did. He likely won't show up to this meeting today as the police arrested him last night."

"He'll be dismissed. You won't have to worry about him harassing you anymore." Dr. Walker's words are sympathetic.

"Thank you."

When a wave of relief washes over me, I know that this isn't over yet, and the worst is yet to come.

"But that's not all, Dr. Walker. Marcel was recording Chelsea. He wanted to use what he was doing to her as evidence against her at the hospital. He was aiming to have her fired."

"Fired? Sorry, I'm not sure I'm following."

Cameron explains the situation to Dr. Walker, and in particular, how Elizabeth Atkins is involved.

"She was the mastermind behind the whole incident," Cameron finishes.

"Elizabeth? That can't be right. She's an amazing surgeon and well-respected in this hospital and in the wider medical community."

Nerves return as Dr. Walker sits there in disbelief.

There's a knock on the door. Craning my neck, I see Dr. Atkins walk in and sit in the chair closest to Cameron. Her evil yet charming grin plastered on her face. I liken it to an evil Disney character who thinks they've won.

But you haven't won yet, Elizabeth.

Cameron and I will fight you every step of the way.

While I want to give off a confident persona on the outside, on the inside, I'm a mess. It's one thing to discuss the situation without Marcel and Dr. Atkins here, but now that she's sitting in the room, my voice is all but lost, and I'm turning into Jell-O.

I'm not sure I'm strong enough to come up against a woman like Elizabeth Atkins.

Thank God I have Cameron by my side.

CAMERON

Watching Elizabeth stalk into the office and sit down next to me almost has me cringing.

Unlike Chelsea, I can't bring myself to look at the woman. I can only hope that Dr. Walker hears us out and does the right thing in this situation and dismisses Elizabeth on the spot. In my opinion, he doesn't have a choice.

"Good to see you, Elizabeth," he starts, and instantly the hairs on the back of my neck begin to rise.

"Maxim, you look well today," Elizabeth replies, her tone almost flirty.

"Can we get on with this?" I groan. I don't want to have to spend a second longer with that woman than I have to.

"All right." Dr. Walker blinks several times before switching his gaze to me and then to some paper in front of him. "Elizabeth, you're being accused of trying to set Dr. Mitchell up with your intern. What do you have to say about it?"

"What? Maxim, really? Set them up? Hardly. Chelsea looked like she was more than happy to date Marcel."

"You know what we're talking about, Elizabeth. Have you not noticed your intern isn't here today? He was arrested for sexual assault last night as he held Chelsea against her will at her apartment." My tone is clipped, but I'm struggling from getting too angry at the situation right now.

Glancing at Chelsea, her shoulders have dropped, and she's looking at her clasped hands in her lap. She looks absolutely amazing in what she's wearing today, but I know now is definitely not the time to be checking her out.

She's told me she is not good with confrontation, and I'm more than happy to speak for her, but I'm hoping she adds to the conversation as well. Otherwise, it may be somewhat suspicious that we're more than in a resident-supervisor relationship.

"He what?" She gasps, feigning shock. "Well, if that's what he did, then yes, I support his dismissal."

"Are you forgetting the part where *you* put *him* up to it to get Chelsea fired?" I add.

"I what?" she shrieks. "Maxim, I did no such thing. Why would I?"

Why does she get to call him Maxim in such a professional setting?

"We have proof, Dr. Atkins. Marcel recorded it all," Chelsea mutters.

Elizabeth leans forward and throws Chelsea a look of disgust in an attempt to cover up her agenda before sitting back into her seat. "I wouldn't do such a thing, ba... I mean Dr. Walker."

Dr. Walker's eyes widen at the almost word Elizabeth says. If I didn't know better, I could've sworn she almost called him babe. But she does use that word with some of the staff around the hospital, so perhaps it's was a Freudian slip.

"Do... Do you have proof of this recording?" Dr. Walker asks after clearing his throat.

"We do. It's on my cell. I sent the recording to myself before he was taken away by the police." I pull my cell out and place it on the edge of Dr. Walker's desk before opening the recording and playing it.

As the recording goes on, my gaze shifts to Chelsea, who's looking extremely uncomfortable as the situation replays.

"I can't listen to this," she mumbles.

"Only a little more," I whisper back.

In the space of ten minutes, the recording finishes thanks to Dr. Walker wanting to fast-forward on some of it, much to Chelsea's relief.

Placing my cell back into my pocket, Elizabeth scoffs next to me. "That doesn't prove anything. Only that Marcel tried to blame his actions on me. Maxim, I have nothing against Chelsea or Cameron. I'm not sure where this has all come from, but it needs to end. Our hospital should be a cohesive unit, and we can't have stupid rumors and innuendo floating around."

My head flicks toward Elizabeth in astonishment. How can she deny all of this?

"I agree," Dr. Walker says, and my head snaps to him.

What?

He can't be fucking serious.

"You agree?" I croak, trying to wrap my head around the idea that he doesn't believe any of this to be true.

"There isn't any hard proof that Elizabeth was behind this. It's all hearsay."

"This is crap," Chelsea adds.

"I'm sorry this happened to you, Dr. Mitchell, but this isn't on Dr. Atkins. Dr. Bountheim will be dismissed right away, and I encourage you to pursue your assault claims against him."

"He was only a pawn in all of this," Chelsea mutters before straightening herself up. "Dr. Atkins threatened me in the stairwell a few days ago as well. Perhaps you don't think that she's capable of something like this, but she has a vendetta against me, and I do think that whatever Marcel said about her is accurate. She wants me out of the way so she can *work* directly with Dr. Chase." She uses air quotes around the word 'work.'

Chelsea's words are clear, and her sentences are well articulated. Any nerves she had from earlier have dissipated, and I'm proud of her for standing up for herself.

"Why wouldn't I want to work with Dr. Chase. He's one of the best, and I feel his talents are being wasted supervising a resident like you." Elizabeth waves her hand as though dismissing Chelsea's statement.

"You've obviously never seen Chelsea at work then... she has amazing potential," I add.

"Thank you, Dr. Chase," Chelsea whispers before pulling a card from her pocket. "This is the police officer who came to my apartment. He has my full statement as well as Dr. Chase's."

"I don't need to speak to the police, I can make up my own mind," Dr. Walker grumbles. "Look, I have an extremely busy day today," Dr. Walker begins. "I don't believe there has been any foul play on Elizabeth's behalf. She's an outstanding doctor here and a wonderful woman in herself."

"You're wrong," I correct him.

"That's your opinion, Dr. Chase. I suggest you all try to find a way of working together, or it may be last in, first out."

Did he just threaten my job?

Fuck. This couldn't have gone any worse.

Looking at Chelsea, her head is bowed. Her reaction is exactly how I feel, although my blood is about ready to boil. How could Maxim be so blind to Elizabeth's antics?

Standing up, I don't bother to thank Dr. Walker for his time. He didn't resolve anything at all. Chelsea stands with me, and we both walk from the room, leaving Elizabeth and Maxim.

Heading back to our locker room, Chelsea's quiet and definitely holding back her feelings on this situation. One thing I do know is that she'd be just as disappointed as I am with this outcome.

"Spill?" I encourage as we walk through the door. No one else is in the locker room right now.

She frantically shakes her head. "It's too dangerous for me to do so." Her eyes dart around the room.

"Dangerous?" I ask.

"As in, if I start to tell you how I'm feeling, I may not be able to stop myself, and it's completely inappropriate to be saying them at the hospital."

"I understand. I'm sorry things didn't go to plan." Dropping my head, I can't make eye contact with Chelsea right now. I feel as though I've let her down.

"It's not your fault. I thought she'd crumble when we told her that Marcel spilled the beans."

"Me, too," I add.

Opening my locker, I gather my things and close the door. I notice Chelsea is madly searching for something in hers.

"Shit," she cries. "I can't find my cell. My pager is here but not my cell."

"Where did you last have it?" I ask.

"Before the meeting. I'm sure I put it in my pocket with the police officer's card."

"Could it have slid out onto the chair?"

"It must have. Can I run back and grab it, and I'll catch up to you as you do your rounds?"

"Of course," I reply.

Watching her take off back toward Dr. Walker's office, I run my hands through my hair in frustration. Sure, we've eliminated one problem today in Marcel, but he was Elizabeth's pawn, a willing participant. We failed to catch the ringleader.

Frustration builds within me, and unsure of how to rid myself of it, I lightly punch at my locker. It'd be completely stupid to do that at full force. My hands are my livelihood.

As I pace, I start thinking that a coffee would be great. Figuring it's better to drink water right now than to hype myself up on caffeine, I turn my pace into a walk and grab a bottle from a nearby vending machine before heading back to the locker room.

Cracking the bottle open, I slide to the floor and guzzle half the liquid before taking a break. My eyes close as I try to allow the tension to escape my body. My bedside manner will be completely unacceptable if I see patients now. I'm best to be a few minutes late and calm myself the best I can.

After my emotions calm, I feel I can complete my job and change into some scrubs. I slide my lab coat over my arms and jerk my shoulders, trying to get it comfortable.

Not only has today's outcome affected the hospital, but it's completely dampened the chances of Chelsea and me getting back together.

I'll have to accept that Elizabeth is here to stay and that if she tries any shit again with either Chelsea or me, we'll have to get some form of video proof or something much stronger than a recording.

My cell sounds as I begin to leave the locker room, and I dig it from my pocket, expecting it to be Chelsea, asking where I am.

Instead, it's Matthew.

Matty: *Your contract is as tight as a dolphin's ass. No way around that clause that I can find. Sorry dude.*

Replying with a quick 'Thanks,' I'm regretting checking the text now as I'm even more furious than before.

This day had started with such high hopes, and now I'm at rock bottom. If only there were a reset button on the day.

CHAPTER
36

CHELSEA

Running into Dr. Walker's office, I accidentally startle his PA, Maryella.

"Sorry, I begin. "I think I left my cell in the office."

"He's still in there with Dr. Atkins," she mumbles. Her response doesn't answer what I originally stated.

Maryella looks miserable and as though she's shed a few tears given the light smudge of her mascara.

"Still?" I repeat. It's easily been ten to fifteen minutes after we left.

Looking toward his office, I notice a fine gap between the frosted panel and the window frame.

Maryella shrugs her shoulders before a grin spreads across her face. "Ava told me you're coming out with us tonight. That's awesome."

"Yeah," I reply, half-listening to what she says. My attention is completely focused on this clear gap in the glass. I could've sworn I just saw Elizabeth walk up to Dr. Walker. "Do you find it strange that you can see into Dr. Walker's office through this small gap between the frosted glass?" I ask Maryella

"What gap?" she asks, her eyes widen before softening again. "I had no idea there was a gap. My distance vision is pretty poor. Ava's always on my case for me to get glasses, but they wouldn't suit my face." She fakes a chuckle at the end of her sentence—strange reaction.

Walking over to the office door, I peer through the gap as I wait for Maryella to call him through the intercom. My eyes bulge from my head as I can clearly see Elizabeth sitting on Dr. Walker's lap. Her hands wrapped around his neck. As he brings his hand toward her chest, I lean back. I don't want to see this.

Oh. My. Goodness.

Quickly moving away from the door, my mouth is wide open, and I'm unable to close it. I'm trying to process what I've just witnessed.

It must be some kind of error. Perhaps I hate Elizabeth that much that I'm seeing things.

But I wasn't. I wouldn't have imagined him palming her breast.

"Are you okay, Chelsea?" Maryella asks.

"Yeah, yeah," I croak, my mouth dry, and I'm in desperate need of a drink.

I blink several times before rubbing my eyes, but there's nothing wrong with my sight. I definitely just witnessed something that I shouldn't have.

"Wait... did you come back for your cell?" she blurts out.

"Yeah, that's what I mentioned when I first got here," I reply.

"Sorry, don't even remember you mentioning it." She holds up the cell, and I nod at relief in seeing my device.

"That's okay. You seem to have so much on your mind. I'll just take it. I've got to get back to rounds."

"You have no idea, babes," she answers before the phone on her desk begins to ring.

Taking the device from her, I whisper, "See you tonight, Maryella."

"See you then, Chels," she calls before scooping up the receiver.

As I walk away, I ignore her use of my nickname and walk in somewhat of a daze to where I'm meant to meet Cameron on the ward. My cheeks feel as though they are on fire. Have I just witnessed something that I shouldn't have seen at all?

Ducking into a bathroom on my way, I gently pat water onto my cheeks to try to cool them down.

Staring at myself in the mirror, the images play over and over in my head. It definitely isn't something that my mind made up—it happened right in front of my eyes.

A lady walks into the bathroom and gives me a kind smile as I grab a paper towel and pat dry my face.

Placing the paper into the trash, I leave the bathroom and continue on my way to the ward.

Walking through the doors, I head straight toward the nurses' station, hoping that Pamela is on and able to tell me where Cameron is currently located.

Luckily, she is, and I don't even have to ask. She points toward the room and hands me a clipboard. "Thank you," I mouth. Shit, he's had to do many of the reviews on his own.

Taking a deep breath to calm myself, I walk into the room and give the patient a warm smile before Cameron twists his head to see me. His eyebrows furrow slightly as he looks at me before continuing to tell the patient that his incision is looking good, and he may be able to go home tomorrow. Nothing beats seeing the look on a patient's face when you tell them that news.

After leaving the room, Cameron asks me to step into the storeroom with him.

Crap, is he going to give me a lecture about leaving him to do all the reviews on his own. I know he normally insists on me being with him.

He closes the door behind us. Before he starts his tirade, I jump in, "I'm sorry I took so long. Elizabeth and Dr. Walker were still in the office, and his PA was off in her own world, and then I saw her sitting on his lap, and then Maryella remembered he'd already brought my phone out." The sentence falls out of my mouth in one long, breathless motion.

His eyes are wide as he tries to decipher what I've blurted out. "Hey, hey. Calm down. What happened?" he asks. "What did you see?"

"When I went back to the office, Maryella, the PA, who's also Ava's cousin, said that Elizabeth and Dr. Walker were still having a meeting." I swallow harshly before continuing, "I waited at the office door for Maryella to announce me, and there's a slight gap between the door and where the frosted glass starts. It's like a clear panel. I couldn't help but look. Elizabeth was sitting on Dr. Walker's lap with her arms around his neck." Sucking in a deep breath, I try to calm myself. I hadn't wanted to share the information with Cameron here. I'd have much preferred somewhere private, but I couldn't hold it in.

"On his lap? Are you sure? I thought he was married?"

"I don't know, but I know I definitely saw her on his lap."

"Did you see anything else?" Cameron asks.

"Not really. I moved away in case they could see me through the glass."

"Smart move."

"So, I am sorry I'm late."

"Shh, it's fine." He places his clipboard down on a shelf before his hands slide along my cheekbones as he brings his lips to mine. His gentle caress brings a sense of calm over my body. The feelings I've been desperately trying to suppress rush to the surface once more. But this is not the place.

Enjoying the moment as I allow his lips to massage mine,

even if only briefly before I push him away. "Cam, not here."

"Don't you see... we have proof now that the man who made up such a stupid clause in all our contracts is breaching it himself, with none other than a woman who should've been fired this morning."

His words process through my mind. I hadn't thought of it like that.

"Doesn't mean you can kiss me here. We have no proof. If this morning taught us anything, it's that we need solid proof," I warn. His hands slowly leave my face, and I instantly miss his touch.

"That's true. But this is the hope I was after today, especially after Matthew said the clause in our contracts is iron-clad."

"It's hope, yes, but we need to tread carefully."

"Agreed. We need a plan. Free tonight? I could grab a bottle of wine, and we could discuss." He pulls one side of his mouth into a smile.

A knock sounds at the door, and we both jump an extra foot apart as Pamela opens the door.

"Oh, sorry. Didn't realize this was a conference room now," she teases.

"We needed to discuss a patient's treatment without his wife trying to eavesdrop," Cameron replies.

Pamela laughs. "I think I know exactly who you mean. I believe she was once a nurse. She's always trying to sneak a look at his chart in the nurses' station."

She steps into the storeroom and apologizes as she steps past me, trying to get something from the far wall.

Cameron and I look at each other, unable to continue our conversation until Pamela leaves.

"Don't stop talking on my behalf. I'll grab two of these packs, and I'll be out of here."

"No problem, take your time," Cameron replies. "Chelsea,

251

tomorrow you'll be learning mostly. But I may allow you to assist if it isn't too difficult."

Nodding at Cameron's instruction, Pamela steps past me again before walking out and closing the door behind her.

"Geez, can't have a private conversation anywhere here." Cameron laughs.

"The walls have ears," I reply.

"Anyway, oh that's right... tonight."

"Unfortunately, I agreed to go out with Ava tonight. Maryella, too. Perhaps I can get dirt on Dr. Walker. She seems to know more than she lets on."

"That might be a little risky."

"Not if she gets drunk and spills the beans."

"We need to get back to rounds before we head into surgery, but text me after you get home tonight and see what information you can get out of her."

"Will do."

Cameron holds the door for me as we both leave the storeroom and continue our rounds.

Instead of thinking about the patients or my night out tonight with Ava and Maryella, my mind is fixated on that kiss Cameron gave me—those soft, sweet lips touching mine as his beard tickles my chin.

A kiss I've been longing for.

One I hope to get again and very soon.

CHELSEA

Overjoyed that I've managed to finish work at the rostered time, mainly thanks to a little push from Cameron, I've rushed home to get changed. I didn't feel my business attire from this morning would cut it, and scrubs aren't exactly something that should be worn outside the hospital.

Throwing my bag and jacket on the couch, I kick my running shoes off before stripping out of the scrubs and stepping straight into the shower. Even though this will make me a little late, I'd prefer to have a night out, freshly bathed.

After the quickest shower in history, I choose my favorite jeans and an off-the-shoulder red sweater and team it with my black jacket and low heels from this morning.

Barely-there makeup and a smooth-over of my hair, and I'm ready to go, deciding to drive there rather than Uber it. I'd rather stay sober tonight than have one too many and regret it tomorrow morning.

Parking my car in the lot behind Rick's, I grab the space next to Ava's car, glad that I'm not the only one going to behave responsibly tonight.

Walking around the front, I'm stopped by the burly security guard. "ID?" he asks, his voice deep and raspy.

Digging my card out of the bag, I show him, and he, of course, lets me in. It still gives me a little thrill when I'm asked for my ID. In a strange way, it's flattering.

The bar is quite busy, and the smell of many different types of alcohol nearly knocks me over. I look left and right, trying to find Ava and Maryella. Hesitantly walking a little deeper into the dimly lit establishment, I finally spot them at a booth near the back.

Lifting my arm, I wave, and Maryella spots me first.

"About time," Maryella slurs as I approach the booth.

"Sorry, went home to change," I reply before furrowing my brows at Ava.

She lightly shakes her head before inviting me to sit down.

"What drink do you want, Chels?" Maryella calls over the noise and music in the bar.

"I'm driving," I yell back, "Maybe a Coke for now."

"Ah shit, another party-pooper. Ava's on call," she pouts before heading to the bar. Her green off-the-shoulder sweater flopping about as she stumbles in her heels.

"She was here a good hour before me. I was sure they would've cut her off by now, but they keep serving her." Ava shakes her head before adding, "Mark said he'd call me if it got too hectic like last night," Ava explains.

"Aren't you exhausted?" I ask, worried and knowing she had a long shift last night.

"Yeah... but I'm only on-call until midnight, and then I have tomorrow off. I plan to sleep all day." She laughs.

"Nice. I can't stay late tonight. The first surgery is at eight tomorrow."

"I know you, Chelsea... you came here to hear the gossip,

didn't you?" Ava teases.

"I'm not the gossip type, Ava. You know me better than that."

"Yeah, yeah... well, it gets even better. Wait until Maryella gets back. I'm sure she'll spill it all to you."

Raising my eyebrows at what Ava says, I lean back into the faux leather seat and tap my foot to the music. This song sounds like a mix of country and pop, but I've never heard it before.

Maryella comes back as the song ends.

"Why... why do men suck... suck so bad?" she stammers as she sways before sitting down.

"Not all men do," Ava replies. "Mark is a good one."

"You're lucky, cuz. 'Cause I just tried to talk to a guy at the bar, and then his chick was all over him and told me to fuck off." A sob escapes her.

A waitress puts the drinks down on our table. Four shots and two sodas. Maryella is really planning on getting wasted tonight.

"Don't you think you'd better slow down, Ella," Ava warns. "You'll be in no condition for work tomorrow."

"What work? Maxim fired me this afternoon," Maryella garbles.

"What?" Both Ava and I say at the same time.

"He told me my services weren't needed no more. By services, he meant sex. Apparently, he's been fucking Elizabeth Atkins for the past month."

"That's awful," Ava gasps. "How long were you with him?"

"Months. Since I started, we screwed on my first day, and he liked my boobs because they were lots bigger than his wife's. He told me that I'd have a job as long as I could relieve any tension he felt from his job. We fucked twice a day sometimes. I only discovered he was cheating on me with Elizabeth after Chelsea left the office today. I walked in on Maxim motorboating Elizabeth's tits. Fucking bastard and his dirty bitch. I was meant to be his other woman." Tears run down her cheeks before she grabs a shot and downs it in one go.

Shaking my head in disbelief, I pop my ears to make sure I'm hearing this correctly. Maryella and Maxim Walker have been having an affair for the last few months.

"I'm so sorry, Maryella," I say, reaching across the table and patting her arm.

"Don't be. Thank you for pointing out that little gap. Lucky for me, I filmed them on my cell getting it on with each other as proof. I'm taking it to the board tomorrow. While I never had that stupid non-fucking rule in my contract and neither does he, Elizabeth certainly does. I checked."

A wave of excitement rushes through me. This could be the way to get rid of her for good.

Maryella rests her head on the wooden table after drinking the second shot. "I've got videos galore of us fucking in his office, in his chair, while he was on a call to one of the board members. I sucked his cock when he had a meeting once. I told him I deleted the videos, but he never checked 'cause he was too old to know how." She laughs as she closes her eyes.

"Holy shit," I mouth to Ava.

"Told you it was good," she mouths back.

"Oh..." Maryella blurts out, partially sitting back up again. "I know so much shit about that hospital. The board wants to fire Maxim because he's crap. Oh, and did you know the board wants to get rid of that fucking rule, too, you know... no fucking between staff crap? 'Cause like there are heaps of married couples at the hospital, and they aren't ev..." She rests her head against the cool of the wood as her eyes flutter closed and she drifts off. Watching as she sleeps for a few moments, I turn my attention to Ava, whose grin is growing by the second.

"I'm so excited, I could fucking burst. Mark and I won't have to hide anymore."

Neither will Cameron and me.

"That's excellent, Ava. I'm so happy for you. Not that you really hid, though." I laugh.

"Well, you know what I mean."

That I do. I'm over the moon for Cameron and me, providing the board does scrap the rule after Elizabeth and Maxim are fired tomorrow.

Maryella startles before reaching across the table to grab the other two shots.

"I don't care about that hospital anymore. I don't owe him shit. He told me that he found better pussy with Elizabeth. At least she can't get pregnant, unlike me. Who tells a girl that, like one who they said they loved? He told me he was moving out of his house this week, and we'd get an apartment together. Fucking lies."

"He's a jerk, sweetheart," Ava soothes, reaching her arm around her cousin. Maryella rests her head on Ava's shoulder, and within seconds, she's snoring.

"She knows how to choose them," Ava quips, the last word of her sentence echoing through the bar in the lull between songs. "This is the second married guy that I know about."

Ava leaves Maryella on her shoulder as we drink our soda and discuss the scandal about to explode at the hospital before she asks one of the security guards to help get her cousin into her car.

"Nooo," Maryella cries. "We just gotted here."

"And you need to sleep this off," Ava answers. "Are you okay to get home?" she asks me.

"Yes, no problem at all. My car's parked next to yours. I might head out now, too, anyway."

Grabbing Ava and Maryella's handbags, we slowly walk out to the car, the burly security guard from earlier effortlessly walking Maryella.

"You must do this a lot?" I ask the guard.

"Not as often as you think," he replies. "I'm happy to do it as long as they don't puke on me."

Laughing at his comment, I look at Ava realizing it could be a possibility.

"Ella, you aren't gonna puke in my car, are you? Mark just paid to have it detailed."

"I'm fines," she slurs.

"Ava, I have some sick bags in my car. I'll give them to her."

"Thank you, Chels, you're a lifesaver."

As the guard sits Maryella in the passenger seat of Ava's car, I race around and grab the sick bags from the glove compartment. My mom gets carsick from time to time, especially when reading her cell, so it's always handy to have some in there.

After saying goodbye to my friend, I wave them off before jumping in my car and locking all the doors. Even though there are people around, you can never be too safe at night.

Toying with the idea of calling Cameron now, I finally pluck the courage to send him a quick text as he asked me to.

Me: *Lots of information. Can I call?*

He doesn't reply straight away, and I begin to assume he's gone to bed.

As I start my engine, my ring tone starts to sound through the sound system.

"Hello?" I answer, the number not showing up on the screen.

"Hey, Chels, it's me." Cameron's voice has butterflies erupting in my belly.

"Hey. Finished for the day now?" I ask.

"Yeah, in the car, heading home. Where are you?"

"Sitting in Rick's parking lot about to go home."

A roar of laughter almost deafens me. "Your girls' night didn't last long."

"Maryella was drunk by the time we got here. Ava had to take her home but not before we got some *very* interesting information out of her."

"Do share," he replies.

"Not on the phone. I'll meet you at yours, in say, fifteen minutes?" I brazenly ask.

"Sounds good."

Ending the call, I sit and stare into the darkness ahead of me as my mind begins to overthink what going to Cameron's house means.

We can discuss the information Maryella has divulged and nothing more. But that kiss earlier—that told me he still loves me and has my heart beating a little faster.

His kiss reignited my feelings for him, even though they were never really that far from the surface. I love Cameron, and even though the non-fraternization clause is still in play, life is too short to worry about every little what-if. Ava has the right idea—scream that love from the rooftops, and who cares who hears?

Cameron needs to hear me say this—tonight.

CHAPTER 38

CAMERON

Tapping my fingers on the steering wheel, I listen to my father talk about how my mother is annoying the hell out of him again. He calls me from time to time late at night after a shift and loves to hear details of surgeries I've performed that day. Sometimes I think he's living vicariously through me.

But today is different. He had a follow-up appointment with his specialist, and he's ringing to not only inform me that he doesn't need to go back for another six months but that my mother is on the rampage and insisting he go back earlier than that.

"Can you talk to her, Cam?" Dad asks.

"I'm not sure she'd listen to me. Wasn't she there with you, Dad? Like she'd have heard him say it?"

"She was, but you know what she's like? She's overly cautious. I'm fine. The doctor says I'm fine. How would Marla know more than us?"

"She's looking out for you. I think it's sweet."

"Wait 'til you have a wife nagging at you... then it won't be so sweet."

"Nagging," I hear a screech down the line.

"Damn, I woke her up." Dad chuckles. "Talk soon, Cam. Love you."

"Love you, Dad."

As the line goes dead, I shake my head, knowing that my dad's probably getting a lecture right now. I'm grateful he called. It took my mind off Chelsea coming over for the best part of the drive home.

Pulling into my driveway, I switch my engine off before jumping out and running inside. There's no time for me to put my car in the garage tonight. I have a house to clean up and fast. While normally I keep a pretty tidy home, I've let my guard down the last few weeks. I haven't had any visitors either, not even my parents, so I figured it didn't matter so much until now.

Chelsea's on her way over here. Maybe ten minutes out, and I can't have her seeing this house in such a state.

Grabbing a basket, I throw all the dirty clothes items that I find into it before racing to the laundry and throwing them in the washer. Out of sight, out of mind. Right?

After straightening the cushions on the couch, I collect the few pairs of shoes scattered on the floor before running into my bedroom and throwing them in my closet.

As I begin to stack the dishwasher with my breakfast plates, I hear a knock at the door. Luckily for me, the kitchen isn't too bad. It's the one area of the house I keep clean since you can't leave food scraps lying around.

Wiping my hands on a towel, I walk toward the front door and pull it open. Chelsea's standing there looking as amazing as ever. I don't think I've seen this outfit on her before. It accentuates every curve of her body in just the right way.

"Hey." I beam.

"Hi," she quietly replies.

"Come in... care for a wine?"

"Please."

Showing her to the couch, I grab two wine glasses from the cupboard before fetching the bottle of white from the refrigerator. As I pour the wine, I glance at Chelsea sitting very upright and proper as though she's nervous or uncomfortable about being here.

"All okay?" I ask as I replace the wine cork.

"Sure is. Hope you don't mind me calling so late."

"It's fine. I told you to call me, remember?" Chelsea turns her head slightly as a small smile plays on her lips.

Carrying the glasses of wine over to the couch, I place them down on my glass table before sitting next to her, making sure to keep a little distance. I wouldn't want to come on too strong and make her any more nervous than she already is.

"So..." I begin.

"So," she repeats.

"What did you find out tonight?"

"So much." She twists in her seat, and any unease she was feeling has instantly left. Her eyes light up as she begins to tell me the story. "Turns out Maryella was in a relationship with Maxim. They were having an affair for months, ever since she started working there. Well, after I saw him with Elizabeth earlier and told Maryella about the gap in the frosted glass, she saw them."

"She'd never seen them before?" I ask, scruffing at my beard.

"No, apparently not. She said she's near-sighted and needs glasses, but she's too vain to get them."

"Right."

"So... she confronted him. Maxim dumped her on the spot and fired her because he found umm... something better in Elizabeth."

"Wow... that's harsh."

"You didn't hear the real way he apparently said it to Maryella. *That* was harsh."

"I haven't known him long, but my father knew him before he was made Chief, and he said he was a hard-hearted man."

Chelsea nods before grasping at her hair, tightly wound at the base of her head. She gives it a wriggle before pulling it out. The look of relief washes over her face as her hair cascades over her shoulders.

"Anyway, so Maryella, even though she was completely wasted, said she has videos of them in compromising positions, and even when he was on phone calls or in meetings, she was hiding under his desk, and she has videos of that. On top of all of that, she has a video of Maxim and Elizabeth getting it on."

"Holy shit," I gasp. My eyes widen at this information, and I wonder if Chelsea understands the impact this may have on the entire hospital.

"She's requested a meeting with the board tomorrow."

"Hopefully, she's not still wasted when she shows up. Otherwise, they'll ask her to leave."

"Hopefully not."

Chelsea picks up her wine glass and takes a short sip, followed quickly by another.

"That would've been a lot to absorb tonight." I collect my glass from the table and have a short sip.

"It was. Although, something just dawned on me," she mumbles before taking another sip of wine.

"What's that?"

"She was drunk, right? What if this has all been fabricated? She's technically a scorned lover."

"Alcohol can be a bit like a truth serum... things are said when drunk that shouldn't come out, but I can't imagine it being made up."

Chelsea nods. "Probably not, especially if she's got the meeting already lined up with the board." She places her wine glass back on the table before twisting even further around to face me. Her leg bends and rests against the couch as she flicks her foot under her other knee.

"What's the matter, Chelsea? You've been... I don't know... off... since you got here. I thought hearing the information that Maryella gave you today would've made you extremely happy."

"It has. I had a plan, I guess you'd say, in my head of how tonight would go, and now that one little thought of Maryella making the whole thing up has me back peddling." Her gaze drops to her lap, and she begins to fiddle with the strap of her shoe.

"Plan? Hold up... what are you talking about?" I ask, my brows knitting together as I reach out and gently touch her knee.

What's she trying to tell me here?

"It doesn't matter." Chelsea lifts her head and smiles before standing up and walking to my rear glass door. She gazes up at the sky, the moon casting light over the courtyard. "It's so pretty tonight."

"Chels, don't change the subject."

"I'm not. I shouldn't have mentioned anything."

"You didn't. That's the point. If you need to say something, say it. We're both grown adults here." Standing from the couch, I take a step toward her, the coffee table between us.

"I told you, it doesn't matter."

"Chelsea," I exclaim, raising my voice slightly.

She spins around to face me. Her expression is of shock but quickly turns into worry as her eyebrows come together, and she nibbles on her lip. "I came here tonight to tell you that I love you. That I want us to be together, and I don't give a shit what the hospital says about it."

"You what?" I ask, hoping I've heard her right.

"I want to be with you. If we have to hide because of some fucked-up rule, then so be it. But I need you, Cameron. There's been a hole in my heart since we broke up, and after hearing how Maryella was treated tonight, I realized that when you find real love with a good man, you don't let it go. I can't go another day without you. You're the love of my life."

A grin spreads across my face, growing so wide my cheeks begin to ache. "You're all-in?"

"I am as long as you are?" she answers.

"Definitely."

Stepping around the coffee table, I close the gap between us before scooping Chelsea into my arms and smashing my lips against hers. I think I catch her off guard by the kiss as she gasps into my mouth.

Our lips move in a steady rhythm for several moments before we break apart, and I hug her tightly against my chest. She nuzzles against me as Chelsea releases a satisfied sigh. I've been craving to have her in my arms again, and it's finally happening.

"God, I've missed this," she mutters.

"Me, too," I reply.

Guiding her back to the couch, we both flop down on the comfortable cushions before wrapping our arms around each other.

"My plan was to come over here, tell you I need you back, and then rip your clothes off." Chelsea laughs.

"Hey, I'll be on board with that idea."

"Will you now?" she teases as her hand runs along the buttons of my shirt.

She slowly flicks them open, one after another, before pushing open the shirt and running her hand along my chest.

"You want to take it slow, do you?" I ask, my cock already tenting in my pants.

"Maybe I just want to tease you," she replies, gazing up at me and nibbling on her lip.

"That little lip action right there makes me want to carry you to my bed now and do what I've wanted to do to you for weeks."

She nods her head as she gives me a cheeky smirk.

Standing up, I scoop Chelsea into my arms and take her to my bedroom. As I lay her on my bed, she's everything I ever wanted in a woman—smart, gorgeous, and driven. I can only thank my lucky stars that she finally saw reason and agreed to become us again.

Pulling my arms out of my shirt, I bend down over Chelsea and place my lips on hers before sliding myself onto the bed. I rest my head on my hand and sit up on my elbow as my free hand runs down her sweater.

While we may not be able to shout our relationship from the mountains, it's enough to be with her again, and I'm going to enjoy every single moment I have with her tonight and for the rest of our lives.

CHELSEA

The silence is broken by an unusual sound as a warm arm slides across my body, bringing a smile to my face.

My eyes spring open as I realize the incessant buzz is my cell alarm. How can it already be morning? I want to enjoy this a little more before we get up.

"Damn," Cameron croaks from next to me, his hand gently massaging my breast.

The sound of both Cameron's and my alarms going off simultaneously can't destroy the amazing buzz I'm feeling this morning. We spent the most incredible night together, making up for the lost weeks. But today, we're back to reality.

His hand travels down my stomach and rests between my legs as his fingers begin to tease me.

"Mmm," I moan. "Is it wise we start something now, given both our alarms are going off?"

"Trust me, it'll be quick. I'd like to make you go off this morning, too," he whispers.

He was right. It didn't last more than five minutes, but it was the best start to the morning I've had in a very long time.

By the time the alarm begins to chime again, Cameron returns from the bathroom with a warm face towel and places it gently between my legs.

"Thank you," I say as I take the face towel from him and clean myself up. "How about you shower, and I'll set the coffee machine, and then we can swap?"

"Sounds good." I know that if we were to step into the shower together, we'd definitely be late for work, and that can't happen today. I want to be there to support Maryella, but Cameron and I also have a big surgery.

Once we've both showered and dressed, me, unfortunately, wearing last night's clothes, we stand at his kitchen counter, and it's almost awkward.

"What?" I blurt out after he gives me a little smirk for the fifth time.

"Nothing." He takes another sip of coffee.

"Why do you keep looking at me?"

"Because I can't get over the fact that you're here again. You're my girlfriend again. You're my everything again."

"Aww... I love you, Cam."

"I love you, too." He places a quick peck on my lips.

"Waking up next to you felt so right this morning, and I want to do that more often."

"Deal! Care to move in with me?"

My eyes widen in shock. "What did you say?"

"Would you like to move in with me?"

"There's a big difference between getting back together and living together," I mumble.

"True, but we both agree that this is a forever type deal, correct?"

"Yes, definitely."

"Well, then, the obvious step is for us to move in together and see where life takes us."

Thinking about his suggestion for a moment, excitement bubbles in my stomach. But I also need to be practical. "I'm not saying no. Can I ask that we don't decide until we find out what happens at this board meeting today?"

"Of course." He grins as he waves a hand in the air. "I do feel there may be more to this board meeting that you haven't told me, but I trust you. If you feel the outcome of this meeting will help to make our decision easier, then yes, we'll discuss this further tonight."

"Good. That's settled. Now let's get moving. I'm excited about many things today."

Deciding not to push our luck, we drive our own vehicles to the hospital and arrive within five minutes of each other with me walking through the doors first.

Noticing Maryella in the foyer, I walk over to her to check how she is.

"Hey."

"Hey," she replies as she fumbles with some papers and a folder.

"How are you after last night?" I ask.

"A slight headache, but I'm fine. Thanks to you and Ava for cutting me off when you did. I'm not sure I'd be this good if I weren't stopped."

"That's not a problem. Are you prepared for today?" I hesitantly ask.

"Yes. I've been up for hours. I printed photos, texts, and my edited contract, and, of course, I have my videos."

A wave of relief washes over me. Everything I was concerned about last night is true, and she's presenting evidence against Maxim Walker.

"Do you need anyone to go in with you?"

"Thank you for the offer. Ava is coming in on her day off, and she'll be my support person."

"I've got my cell with me, so make sure you get Ava to text me when it's all over."

Maryella nods before puffing out a breath.

"Tell yourself... just say the facts and present your evidence, and you'll be fine."

"Thanks, Chels. I appreciate your support."

"And I appreciate you being brave to fight against two people who think they are untouchable."

"It has to be done," she replies.

"I have to head to surgery now. Good luck."

"Thank you."

Heading off to the locker room, I notice Elizabeth at her open locker and think twice about heading inside.

I'm not hiding from her, though. You don't hide from bullies. Instead, I walk straight up to my locker and open it without even casting a glance her way.

"Good morning, Chelsea," she mumbles.

A chill washes over me as her voice fills the room.

Be polite—one-word answers. Then walk away.

"Morning," I reply.

"Good luck with your surgery today. You'll be great."

Has hell frozen over?

Why is she being so nice to me?

"Thank you."

Closing my locker, I grab myself some scrubs and my lab coat and decide to get changed elsewhere. With any luck, she'll no longer work at this hospital in a few short hours.

After changing, I head back to the locker room to put my clothes away, and Elizabeth is nowhere in sight. I breathe a sigh of relief. I don't like ignoring or avoiding people, but with that woman, you never know which personality you may get at any given moment.

Cameron walks in as I close my locker.

"Hey, you." He beams as he walks to his locker and places his belongings down before collecting some scrubs and his lab coat. "Any news about the board meeting yet?"

"No, I think it starts in a half-hour, but I saw Maryella in the foyer on the way in. She looks nervous."

"I don't blame her. You would be, too, if you were to speak in front of the people who run this hospital."

"True."

"But more importantly, are you ready for this surgery?"

"For sure. I'm so excited to learn."

"Well, the patient has been given their pre-meds and will be brought up here in about a half-hour. Want to grab a coffee before we start? It could be a long procedure given that we won't know how serious it is until we open him up."

"Sounds like a plan."

Five hours later, and both Cameron and I are washing up after a successful esophagectomy surgery. A surge of adrenaline is coursing through my veins, and I can't stop smiling.

Cameron laughs as I take off my face mask. "It's a good feeling, isn't it?"

"It is. I'm exhausted, and my feet are killing me but knowing that we've given this man some quality of life is something you can never get enough of."

"I agree. It's the reason why I wanted to become a surgeon."

In all the excitement and stress regarding the surgery, I'd completely forgotten about the board meeting. I feel my cell buzz against my leg. "Shit. The meeting," I whisper to Cameron.

"Any word?"

Pulling out my cell, I notice there are four text messages waiting.

"The texts are from Ava. But she doesn't elaborate on what's happened."

Me: *Ava, what happened?*

I instantly start to see the three dancing dots on my screen.

Ava: *Are you out of surgery? I'm still at the hospital.*
Me: *Yeah, only just. I need to do a follow-up, and then I'll meet you at the cafeteria... say fifteen minutes.*
Ava: *See you then.*

Speaking directly to a patient's family is something I'm still not yet used to, although Cameron says I'm a natural. He makes it look so easy, but I sometimes feel like a bit of a bumbling idiot.

Perhaps it's that my train of thought isn't one hundred percent on the job. Now that I've spoken to Ava and know there's an outcome for the board meeting today, I'm desperate to know what's happened.

"I'll come with you," Cameron replies after I tell him where I'm going.

"You don't have to, Cam." I think a part of me is still slightly worried that it blew up in Maryella's face, and we're still all in the same position.

"But I want to. Plus, I think it's time I met Ava as your boyfriend and not as your supervisor."

"Really?" I ask, my grin growing by the second.

"Sure. Why not? I'm also hoping you're free for dinner on Saturday, so you can meet my parents."

My goodness.

Bubbles of excitement mix with nerves at the suggestion.

Before I can answer, Cameron jumps back in, "If it's too soon, then that's completely fine."

Clearing my throat, my smile begins to return. "No, no. Not at all. I'd love to meet them."

"Great."

"Maybe you can meet mine when they get back from their trip?" I ask.

"Of course. I'd love to meet them."

Puffing out a breath, I gaze into Cameron's eyes, not caring who sees. "This is really happening now, isn't it?"

"It is... so if you want to back out—"

I cut him off. "Hell, no."

Cameron chuckles. "Good."

He escorts me down to the cafeteria. We decide against holding hands, just in case, but as we spot Ava toward the back and see that she's sitting on the other side of the booth to Mark, a rush of disappointment envelops me.

"Why do I get a bad feeling about this?" I mutter to Cameron.

CHAPTER 40

CAMERON

Desperately wanting to reach out for Chelsea's hand, I stop myself.

"It'll be fine, Chels. Keep breathing," I encourage as we walk over to Ava. She looks as though she only has Dr. Fisher with her.

The cafeteria is relatively busy. Most tables are taken with a mixture of staff, patients in wheelchairs or with drip stands, and visiting family members. This probably wasn't the best place for everyone to meet up, considering the nature of the issues we're here to discuss.

"Hey," Chelsea says as we grab a couple of nearby chairs and sit at the end of the booth.

"Hey," they both reply.

Ava slowly twists her head, and her eyes widen as she realizes I'm with Chelsea.

"Dr. Chase. I didn't realize you were coming as well." Her eyes dart between Chelsea and Dr. Fisher. "Umm, the nature of this conversation is rather... umm... personal."

"Ava, it's fine. He's... ahh... with me."

"With you?" she repeats.

"Yeah, with her," I answer as a smile spreads across my face.

Chelsea does the same as Ava's mouth drops, and she reaches across and playfully slaps Chelsea's arm. "You shit. You never said anything. I mean, I knew you had a spark, but I didn't think you'd act on it."

"Shh," Chelsea warns. "We don't want the world to know yet. You're the first one."

"Like first?" she asks.

"Yes, besides us, you and Dr. Fisher here are the only people to know," I respond.

"Holy crap. That's so awesome."

"Thanks, we think so, too." Chelsea beams before nudging me.

"Aww, look how cute they are," Ava squeals and reaches across the table to Dr. Fisher.

"So, what happened today? I'm assuming it didn't go well," Chelsea states.

"What makes you think that?" Ava asks.

"You don't look over the moon. I thought you'd be all over each other in celebration."

"No, it has nothing to do with that," Dr. Fisher begins. "I'm on duty. There's a good chance we have patients in this cafeteria, and I feel it'll look bad for my practice if we are seen, umm... canoodling."

"That's understandable," I reply.

"So, what happened then?" Chelsea asks rather impatiently. I understand her need to know. We both want Elizabeth gone from this hospital. Hell, after yesterday, I'd love to see the back of Maxim Walker too.

"Maryella was amazing in there. She was cool and calm and stated all the facts. While she showed them pictures and texts, they said seeing the videos wasn't necessary. They will be speaking to Dr. Walker, and a decision will be made by two this afternoon. They will call Maryella with the news, and she'll text me. She won't get her job back, but she didn't do it for that, anyway. She's already got an interview at another office."

"She'd make a good receptionist, I think." Dr. Fisher grins.

So many questions run through my head. What about Elizabeth? Did she get reprimanded?

It's as though Chelsea reads my mind. "I'm so glad she didn't let her nerves get the better of her," Chelsea comments. "But what about Elizabeth?"

"While Maryella brought her up, the video she took yesterday of them together wasn't clear enough to see it was her. They'll question her, but unless either she or Dr. Walker admits to it, she won't be touched."

"Shit," I cringe.

"Fuck," Chelsea whispers. "She escapes again."

"Who knows, they may put their foot in it during their interviews," Dr. Fisher adds.

"You know what the best part was..." Ava starts, slightly bouncing on her seat, "The board voted for that stupid clause, you know the non-fraternization one, to be removed from all past and future contracts with the staff at this hospital. Their lawyers will amend it today, and they said it will take effect immediately."

"Yes," Chelsea cries, louder than anticipated. She looks around the cafeteria at the people looking our way as her cheeks flush pink. "Oops." She laughs.

"Isn't that fantastic," I exclaim. "I'm sure there are many couples in the hospital which will be ecstatic when that gets out."

Chelsea throws her arms around my neck and places a kiss on my cheek. "I'm so glad we don't have to hide now. We can shout us from the rooftops."

"I think you've already done a good enough job of that today." I laugh.

Chelsea's grin slowly disappears. "We still have the problem with Elizabeth," she grimaces.

"We can work that out," I reply.

Checking my watch, we should be heading to the next scheduled surgery. It's only a hernia, and one I was hoping to surprise Chelsea by telling her she can do this one on her own today.

A pager begins to chime.

"Shit. It's me," Dr. Fisher says. "Breech delivery. See you all soon."

Moving my chair out of the way so he can pass, we watch as he runs out of the cafeteria.

"We'd better get going soon, too, Chelsea. Our next surgery is in less than an hour from now."

"I'd forgotten about that. Got caught up in all of this," Chelsea utters, screwing her face up.

"I'm going to head to Maryella's, anyway, and see how her interview went. I'll text you when I hear anything."

"Thanks."

After grabbing some food to go, Chelsea and I head to the staff room to eat. My colleague, Daniel, is sitting in the staff room finishing up his lunch. We greet him before we sit down and dive into our food. I don't know about Chelsea, but I'm famished.

As I take my first bite, Daniel's intern comes running in and whispers something in his ear.

"No idea. Cameron, do you know anything about Elizabeth and Maxim getting fired?"

My eyes widen, and I almost choke on my pasta. My gaze moves to Chelsea, who has frozen mid-sip of her drink.

"What?" I cough.

"Dena, tell them what you heard," Daniel instructs his intern.

"We had a meeting just then, and we were told that we'll be getting a new Chief and a new attending who will be in charge of the interns."

"What happened to Dr. Walker and Dr. Atkins?" Chelsea asks.

"I'm not sure. But we were told they no longer work here," she replies.

"Wonder what's happened there," Daniel says after dismissing his intern.

Both Chelsea and I know what happened, and from my point of view, I couldn't be happier right now. Both Maxim and Elizabeth got what was coming to them.

While my silent celebration calms down, I get back to eating my food as Daniel gets up and leaves.

"I can't believe this," Chelsea whispers.

"Neither can I. But we may need to wait until we get some kind of formal notification. I wouldn't want to get too excited only to have it be fake news."

"Agreed."

We finish our meal and head to the locker room to freshen up before the next surgery. Collecting a new pair of socks and a bag from my locker, I sit down on the small bench between two banks of lockers and change my socks before placing the used ones in the bag.

Chelsea walks over and straddles me on the bench.

"I have dirty socks here," I warn her.

"I don't care."

She wraps her hands around my neck before placing her lips on mine, the passionate kiss catching me off guard.

"What was that for?" I laugh.

"Because I can... now." She grins.

She gets off my lap and continues to get herself ready for the next surgery while I remain seated for a moment.

Her cell chimes and she digs the device from her pocket. "It's

Ava, and it is true. They are both gone."

"Wow. It's unbelievable."

"No, what's unbelievable is the lengths you two would go to, to get a great surgeon like me fired from a top hospital," a female voice growls from the doorway.

Elizabeth.

"We did no such thing," I protest.

"Save it. I know it was the PA who saw, but I'm sure you both are ecstatic to see me go... and poor Maxim, too. He did nothing wrong here."

"You both did, Elizabeth. You know that. But I wish you all the best for your future," I offer, only half meaning it.

"Pfft. You couldn't care if I rot on the road," she spits.

Elizabeth walks over to her locker and opens it before placing a few items inside a bag.

"I'm looking forward to our fresh start in New York," she spouts before turning on her heel and leaving the locker room.

Chelsea breathes a sigh of relief as she disappears into the corridor.

"Hopefully, that's the last we see of her," I add.

We both nod before standing.

Walking over the Chelsea, I wrap my arms around her neck and place several kisses on her cheeks.

"Providing there are no emergencies after this, want to come back to my place for dinner tonight?"

"Sounds like a date."

A date... why didn't I think of that?

"You know what... let's make it a date. A proper date. After work, go home and get dressed up, and I'll take you somewhere nice."

Chelsea's face lights up, and she nods several times.

Now that we can be seen together in a public setting and not care who sees us, I'm going to make it up to my girl and take her to as many fancy restaurants as they have in San Francisco. After all, I need to spoil my girlfriend.

CHELSEA

Pulling up outside my apartment, I instantly notice the front door has been repaired.

About freakin' time.

After fumbling with my keys to unlock it, I race up the stairs as my excitement about tonight almost has me giggling like a teen.

After a very quick shower, I pull out an old favorite, my mid-length black dress with the long floral sleeves that flare at the cuff. It's fun and flirty but still nice enough to wear to a restaurant for dinner. It's one of the last dresses I have left in my wardrobe from when I was in college. Luckily, it hasn't gone out of style.

Slipping it on, I straighten it up before admiring it in the full-length mirror.

"Not bad," I tell myself.

After fixing my hair into loose waves and applying a little makeup, I slide my feet into my heels before placing my cell and wallet into a black purse.

"I hope this is enough," I mumble to myself as I check over my outfit.

Glancing at my bedside clock, I gasp when I see the time. Cameron will be here in a matter of minutes. I toy with the idea of packing a bag for tonight on the off chance I'm invited to stay at Cameron's. After several minutes of tooing and froing, I throw a pair of pajamas in a small bag, some sweats, and a toothbrush as well as my brush. I'll leave it near the front door. If he doesn't mention anything about staying over, then I'll leave it behind.

Closing the drapes in my bedroom, I switch the light off and head to the living room, where I place the bag at the front door. Not wanting to get achy feet before we even begin our date, I carefully sit on the couch, trying my hardest not to crush my dress.

My foot bounces in time to the seconds ticking on my wall clock, the rhymical sound echoing through my eerily quiet apartment. Sure, I could switch the television on, even if only for background noise, but Cameron is a stickler for time and will be here at any minute.

As though he heard my thoughts, a buzz of the intercom sounds through the apartment. It's been out of use for so long now, I'd almost forgotten what it sounds like.

"Ah, it's nice to see it is working again," I utter as I jump from my seat and race to the wall near the door.

Pressing the button, I lean forward and say, "Hello?"

His familiar voice brings a smile to my face. "I believe you have a hot date tonight, Dr. Mitchell."

Giggling into the intercom, I reply, "Yes, yes, I do. Is he here yet?"

"Cheeky." He chuckles.

"Come on up." I'm still laughing as I press the unlock button.

Peering through my peephole, I wait for my handsome date to come into view. He must have run up the stairs as he appears in no time at all. Pulling the door open, I'm greeted by a beaming smile and a huge bunch of flowers. I notice he is carrying a bag in his other hand.

"Don't you look stunning," he comments as he holds out the flowers for me to take.

"Oh, stop." My cheeks warm at his compliment. "Thank you for the flowers. They are absolutely beautiful."

"I remembered you don't own a vase, so I bought you one, too. I actually bought it a few weeks ago for your birthday, but now seems like the perfect time to give it to you." He holds up the bag.

A chuckle escapes me. "That's fantastic."

"Think of it as an early birthday gift."

"Only three months out." I laugh.

"It's better than me forgetting, isn't it?"

"Of course. It also helps that our birthdays are two weeks apart." A giggle escapes me. I'll never forget his birthday.

Cameron follows me to the kitchen counter and places the bag down before pulling out a large rectangular box. I place the flowers flat on the counter, knowing that I have a vessel to hold them now.

"I know it's not wrapped fancy, but the box is pretty."

"Reusable gift bags and boxes are perfect, less paper waste that way."

He slides the box in front of me. I carefully remove the lid and place it down next to the box before removing some of the bubble wrap.

A beautiful, tall glass vase fits perfectly inside the box, the etched pattern detail is stunning. I notice some words along the bottom of the vase, and I carefully remove the vase from its packaging.

Holding it up closer to my face, I see 'May this vase always hold flowers as gorgeous as you. Cameron and Chelsea <3.'

"Oh my goodness..." I gasp as I carefully stand it on the

counter. "That's stunning."

"It's a promise. I'll always keep it filled with beautiful flowers for my beautiful girl."

My heart flutters at his words, and I feel the need to pinch myself to make sure this is real.

After placing the flowers in the vase, I look around for somewhere to display the arrangement before deciding that it's best to leave it where it already is on the other end of the counter. That way, I'll see it the moment I walk into the apartment, and the vibrancy of the flowers brightens up that end of the apartment nicely.

"Ready to go?" Cameron whispers as he walks up behind me and places a kiss on my cheek.

"Sure."

Cameron takes my hand and leads me to the door.

"This your bag for tonight?" he asks.

"I didn't want to presume but thought I'd better pack something on the off chance."

"Oh, you're coming back to mine," he rasps, sending a chill up my spine, and goosebumps form on my forearms.

After a short drive we park the car, we arrive at the restaurant and head inside. The soft lighting and neutral colors of the tables, chairs, and linen provide a romantic ambiance. Having been to several nice restaurants in my life, I've never been to one on a date. There's something about a man wining and dining you that has me feeling a little giddy.

We're shown to a table for two near a window. As the waiter steps forward to pull my chair out, Cameron stops him.

"Please, let me."

"Of course, sir," the waiter replies, stepping aside. My back is to the front of the restaurant, giving a more intimate feel to our date.

"Thank you," I whisper to Cameron, thankful the flush of my

cheeks is concealed by the muted light.

Cameron sits opposite me, and we're handed the menus before the waiter pours us both a glass of water and places the slender bottle in the middle of the table. He then leaves us to read over the menu. I read each item, one by one, seeing which I feel like tonight. Although, in this very moment, I could eat just about anything. I'm starving.

"Like it?" Cameron asks, catching me off guard.

"The menu?" I reply.

"No, the restaurant." Cameron chuckles.

A snicker escapes me. "Oops. It's fantastic. I haven't been here before."

"Neither have I."

"See anything that tickles your fancy?" I ask.

"Besides the stunning woman in front of me?"

A smirk spreads on my face before I look away. "Cam."

"The beef looks good, as does the chicken with the cream sauce."

I nod. "I saw the chicken, too."

"How about we both get that and a nice white to go with it?"

"Sounds great."

Cameron calls the waiter back and orders for both of us, pronouncing the dishes' fancy names as though it's a second language. The restaurant is more than half-full tonight, and as my stomach growls, I begin to hope that the meal won't take too long to arrive.

Conversation flows as easily as ever between Cameron and me, although concentrating more on our families and our childhoods, something we haven't really spoken about before.

"So, my parents weren't surprised when I told them we were together," Cameron blurts out.

"What? You told them already?" I gasp.

"Apparently, I speak about you… a lot. Mom had an inkling for quite a while. I didn't realize I included your name in my conversation so much."

I begin to chuckle.

"What's so funny?" he asks.

"My mom said the same thing." I laugh.

"So, you told your parents?"

"Only Mom," I admit.

"I only said something, so it wasn't awkward when we arrive for dinner next week."

"That's what I thought, too," I reply. "All I ask is that you don't call me Chels in front of Mom and Dad... you'll lose brownie points." My lips twist into a smile.

"I wouldn't dream of doing that," he replies from behind his wine class. As he places it back down, his attention is drawn to behind me. "This looks like our meals."

Breathing a sigh of relief, I watch as the waiter places my meal in front of me before serving Cameron. Leaning forward slightly, I breathe in the aromatic fragrance of my meal as my mouth begins to water. Gazing up at Cameron, I notice he's doing the same.

He lifts his glass, and I follow.

"Here's to us."

"Here's to us."

The meal tastes as good as it smells, if not better, and before we know it, Cameron and I have finished in surely what has to be some kind of a record.

"You must have been as hungry as I was." I laugh.

"Certainly was. Dessert?"

"Please."

We decide on a rich chocolate dessert, the waiter suggesting we share one, and I'm so grateful we listened to him. A beautiful finish to our meal, but a small amount was more than enough for me.

Watching as Cameron struggles to finish the dessert, I take the last sip of wine as a person comes to a stop beside me.

"Always knew there was something going on between you two," the female voice trills.

Cameron's face instantly drops as his spoon teeters on his fingertips. Closing my eyes, I know that voice, yet I don't want to look up to see if I'm right.

But I sneak a glance and my suspicions are confirmed.

Elizabeth.

"You look lovely, Chelsea," she offers, her lips struggling to twist into a small smile.

Maxim Walker appears behind her.

"Cameron," he sternly offers.

"Dr. Walker," Cameron replies.

"Come, darling, let's take our seat," he encourages Elizabeth, trying to guide her away, but she stops him.

"You may have gotten what you want with both of us leaving, but all it would take is one phone call, and your relationship will be all over the hospital, and you'll be following suit," she seethes.

Sitting up a little taller in my seat as a wave of confidence washes over me, I know I now don't need to hold my tongue around this woman anymore. She's nothing to me. "But didn't you hear, *Elizabeth*..." I begin. "The hospital lawyers changed that clause in the contracts today."

She stands up straight before turning to Maxim, who takes a step forward and leads her away. I can just hear her asking him if he knew of the changes before they were out of earshot. I'm extremely grateful that they are seated on the other side of the restaurant away from us, and we're almost finished.

Cameron shakes his head as he smirks. "I'm so glad you said that to her. I was thinking something along those lines, too."

"God, I hope we never have to see her again."

"Hopefully not."

"Do you think she deliberately came to the same restaurant as us tonight, maybe to try and cause trouble?" I ask.

"Who knows. Maybe she overheard me making the reservation, but we won't let them ruin our night."

"Never."

Bringing my water glass to my lips, I have a small sip of water as Cameron takes one more bite of the dessert before pushing the plate aside.

"Before we head home, I wanted to ask you something." Cameron collects the napkin from next to the plate and wipes at his mouth.

My eyes widen as I gulp. My skin tingles as a mass of thoughts runs through my mind. What could he possibly want to ask me?

"Chels," Cameron starts before puffing out a breath. He reaches across the table and grasps my hand.

"Yes?"

"Chels, I was wondering... would you like to officially move in with me?"

The breath I hadn't realized I was holding leaves my lungs as I place my free hand on my chest. "Oh, wow," I reply.

"I asked you only a short time ago but thought now would be a good time to ask again. What did you think I was going to ask?"

Shaking my head, I silently laugh. "Nothing... I'm not sure. Sorry."

"I wouldn't ask you to marry me in a crowded restaurant with two people I despise here." He chuckles.

"That wasn't it. Anyway, my answer is yes. Yes, I'll move in with you."

"That's music to my ears."

Cameron calls the waiter for the check as I slide some money from my handbag.

"Put it away. I told you I'm taking you out, and that means I pay."

"That's very sweet. Thank you."

"My pleasure. Now let's pay so I can take you home... to *our home.*"

'Our home' has a nice ring to it.

This is a huge step for us, and even though I've never lived with a male besides my dad, it felt as natural as anything to answer yes. This feels like the perfect progression for Cameron and me. I'll forever appreciate my cousin shuffling her wedding party around and pairing me with Cameron, but I'm indebted that fate stepped in, and Cameron ended up being my new supervisor.

While the road for us getting here has been far from smooth, I now have my Doctor Dreamy in my arms, and I'm never letting him go.

EPILOGUE

CHELSEA

Six Months Later...

Stringing the final row of fairy lights onto a tree branch in my parents' yard, I climb down from the stepladder and admire my handy work. It's Mom's birthday today, and her only request for decorations was a backyard full of twinkle lights.

Tonight is bittersweet for me. In one way, I'm so happy that my parents are off on yet another adventure, this time heading to Hawaii before traveling to Australia, New Zealand, and Fiji for their wedding anniversary. But I'm also sad that this will be the final party we have in this backyard before the house is sold.

After my parents return from their trip, they're putting the house on the market and buying an RV. They plan to travel not only all over the US but head to Canada as well. It seems as though the travel bug has bitten them both hard.

The fairy lights I've just hung have slipped slightly, and I stretch up to correct it but can't quite reach.

"Here, let me," Cameron says from behind me.

"I knew marrying someone tall would come in handy." I grin.

"Shh, it's meant to be a surprise, remember?" he warns.

Rolling my eyes, I shrug at his comment. We never intended on getting married out of the blue. Hell, Cameron never officially proposed.

We went for a drive last Monday after a long night shift that turned into most of the morning and ended up at our favorite spot at Mount Tamalpais. Only it was occupied this time with a couple and their bridal party.

As we sat in the car and watched the loved-up couple take a million photos, Bruno Mars' song,

"Marry You," played on the radio. Of course, I sang along as it's one of my favorites. The final bars of the song played, but Cameron kept singing. At first, I laughed thinking he was being silly, but then he twisted in his seat and said, "I think I want to marry you," before turning back in his seat.

Thinking nothing of it, I casually said to Cameron how nice it would be for that to be us one day. His reply was the lyrics again, "I think I want to marry you."

He grinned, and I grinned before tears sprung in my eyes. He never officially asked, but we both knew in that moment that we wanted to get married.

"What about today?" Cameron suggested.

"Why not?"

Neither of us wanted a big, over-the-top wedding like Sara and Matthew's, so a civil ceremony sounded just right.

He drove us back to the courthouse. We got our license and were married in our scrubs within two hours of deciding to become Dr. and Dr. Chase. After our ceremony, we went home and slept for a while before getting up and enjoying our single day off at home and getting takeout for dinner.

It was low-key, extremely intimate, and perfect for us.

Cameron is now my husband, and I wouldn't have it any other way.

As nice as it is in our own little bubble, we knew we'd have to share our news soon and thought it'd be a great idea to surprise both of our parents tonight at the party. Once the initial shock subsides, I can only imagine the first words from my mother's mouth will be about babies, but that's not on the cards just yet.

"What's the surprise?" Mom asks from behind us.

Playfully grasping Cameron's button-down shirt, I close my eyes for a split second before spinning around to my mom. A smile is plastered on my face as I reply, "Nothing."

"Hmm," she groans, knitting her brows together. "You'd better not be pregnant, and you're hiding it."

"Oh, for goodness' sake, Mom."

"Nothing like that, Hen. You'd be the first to know," Cameron adds.

"Well, I think you two will make amazing babies, and Dad and I aren't getting any younger."

"Neither am I," Cameron laughs. I gently tap his chest, not wanting him to encourage Mom anymore.

"Cam, do you mind helping Alan with the chairs from the garage, and Chelsea, you can come with me? We have food arriving shortly."

Placing a quick kiss on Cameron's lips before Mom drags me away, we head into the house and collect the serving plates Mom wants to serve the food on for tonight.

The guests aren't due for at least another hour. There are roughly thirty people attending, but I'm sure Mom ordered enough food to feed all the staff and patients at the hospital as well.

"Do you really need all of this, Mom?" I ask, looking at the twenty-five serving platers scattered over the kitchen.

"Well, we had to have some vegetarian for your aunt, Sara had to have something that was completely cooked, otherwise it'll make the baby sick, and Agnes is a celiac and needs gluten-free. So, I catered for everyone's needs."

I nod at my mom's explanation. "That's lovely you thought of everyone individually."

"I even got you your favorite chicken sushi."

"Thank you," I squeal.

"You're welcome, darling. I have to admit, I'm going to miss entertaining here. It's the perfect house for it."

"It is. But I'm sure you'll enjoy entertaining just as much in the RV."

"It won't be the same, but I'm looking forward to the new adventure it brings."

A tear wells in my eyes, knowing that my parents won't be a short drive away anymore.

"Oh, don't you get emotional. It'll start me off again," Mom blubbers before scooping a tissue each for us and throwing one to me.

This isn't me—I don't get emotional in situations like this.

"I can't help it. I grew up here, Mom." She stares at me for the longest time. I get the feeling she wants to say something but doesn't.

Mom shakes her head quickly. "But look where you live now. Cameron's home is beautiful."

"It is... but this will always be my home, too."

The knock on the front door startles us both. As I walk toward the door, I wipe at my eyes, desperate to try to save the small amount of makeup I'm actually wearing.

Pulling open the door, I invite the caterers inside and

instantly notice that Cameron's parents are walking up the front path.

"There's our girl," Cameron's mom calls.

Laughing at her comment, I'm so glad they welcomed me into their family with open arms. People often complain about their in-laws, but I've been blessed with this pair.

"Hello," I reply as they approach the top of the stairs. I hug them both before inviting them inside the house.

"I can't get over the layout of this home," Cameron's mom gushes.

"When Mom and Dad remodeled, they put a lot of thought into the layout. This was meant to be the home they grew old in." I stifle a sob before patting at the tear at the corner of my eye.

"Oh, honey," Cameron's mom sympathetically says before hugging me.

"I'm not even sure why I'm crying. I'm not an emotional person... I—" I stop myself from continuing my sentence. I almost said that I didn't even cry when I married Cameron. That's not the way we want to tell our parents.

"You're not pregnant, are you?" Cameron's dad jokes.

"No," I reply before my face drops and worry kicks in.

Shit. I can't possibly be pregnant.

"I think she'd know if she were, Dennis. She's a doctor, after all," Cameron's mom says, defending me.

Showing them through the house, I leave them with Cameron and my parents before collecting my handbag and heading to the bathroom.

Dennis' comment is playing over and over in my head. While Cameron and I are still somewhat careful with contraception, we have had a few slip-ups since I ran out of pills. I accidentally let my prescription for the pill lapse two months ago and haven't gotten around to sorting that out again. You'd think with working at a hospital I'd remember to arrange it, but my sexual health is the last thing I think of when I'm working.

We've discussed our situation multiple times. Cameron would love nothing more than to be a dad as soon as physically possible. I wanted to wait until after I scored a permanent surgical placement at the hospital, but we both agree that if anything happens, then we'll be fine with it.

After locking the bathroom door, I place my handbag on the countertop and retrieve my cell from my bag. I scroll through my calendar, checking to see when my last period was and then count forward—smack bam in the middle of the four days of nonstop hernias and thyroid surgeries.

Nope, definitely didn't have it then.

Shit.

We've had a couple of scares in the last six months, so I shake my head, knowing this is likely to be another, although we haven't been as careful with contraception as we should be. The long hours, lack of sleep, and stressful situations can really wreak havoc on your body and cycle anyway.

Pulling a pregnancy test from the pocket of my handbag—a leftover from the last time I checked while at work—I shrug my shoulders. It'll only be two minutes to know a yay or nay. Why not?

It's not until I've taken the test that goosebumps form on my skin. Replacing the cap, I place it flat on the counter in front of my handbag and watch as the pink washes across the viewing window.

Each time I've previously done the test, it has only been a day or so later and a just-in-case type situation. But this time, my stomach is in knots as I don't really know how late I am.

Placing the toilet lid down, I sit on top and take some slow, deep breaths to calm my nerves. I can just see myself in the reflection of the mirror. My cheeks are tinted pink. Scooping up my cell to check the time left, I can't help but admire the handsome doctor on my screen—the one man who makes me weak in the knees, the one I'm lucky enough to call my husband.

A knock at the bathroom door makes me jump.

"Won't be a minute," I call out.

"Chels. It's me. All okay?" Cameron calls out. "You disappeared in there quite a few minutes ago now."

Slowly standing, I take the few steps to the door and unlock it, pulling it open only slightly.

"Come in here," I whisper.

Cameron's brows furrow before he nods, pushes the door open, and steps inside.

CAMERON

Locking the door again behind me, Chelsea moves to stand against the vanity as though she's trying to conceal her handbag.

"People will assume things if we're in here too long," I joke. "But in all seriousness, is everything all right?"

"I'm fine. Your dad said something earlier, and it made me think."

Inwardly groaning, I begin to think of what he could've possibly said to make Chelsea upset. She's still not used to his blunt humor.

"Crap, what did he say? Did he upset you? He says things without—"

Raising her hand, she stops me from talking. "It wasn't anything bad. I was a little upset about my parents selling the house, and you know, I wouldn't normally get upset over something like a house."

"Yeah, that's strange." I nod. Chelsea's usually quite good at keeping her emotions in check, whether it be at the hospital or home.

"So, your dad commented about me being pregnant. Of course, I laughed it off, but thinking about it, I can't remember when my last period was."

My eyes widen in surprise as I feel my lips involuntarily pulling into a smile.

"So, I came in here to do a test. I had a spare from the last time."

"You do keep everything but the kitchen sink in that bag." I chuckle.

"True."

"And?" I whisper.

"I'm still waiting. I can't bring myself to look at it." Placing her hand behind her back, she fumbles before slowly extending her hand toward me. A thin, white stick—a pregnancy test. Her fingers conceal the result panel.

Reaching for it, I stop short. "Oh, wow. Do you think it's a possibility?" I ask, not sure what else to say.

My heart is beating so much faster than it should be as I begin to hope that the test is positive.

"I don't know." She shrugs before a soft laugh escapes Chelsea's mouth. "We're both doctors. You'd think we'd know if we've made a baby or not."

"Here," I mouth as I take the test from her hand.

Slowly turning it over, I take in the pink lines—one solid one and one fainter. But it's definitely there. My eyes go back and forth between the two lines, trying to make sure this is truly happening.

A mixture of relief and nerves washes over my body before I begin to wonder how Chelsea will feel about this.

Chelsea nervously taps her fingers against each other as I fear my expression will give away the result. Lifting my eyes to meet hers, my lips pull into the biggest smile as my cheeks instantly begin to ache. I need to put my wife out of her misery.

I'm going to be a dad.

Inside, I'm jumping around like crazy, but on the outside, I need to find out how my wife feels about this first.

"We're having a baby," I whisper.

Holy shit. Those are words I've longed to say.

Chelsea's hands begin to shake as she absorbs what I tell her. She clasps them close to her chest. Searching her face for any type of reaction, I get nothing.

Geez, this can't be good.

"Chels..." I mutter, placing the test down on the counter, "...are you all right? I know this is a shock."

Clearing her throat, she opens her mouth to speak, but no words come out. Chelsea quickly spins around before turning on the faucet. Rubbing her back, I worry she's going to be sick, but instead, she has a small sip of water.

As she turns back around, I wipe a drop of water from her chin and encourage some kind of reaction from her.

"Chels, if this isn't something you want right now, then we can discuss that."

The sentence hurts to say, but if my wife isn't ready for a baby, then we need to have a talk about the options we have.

Chelsea's eyes widen before she shakes her head. Opening her mouth, this time the words aren't trapped. "Wow."

"Wow, indeed."

"If your dad hadn't said anything, I could've been one of those women who had no idea they were pregnant until going into labor." She laughs.

"I'm sure it wouldn't have come to that. But are you... happy about this?" I tentatively ask.

A small smile appears on her face as she slowly nods. "I think so. Not ideal timing, but there will never be that perfect time."

Stepping forward, I wrap my arms around my wife and pull her close. Placing a soft kiss into her hair, I can't help but say, "I'm going to be a dad."

Pulling back, I lower my lips to her and place a soft kiss. "I love you so much, Chelsea."

"I love you, too."

Deciding to keep both the baby news and marriage to ourselves until after the party, I ask my parents to stay until after all the other guests have left.

Chelsea manages to get away with not drinking tonight by telling the two people who asked why that she's got a stomach condition and needs to limit her alcohol intake. I guess being doctors, people don't question it.

Her cousin, Sara, and my best friend, Matthew, are the last to leave. Sara takes Chelsea's hand and places it on her belly. "Skyla wants to say goodnight, too." They are having a little girl in a few months, and they've chosen the name Skyla as it means scholar, which Matthew wants his daughter to be.

"Good night, cuz," Chelsea says as she kisses her cousin on the cheek before placing a soft kiss on her growing belly and whispers, "Good night, Skyla."

"See ya, man," Matthew says, offering me a firm handshake. "Come over when you're ready tomorrow." It kills me not to be sharing our news with my best friend yet, but I plan on doing that in the morning.

Waving goodbye to them, I walk up behind Chelsea and slide my hands around her waist, gently placing them close to where our baby is growing. Whispering into her ear, I grin, "That will be us soon."

Chelsea nods before nuzzling into my neck.

"Come on, Chelsea. Let's start cleaning up," her mom calls after we close the front door.

"Mom, leave that for a minute, and let's all pour a drink."

"All right," her mom replies and fetches six fresh glasses, pouring each of us a small amount of leftover champagne. Chelsea steps forward and reaches for the orange juice but stops just short, instead letting her mother pour her a glass of bubbles. It'll ruin the surprise we have for them.

Raising her glass, Chelsea toasts, "To safe travels, love, and many exciting new adventures."

As everyone repeats her toast, she reaches up and places her lips on mine. I'll never get enough of her sweet kisses. Our eyes connect, and she gives me a little nod.

Now's the time.

"So, we have some news for you all," I start.

Henrietta gasps before placing her glass down on the kitchen counter.

"Earlier this week, Chelsea and I decided to get married," I announce.

A chorus of "oh my gosh" and "congratulations" echoes through the kitchen.

"That's not all," Chelsea adds. "We went out the same day and made it official."

"What?" her mom shrieks.

"It was spontaneous and perfectly fitting for us, given our whole relationship has been that way," she explains

"But a wedding, Chelsea..." Henrietta cries. "Dad and I would've loved to have given you away."

"We haven't decided fully yet, but we'd still like to have a wedding. However, some news from today may change that slightly."

Gazing up at me, I nod. I'll leave the slightly bigger news for Chelsea to share.

"We found out a little earlier today that we're having a baby."

"Ahh," sounds from both of our mothers, who rush forward to hug Chelsea and me before extending their arms and holding each other tight. My mom has tears running down her face, and I'm sure I heard Chelsea's mom sob.

"Chelsea, you told me you weren't," her mother exclaims over her sobs.

"I didn't know then," Chelsea replies.

Our dads walk over to us and offer their congratulations.

"I knew I was right." Dad grins at Chelsea.

"That's what made me think about it," she replies.

"Did you find out here?" Chelsea's mom asks, wiping her eyes and stepping away from my mom.

"Yes, just before the party."

While Chelsea's deep in conversation with my dad and the mothers about finding out she was pregnant, I take Chelsea's dad, Alan, aside, and I whisper to him, "Perhaps we can discuss me purchasing this house from you. I'd like to raise my family here, and there's already room out front for your RV."

He grins before nodding his response and turns back to the conversation. I just know that this will be the perfect gift for Chelsea.

The idea to purchase Chelsea's parents' house has been on my mind since they first announced they wanted to sell. It's much bigger than mine and slightly closer to the hospital. But it has a yard, and it'd be lovely for our children to grow up in the same space as Chelsea did.

Her mom walks back to her drink before snatching Chelsea's from her. "You need orange juice, missy," she scolds.

After handing Chelsea a fresh glass, she holds hers in the air. "To our connected and growing families."

Clinking glasses with my wife, I give her a little kiss.

Fate brought Chelsea and me together and has had a helping hand in this relationship over the past almost year. I'll forever be grateful that we hooked up that night, and while the road to us being together was far from smooth, it only proved how much we really love each other, and that's something special.

ACKNOWLEDGEMENTS

Kat, thank you for everything, from being my sounding board to your marketing help. I can never thank you enough for all you do for me.

Jessica, thank you for being amazing. Thank you for being an amazing Beta reader for me. I appreciate you and our friendship so much.

Dana, thank you for being a wonderful Beta reader. Can't wait to catch up with you soon.

To my family and friends, thank you for all your support. It means the world to me.

To Kay, Nicki, and Kim at Swish Design and Editing. Thank you for the amazing work you do.

To Sarah Paige at Opium House for my amazing covers. Thank you for working your magic yet again.

And lastly, to my readers, thank you for your support and encouragement. I hope you've enjoyed Cameron and Chelsea's story.

Love you loads,
Alana xx

Thank you for reading, more information can be found below.

BOOKBUB

Connect with me on Bookbub.
https://www.bookbub.com/authors/alana-jade

GOODREADS

Add my books to your TBR list on my Goodreads profile.
https://www.goodreads.com/author/show/18177818.Alana_Jade

AMAZON

Click to buy my books from my Amazon profile.
https://www.amzn.com/Alana-Jade/e/B07FK8XZNP

INSTAGRAM

@alanajadeauthor

Alana Jade

EMAIL
alanajadeauthor@gmail.com

FACEBOOK
https://www.facebook.com/alanajadeauthor

About THE AUTHOR

Australian author, **Alana Jade,** was born and bred in Sydney. Alana has loved writing since she was a child. She's a wife and mum to six children who are her everything, and fur-mum to one spoilt pug called Harper. When she isn't busy with her family or writing, you'll likely find Alana watching an episode of *Friends* or scrolling through Facebook.

Made in the USA
Middletown, DE
30 April 2022

65048072R00176